A ROSE O'BRIEN SERIES - BOOK 2

SAVING Foxy

S. S. DUSKEY

ALSO BY S. S. DUSKEY

A ROSE O'BRIEN SERIES:

SAVING LILY-BOOK ONE

THE ROSE O'BRIEN TRILOGY:

SECRETS IN THE KEYS

DECEPTION IN THE BITTERROOT

REDEMPTION IN THE TAHOE BASIN

Printed in the United States of America
First printing, 2025
Cover design and author photo by Debbie Driggers
Editor - Carrie Padgett
Publishing Coordinator - Sharon Kizziah-Holmes

SakiRose Publishing
Hamilton, MT

www.ssduskeyauthor.com
www.instagram.com/ssduskey
ssduskey@yahoo.com

ISBN - 13: 979-8-9893427-1-6

DEDICATION

This book is dedicated to Randi Zimmerman. You will forever be my ray of sunshine. #CancerSucks.

ACKNOWLEDGMENTS

I would like to express my gratitude to Steve Weinstock, Charisse Rose, and Teri Albrecht for their expert contributions. Debbie Driggers deserves enormous thanks for her ongoing, exceptional work designing my book covers.

CHAPTER 1

◆

THE CHOPPER DESCENDED on me like a hawk hunting its prey, buzzing and chuffing, then swiftly pulled up. As the chap on the ground gained on me. My heart pounded in my throat as I ran. But the damned ninety-degree temps with 99 percent humidity—that felt as though it were one hundred percent—made it next to impossible to run any faster.

Gotta love Florida June weather. And it was only 9 a.m.

How do I end up in these situations?

"O'Brien, you can run, but you can't hide. I'm better than you," sneered the maniac.

I scanned my body. How many times had I been shot? I couldn't count. As I spun to see where my enemy was, I tripped over a branch and slid down an embankment. Thank God my Glock 9mm and M4 were unscathed. Suddenly, a thought occurred. Were there alligators out here?

Crap on a cracker.

The helicopter returned out of nowhere and was so close the rotors' downwash pounded me, kicking up leaves and branches. Not only did I have to hide from the crazy man chasing me, but also from his partner in the sky.

"Come on, Rose," I muttered.

The second I eased to a stand, I was hit on my backside. Argh! I fell to the ground again. Where was he? He was good. I gave him that much. I scanned the woodlands for a place to take cover. Perfect. Approximately one hundred yards away, I saw a line of overgrown oak trees covered in moss.

"Ready to surrender, Rose?" he hollered in the distance.

"Surrender? Is he kidding?" I picked myself up and continued limping toward the trees.

Bam! Not again. The burning was almost unbearable. I peered at my leg and saw the red dripping. Then I took another in the arm. Crap! I was no match for him.

"Come out, come out, weak little girl. You'll regret the day we met."

"Weak little girl?!" I rumbled under my breath again.

My face felt hot and most likely looked as crimson as what dripped down my black pants. I checked my chamber. I only had three rounds left in my M4, but my Glock was loaded.

Make it count.

Stillness filled the air. The jeering stopped. Damn. I lost his position.

"I'll show him weak. Time to take this jerk down," I growled to no one. Although he was better at this game and had more practice, I was learning to hunt and was a quick study. I searched the forest floor for something—anything—to make a snare trap the way I'd been taught.

Nada! Not to mention time was not on my side. Instead, I got on all fours and crawled to the large oak. I slowly stood and peeked around the massive trunk. In that moment, I spotted him moving in a steady and smooth stride. He looked like Groucho Marx walking with his M4, scanning the forest in the manner of a true soldier.

He was all mine.

A few seconds later, I jumped out and opened fire. I unloaded the remainder of my M4 magazine. Just like in the movies, his body recoiled with every hit in slow motion. After the M4 was empty, I quickly pulled out my Glock, emptying that too.

He lay still on the ground, panting for a brief period, before he sat up, waving his hands in surrender. The chopper returned, but Simon signaled him on.

"What's the matter, Simon? Were you beaten by a weak little girl?" I heckled. "And for the record, I don't regret meeting you. Now get up." I removed my helmet and walked over.

"Well played, Rose." He threw off his protective helmet, too. "I forgot how these Simunition rounds hurt. And kudos for not revealing where you were hiding." He gave me a handsome toothy smile with his dimpled chin as he shot me in the leg with his Glock 9. One round to the thigh. Point-blank range.

"Ouch! That's dirty, Simon." I clutched my leg and winced. "I have no padding there. And you're not supposed to hit that close. Where's the safety in that?"

"Come on." He stood. "It's not that bad. I only nicked you in the outer thigh. I know what I'm doing. It's your fault for getting too close to the enemy. You had no idea how many rounds I had remaining … and safety? What you did? Unloading on me like you were John Wick? Now that's dirty!"

"You're far from helpless. And you're correct. I had no business shooting the bejeezus out of you," I said. "I've been shot in that leg before … with real bullets. You hit scar tissue." I whimpered, limping away.

"Rose, sorry," he shouted from behind.

"Ha! Gotcha," I spun. "I was actually shot in the other leg. But it seriously hurts. I'll undoubtedly be super bruised. Thanks for that. It's shorts season." I squinted. "Ah, damn. I have that thing tonight. The fundraiser on the boat. I was going to wear a mini dress. Now I have to wear a muumuu."

"Yacht, Rose. What you live on is a yacht," Simon said, catching up to me.

"Potato, potato." I shrugged. "Not after midnight, Sunday." I stopped and dropped my head.

Simon pulled me in for a hug and kissed my forehead. Simon Rose was six feet, four inches of pure muscle. He had crewcut brownish-auburn hair mixed with a touch of black. And lashes I'd kill for. The corners of his brown eyes creased when he smiled. It was a good thing I was happy with my guy, Kevin O'Malley. But Simon was more like an annoying big brother. I wouldn't have had it any other way.

"Why are you going to the party if you're walking away from it all?"

"The fundraiser for the wounded vet foundation has been planned for months," I said. "I'm not that kind of person. Besides, it's for a great cause."

"I get it. And I appreciate it."

Simon and I were silent the rest of the way to Mel's shop. As a former Army Special Forces Operator, Simon was well connected.

The 200 acres of heavily forested land up in Tallahassee we'd been playing on belonged to Mel, an army buddy. Mel allowed his "special" friends to use it for outdoor training.

Since I still had an enemy lurking in the shadows, I'd hired Simon a few months ago to train me to protect myself. Cora Alvarez, former CIA, who called the hit, had a personal vendetta. She supposedly left the Agency, changed her name, and fled the country. Although Grandma, using her contacts, had the hit called off, told me to keep looking in the rearview. So, Simon took me out for Simunition training. Sims for short.

In my prior career, we'd practiced with the non-toxic and non-lethal force on force training. It's commonly used by law enforcement and the military to make it real world, without real bullets. The Simunition rounds mark you up like paintball, but unlike paintball, these hurt. Especially at close range.

Sims training was conducted with a team, making entry into a home, but Simon believed the three of us out in the forest would be reality based. He was big on "what if's." What if I was alone—as he claimed I was most of the time—and being hunted? Simon wanted to see how I would react. He approved and gave himself a pat on the back.

The second we arrived at Mel's shop, I was panting like a husky in a hot yoga class. Since I wasn't keen on getting pummeled with massive bruising, I had layered as much as possible. But the full body protection didn't allow for the humidity. But it was required—and welcomed—since the paint-filled Sims rounds were realistic in that they mark the point of impact and mimicked the weight, feel, and functionality of live ammo. Our guns were real but modified. So, between us three, we triple checked to make sure no live rounds were accidentally put in them.

After we finished cleaning our gear, I couldn't peel off my protective equipment quickly enough. I shrugged out of my top and bent over to remove my tactical pants.

"Hey, I hope you have on shorts. Sheesh." Simon swiftly looked away.

"Yes." I gave him an elbow to the stomach. "And a tank top."

After I dropped my pants, I inspected the bruise forming on my thigh.

Simon put his hand on my shoulder. "Sorry, sister. You're

correct. That's going to be ugly. Good thing your boy toy, O'Malley, is back in Washington."

As I eased onto a log bench and continued to inspect my thigh, Mel came out with a bag of ice, my precious fur baby, Sue, on his heels.

Sue ran at me, full bore, all forty-five pounds of her. And just as she was about to leap into my lap, Sue quickly halted with her nose in the air. She was my service pup and understood immediately I was wounded. Instead, she gingerly hopped next to me and laid her head on my lap.

"It's okay, love muffin." I kissed her nose.

After we said our goodbyes to Mel, we made our way to my helicopter that had landed on the helipad. The pilot, and third member of our training team, was another Army pal of theirs, Tucker Fite. My pilot, Kate Orr, was off on a holiday with her sisters to some exotic island before she began a new job. And she needed some serious R&R after our excitement in Montana. But that's a story for another day, Grandma would say.

Tucker would only be with me another couple of days and needed a gig in between jobs. At Simon's request, I didn't ask Tucker where his next assignment was going to take him. My hunch was he worked as a contractor overseas. Tucker was six feet, one inch, 190 pounds, blue eyes, brown hair, and a strong jaw line. He was a man of few words who grunted … a lot.

Suddenly my phone rang; I fished it out of my shorts' pocket.

"I told you, no cells," Simon scolded. "What if that happened when you were out there? It would've given away your location."

"Sorry, I thought it was on vibrate." I flicked my wrist at him. "Well, hello, Ms. Cazier … what's up?"

Simon beamed from ear to ear, wearing his coy grin. He turned the color of the red paint that was splattered all over us. He leaned in to hear what his new love, Lily, was saying.

I pulled my head away and put her on speaker. "Say that again?"

CHAPTER 2

♦

AS LILY CAZIER pulled out of the physical therapy pool center in Miami Beach, she turned up the radio, listening to a news reporter: *This just in. We are watching a dangerous weather pattern form over the Atlantic. We are looking for severe thunderstorms. There is a potential for this to turn into a hurricane by the time it reaches land sometime late tomorrow afternoon. Folks, we are looking at a major tropical storm that appears to be strengthening. Hurricane season is in full swing, so I don't have to remind you to stock up on batteries, sandbags, wa—.*

Lily reached over and turned off the radio as something unsettling caught her attention. A white SUV, with heavily tinted windows. Lily was certain the same vehicle was parked outside her favorite java café early this morning. Although Lily had only been in Florida for a month, she had her spot. It made her feel all was normal within her world.

"I don't like this one bit." Lily's palms sweat as they clutched the steering wheel. She quickly dialed her bestie.

"Rose. I … I'm being followed," Lily said. "D … do you think they found me?"

"I doubt it. The hit was called off, remember? And you're driving my car."

"I have an odd feeling." Lily caressed an antique locket that fell around her neck. Someone sent it to her in Montana. A mystery still surrounded the sender's identity. It gave her peace as it had lilies etched on the cover. Her mother's favorite flower.

"Okay. I trust your instincts. Can you copy the license?" Rose asked.

"No front plate."

"Drive straight to the police station. If you're being followed, it'll be obvious."

"Shoot, I passed it already. They're doing construction. It'll take me forever to circle back. Not to mention I'm almost on the MacArthur Causeway. Traffic is a nightmare."

"Okay. I assume you're headed to the marina?"

"I was. Should I not?"

"Negative. I have a better idea. The Coast Guard station is a stone's throw from the marina. Pull in. If someone is following you, they'll turn around and continue going," Rose said.

"Not sure why I didn't think of it. My mind hasn't been right for some time."

"Still not sleeping well?"

"No."

"Oh, don't forget we have that *thing* tonight."

"Did I just hear an eye roll?" Lily chuckled.

"You know me all too well."

"What time?"

"Six."

"Did you hear? A major storm's coming. The news reporter said it's gaining strength. Will the yacht be able to handle it?"

"Not really. Khan and TJ are going to make sure it's dry-docked after tonight. But it won't be my problem. It'll be Keith's ..." Rose's voice trailed off.

"I'm sorry, Rose."

"It's all good. It was never my money to begin with."

"I still can't believe Max stored sperm. And what would make him think you'd allow yourself to be inseminated?"

"Don't forget, and raise Satan's child, too."

They shared a laugh, and the line went still again.

"If you need any help packing," Lily said somberly.

"I'm almost done. Thank God I didn't have any furniture."

"What are you going to do?"

"Um ... don't know. We'll chat about it when I see you. Tucker is waiting for us to take off." Rose hung up.

After Lily disconnected, her heart ached for her friend, who was more like a sister. If Max wasn't dead, she would give the jerk a punch. Rose was all too calm about it. Lily was concerned for her.

As the traffic began moving again, Lily peered into her rearview mirror. The SUV was two vehicles behind her. Just as she drew closer to the stop light, she slowed to a turtle's pace. An impatient driver honked and gave her the middle finger salute. But Lily was so focused on her suspected follower, she didn't care. And her next move was bound to infuriate the jerk behind her even more.

She waited for the light to just turn red and punched it. Lily zoomed past her exit to the super yacht marina and waited at the entrance of the Coast Guard. She watched the white SUV gun it through the green light and whip into the marina. It *was* following her. Or was it?

Her breathing returned to normal as she sat a spell, caressing her locket. How she wished her mother were still alive.

CHAPTER 3

◆

AGENT H WALKED the grounds of the Memorial Garden at CIA headquarters in Langley, Virginia. Located between the original headquarters building and the auditorium, it featured a garden with an attractive array of both natural and landscaped flora. Although he couldn't smell, he was informed that the wildflowers had a heavenly fragrance. It was one of several memorials at the CIA compound and paid tribute to all deceased intelligence officers and contractors who served their country.

Agent H groaned as he fondly recalled one of those unnamed operatives. While their names are not etched, they were remembered, nonetheless. The garden was designed as a serene place for the employees to enjoy a respite from the stress of their duties. And with the sunshine today, more staff would be milling about, so he needed to hurry. He walked briskly around the large fishpond, where a surge of water flowed from stone outcroppings.

This is where Agent H made his phone call. Since he had a meeting in thirty minutes, he couldn't drive off the grounds where ears weren't listening.

He dialed.

"I don't have much time," Agent H said.

"Well, happy Friday morning to you too," a woman replied. "Burner phone?"

"Affirmative. I've got another job for you, Juno."

"I'm listening, Hansel."

"Don't call me that. Never liked that name. It's H or Agent H. You know that."

"Just had to, for old time's sake."

"Not funny."

"I'm not with the Agency anymore. I can call you whatever I damn well please," Juno growled. "And you called me."

"Point taken." He paused and watched two staff members approach, nodding as they passed. "I had Gil's apartment turned upside down. As I suspected, he cleared it of any pertinent documents and left in a hurry. As you're aware, he met with Lily Cazier in Montana."

"I remembered you telling me about her. Wasn't he eliminated?"

"Affirmative. But any documents were either taken or destroyed. His laptop included."

"Then why are you calling?"

"When Gil's place was searched, they found a letterhead. He'd apparently penned a letter to a Fran something. The paper's indentation only revealed that much. According to his records, Gil did not have a wife or children. His only family member was his sister who died of a heart attack a year ago. She, however, had a daughter named Francine Fox."

Agent H kept his head on a swivel as the sweat dripped down his neck, soaking his white-collared shirt. It was one of the muggiest days of the year and he chose to wear an all-black tailored suit with black Ray-Ban sunglasses. He looked like Tommy Lee Jones, Agent Kay, from *Men in Black*. Huh. He was H. Jones was Kay and Will Smith was Jay. They just needed Agent I for a full alphabet soup of covert operatives.

H shook his head. He needed to be fully engaged in this conversation.

The stress he was under did not help the sweat situation.

"I'm sending you Francine's information right now," he said in a hushed voice. "I suspect Gil sent her something important. Find it and contact me when you do." He looked at his watch. "June Bug, I don't need to remind you how sensitive this is and it must not be traced back to me."

"Don't call me that," Juno said. "We're not a couple anymore."

"Fair enough."

"And I always operate discreetly."

"I'm aware. Get it done quickly. And keep me posted."

"What did this CIA scientist have that's got so many people running scared?"

"That information is classified. You know that."

"Yeah, yeah. But what are we looking for specifically?"

"It could be a computer chip, USB flash drive ... whatever. You need to take all the documents. Grab her computer too. I'll have them combed. But, under *no* circumstances are you to look at them. Understood?" Agent H looked at his watch. 11:15 a.m. His lunch meeting was in half an hour.

"Yes, *dear*."

"We're back to that." Agent H sighed.

"What do we do with the girl?"

Silence fell on the line.

"I have a meeting. Tell me when it's done." He disconnected.

Juno lay on a lounge chair on the deck of her beach front condo. The umbrella misters cooled her long, tan legs. She fanned the back of her short, brunette cropped hair and took a sip of her lemonade with fresh lemons. She dialed her hired thug.

"Captain speaking," a male with a Latin accent answered.

"Did you get my text on the Fox woman?" Juno demanded.

"Yes. I'm looking at her photo right now. She works at the Dancing Flamingo in Miami Beach?"

"That's what it says. Did you get her address?"

"Yes, yes. I shall go to see her apartment," Captain said.

"It's go to, you will go to—never mind."

Captain laughed.

"Cut the crap. You were only *born* in Cuba."

"It never gets old," he said, sans accent.

"I'm in no laughing mood." Juno groaned.

"What am I looking for?" Captain inquired in a more serious tone.

"Computer, a USB flash drive, microchip. There may also be correspondence from her uncle. A man named Gil Fox."

"What if there isn't anything?"

"Then I suggest you have a *chat* with her."

"Look, I don't mind roughing up assholes. She looks so ...

innocent."

"Are you getting soft on a stripper you've never met?"

"No, my specialty is extracting information. A gal like her … just doesn't seem right," Captain said. "It also says she's a college student."

"You don't sound sure of this job. Do I need to hire someone else?"

"She just looks like my kid sister. They even have the same dyed reddish-orange hair."

"What in the hell is wrong with you? Are you PMSing?"

"That's crass and uncalled for. My team won and brought me extra dough. Jeez. Thanks for killing my vibe."

"Can you handle it or not?"

"Yeah. But I've got another job in Miami in two days. How long will this take?"

"One day max. Like you said, she's probably harmless. Call when it's done. Oh, absolutely you are *not* to look at anything."

"I couldn't care less. That's above my scope of giving a damn."

"Call when you're done." Juno hung up.

CHAPTER 4

◆

AS PROVERBS 21:21 says: *Whoever pursues righteousness and love finds life, prosperity and honor.* That verse popped into my head as I hid—no, make that took a quick breather—from the schmoozing crowd of the rich and famous. If it wasn't for such a good cause, I'd be in my pjs with popcorn and a cheap red, instead of hiding in the corner of the yacht's main salon/dining area.

The marble floor and fancy décor glittered under the lights, making a lovely setting for the foundation's event. The home in California I recently sold was nowhere near this extravagant. I missed it. I also longed for those quiet nights cooking dinner for my late husband. I'd found true love with him. True love, prosperity, and honor.

I sighed and poured another glass of red from a bottle whose name I couldn't pronounce. The vino probably cost more than my first car. I sipped as I attempted to count how much I drank and ate. Good thing Simon wasn't here to see my gluttonous behavior.

I gazed at the ornate and elegant spiral staircase that led downstairs to a guest cabin where I assumed my BFF, Lily, was hiding. Should I escape too? Nah, too many people were watching me. And the owner's stateroom, *my* room, was also blocked. Heavy groan.

I sipped more wine and returned to Proverbs. I knew in my heart of hearts I was pursuing righteousness by giving up billions along with this showy yacht. Surrendering gave me peace, too. If Proverbs 21:21 was accurate, I should find life, prosperity, and honor.

At least I would be walking away with my dignity intact. That was something to feel good about. Right?

It was easier than I expected. This lifestyle was a lot of hobnobbing and fake smiles. While the fundraiser was for a very important cause, I couldn't stand another handshake or air kiss from heavily Botox-injected men and women. It was only 10 p.m., and the intimate party of forty-five felt more like a mosh pit.

I suddenly couldn't breathe.

Sue, who'd been at my side the whole time, put her paw on my jeweled Manolo stiletto and whimpered. She tugged my floor-length black gown and ushered me down the foyer and out the grand entrance. After all, she was a Red Kelpie known for herding. Not before I snatched the bottle of red, though. Couldn't leave that behind.

The instant we left the air-conditioned yacht, the late evening temps hit me. I'm sure the wine didn't help. I stumbled and tripped over my Italian-made gown then had to quick step it down the aluminum ramp. I managed to keep my feet in my heels and one hand around the wine bottle. I hit the concrete walk path, tripped once more and sat with a bone-jarring thunk.

Sue scampered over and plopped beside me, checking for wounds. As I sat stunned, staring at my ripped fancy dress and overpriced pumps, all I could do was laugh. Torn dress and scuffed shoes, but I'd managed to save the tasty vino.

Sue thought it was fun too as she caught a case of the zoomies and ran to the grassy area. She was just as happy to be off the yacht, aptly named the Max One, as I was.

Thankfully for me, out of the eight slips available for mega and super yachts, there were only three of us: no one was close by. Clearly, the other yachts had already been dry-docked or had sailed to safer waters, as is typical during hurricane season.

Sitting there, I quickly scanned the dock, looking for the 24-hour security patrol officer. Phew, he wasn't around; my ego couldn't have handled it. I stood and dusted myself off. I took out my hair clips and ran my hands through my waves and shook my head, laughing at myself again. I walked to the grassy area and sat on a bench, watching Sue run like a crazy dog. She made me smile.

Suddenly, I felt eyes on me. Sue did too. She stopped and came over to me. I scanned every direction but saw no one. Could it have been security? And then there was a person's shadow in the west. I couldn't tell if the figure watching me was male or female. I headed in their direction, but they spun around and began swiftly moving. I removed my shoes and sped up, too.

No sooner had I almost reached our midnight stalker when one of the neighboring yachts blared out AC/DC's "Shoot to Thrill." People were hollering and whooping it up. I turned and saw which yacht was playing it, another trust fund baby billionaire party. I rolled my eyes. Although, the tune was one of my favorites. I pulled the cork out of the bottle, took a swig, and recorked it as I made my way back to my yacht, singing along, shaking my head. No doubt, I looked like a class act.

As I was almost to the Max One, I heard a woman scream. And it wasn't a party scream, more of a blood-curdling one. The shouts were coming from the east side of the dock. I tossed the wine bottle and my Manolo's on the grass and bolted toward the gal, my pup alongside me.

As I drew closer, I was able to see a man close to six feet dragging a woman by the nape of her neck. He looked more like a body builder.

"Kick me again and see what happens!"

"What do you want from me?" the woman screamed.

"Where's the letter?"

"What are you talking about?"

"The one from your uncle?"

"What? You're nuts." She kicked the man in the shin with her pointy shoes. Since it was dark, I could not see their features.

I picked up the pace, as did Sue. She reached them before I did and before I had the chance to call her back, she jumped up and bit the man on the arm. He tossed her off and kicked her. Sue yiped.

My blood boiled. No one harms my dog. I gritted my teeth and bolted. My speed surprised me; I felt as if I were the Bionic Woman. I body slammed the jerk, and he flew. Unfortunately, so did the innocent woman.

The man sprang to his feet like a ninja and took a bladed stance. Pretty quick for someone built like a brick house.

"You bitch," he growled at me.

I stood, ready for a fight, fists up, but he turned away from me and headed for the girl.

"Hey, asshole," I shouted.

He spun around and that's when I gave him a quick upper cut to his nose with my elbow. It wasn't hard to do because he only stood an inch taller than me.

"Ow!" he howled, grabbing his nose. The light from the moon illuminated him enough that I saw blood trickling down his lip. He shook his head and returned a right hook. But I was ready and ducked to avoid his fist.

From my peripheral vision, I saw Sue rushing him again.

"Sue, stop!" I ordered in my sternest voice. I never yelled, but she needed protection. She obeyed, as her momma fought for her.

The guy grabbed the woman by her waist, and she kicked his shin again while I gave him a boot to his kidneys. That is if I wore boots. But I was barefoot, and it smarted.

"Shit!" he yelled.

And just as he turned to face me again, the woman was now on my side. She removed her stiletto and launched it at his face.

He quickly batted the shoe away and shouted, covering his eye.

The gal took off like a frightened fawn. As did the man. By this time, security was not only called to the out-of-control baby billionaire's yacht, but to the fight. The marina had probably never seen this level of chaos as it catered to gazillionaires with their mega yachts and superyachts. So, the unprepared security officers most likely didn't know which commotion to address first. The nearby Coast Guard also responded. Since a larger fight broke out on the kid's yacht at the same time, they swarmed it like flies on dead fish.

"Wow, when Rose O'Brien gets into a fight, the Coast Guard is called." Lily's laugh echoed behind me.

I turned around and Lily stood there, Sue next to her. Lily held my shoes and the bottle of wine. She handed both to me. I uncorked the bottle again and took a swig of wine, then passed her the bottle. Just as she drank, I spotted a woman's black handbag on the grass.

"Hmm, must be the victim's," I said, picking it up.

"Victim? Do you want to tell me what happened? Or should I wait for tomorrow morning's news report?" she said with a laugh. "And by the looks of your clothes and hair, I'd say you were the victim."

"You should see the other guy." I snorted.

Lily chuckled.

"No, I'm serious." I gave her a detailed account of what happened.

Her eyes widened. "You really know how to throw a fundraiser."

CHAPTER 5

◆

FRANCINE FOX, A.K.A. Foxy, fled as fast as her bare feet would allow. She ducked behind a lifted truck in the marina's parking lot and crouched by the rear wheel.

She gasped for air as she scanned her wardrobe. With her sequined thong, matching bra and body glitter, she looked like a stripper. Fortunately, she had grabbed her coat as the weather called for rain. She remembered seeing her kidnapper in the audience. It was odd to her that he wasn't like the rest, just there for a good time. In fact, he wasn't even drinking alcohol.

After her set, she snuck out back to take a quick smoke break in between performances. Foxy was not a smoker, but she had an upcoming organic chemistry exam that she didn't feel prepared for, so she borrowed one from one of the other dancers. The stress of the accelerated summer course she was taking was too much.

The second she extinguished her cigarette, someone stepped up behind her and covered her nose and mouth with a cloth doused in Trichloromethane, also known as chloroform. Chemical formula $CHCl_3$.

Chloroform is a colorless, sweet-smelling organic compound. Oddly enough, it quickly popped into her head as she was rendered unconscious. It was on her upcoming exam. Maybe she was prepared after all. Foxy wanted to follow in her uncle Gil's footsteps and become a research scientist.

When she came to, she was slumped in the backseat of an SUV. Foxy was not bound, but that man from the audience was sitting in the back with her, glaring as he pointed a gun at her. While she originally thought he was incredibly hot, his presence now frightened her.

He kept asking for the letter from her uncle and her laptop. What was he talking about? Foxy's lack of knowledge apparently angered her kidnapper as he knocked her out again, and the next thing, she was being dragged through the marina. Given the marina's high security, how did that happen?

One thing was certain, she appreciated that woman and her dog.

The coast seemed clear, so she peeked her head up then ducked down again.

The man ran past, moaning as he covered his face. He hopped into a black Cadillac Escalade and sped off, tires screeching. After he left the parking lot, she stood and made her way to the gate, too.

Where had her sudden courage come from? Throwing her shoe at that man, that was a badass Wonder Woman move, so unlike her. She shuddered. Maybe seeing how a stranger jumped in for her galvanized her inner Diana Prince.

The gravity of the situation weighed on her. Her costume of thong and bra made Foxy feel naked and more like a streetwalker than a high-class dancer. She had to get home. But her car was still at the Dancing Flamingo.

Since she had no phone or money, a long walk was in her immediate future. She headed back to her Miami Beach apartment across the MacArthur Causeway. People honked at her and catcalled, asking how much. Her cheeks blazed, but she kept her head up.

Brakes squealed as a vehicle came to a stop behind her. The driver honked. She hesitated to turn but when she did, relief rushed in at a familiar face. Her neighbor, Mary.

Thankfully, Mary didn't insist on answers about why Foxy was walking around in her dancing getup. Instead, she talked a mile a minute about the date she'd just been on.

Foxy waved her thanks as she jumped out of the car and approached her entry, then froze.

The front door stood open.

Heart pounding, she stuck her head inside. "Hello? Is someone here?"

Silence.

She inched inside to a scene of chaos. Her studio had been

trashed. Her schoolbooks were scattered around her desk which had obviously been ransacked. Her clothes were strewn all over the floor. The mattress was disturbed, seemingly searched under, and every pillow was slashed open.

What in the world?

A paralyzing thought occurred. It must've been her kidnapper.

He had her purse and phone. He knew where she lived.

Foxy frantically threw some underwear, a pair of jeans, and a T-shirt into a bag and ran next door to Mary's apartment.

Foxy just told her neighbor her place had been broken into, and she didn't feel safe there. Mary offered to let her crash on the couch.

But the thought of staying around the complex made her heart pound and a sweat to break out, so she used Mary's phone to call her friend and co-worker, Stella.

Someone she could trust with her life.

CHAPTER 6

◆

I SAT AT my Mahogany desk in my owner's stateroom, sipping coffee, staring at my resume. My head was pounding too much to fill in the blanks. Instead, I watched the dark clouds roll in as the wind kicked up, while Sue lay belly up, snoring, all four paws in the air. She was woofing and chasing someone in her dreams.

I was fortunate to have hired help. They fed her and let her go out to do her business.

I massaged my temples, wishing away the brutal hangover. I peeked at the time on my cell. The blurry numbers read eight.

"Why did I drink so much?" I said to no one. Or so I thought.

"Hmm. I have a couple guesses." A female giggled at my opened door. Lily.

I turned and gave her a faint smile, flipping over my resume.

Lily walked over and handed me a glass of green goo. "Your chef said this would help."

I took it from her, then quickly set it down and made a bee line for my bathroom. The wind was so strong, I felt the yacht moving. So, I had a talk with the porcelain king. Multiple conversations.

"This is way out of character, even for you, Rose. And I've seen you do some crazy things." Lily stepped in and ran a washcloth under the water.

"Can you be more specific?" I sat next to the toilet and draped the cool cloth across my forehead.

Lily handed me the God-awful looking beverage. I trusted my chef and took a sip. "What the hell is in this?" I scrunched my nose.

Lily shrugged. "It's supposed to work."

I gulped more and tried to stand but was too unsteady. "Man, we must be having some wild wind."

"It's not that bad, yet. It's the alcohol still coursing through your body."

"Oh," I said with a curled lip.

"Soo … do you remember what happened last night?"

"I think so." I shuffled out of the bathroom and back to my bed. "I hope I wasn't rude to anyone."

"On the contrary. Your guests had a good show. I overheard some saying they were impressed, and it was a welcome change to Max's stuffy fundraisers. Others though, not so happy."

"Crap. I hope no one backed out."

"There were only a couple who didn't like your performance. And, in a few days, it won't be your problem." Lily sat next to me. "Is that why you drank so much?"

I nodded and looked at my partially packed suitcases, ready for my departure.

Lily must've seen me staring at my bags. "Where are you going to go? You can come back to Montana with me. Your grandma would love to have you."

"That's not necessary. I sold my house in California at full market value. I reinvested it in high yield accounts."

"I thought your house exploded a year ago."

"It was only partially destroyed. I had it rebuilt a while back with the insurance money. At least my fireproof safe room was unscathed, as were some of my belongings."

Lily looked sideways at me. I guess I never told her about it. Heck, only a couple of people were aware of that room.

"Not to mention, with all my paychecks, I bought stock. So, I have options." I shrugged. "I may buy a van and live in my storage unit or even down by the river."

"Or in your case, ocean." Lily laughed then paused.

"What now?"

"You don't remember, do you?"

I drew back my head. "Noo. But something tells me you're going to enlighten me. How can I not remember? All I had was wine."

"Guess again."

"Huh?"

"When we returned to the yacht, you went down to the galley with a bottle of tequila."

"Oh. Yeah, I did." I would've chuckled but my head hurt. I rubbed it. "I remember now. I insisted the crew do shots with me as a last hurrah."

"Emotions ran high. There were tears and lots of 'I love you's and 'Gonna miss you's."

"Mine or theirs?" I asked with my head in my hands.

"A little of both."

Lily walked back to the bathroom. I heard her rattling around in the medicine cabinet before she returned with a couple of Tylenol. I graciously accepted and sucked them down with the remainder of my hangover remedy.

"I don't ever remember seeing you this way. Although I do recall James telling me that you were once found in a similar condition."

"I was drugged!" I protested. "How many times do I have to tell people?"

"True, but weren't you also caught on video calling your boss a quote, 'Pencil dick, twat waffle'?"

"Yes, but I was set up by Shilo. You remember her? She had a thing for Max. She murdered the therapist my employer ordered me to see."

"Yeah, because you shot and killed a few people."

"I never shot a person who didn't deserve it."

"Are you paraphrasing John Wayne?"

I snickered again and grabbed my head. "I guess I am. Anyway, Shilo was obsessed with Max. There wasn't anything she wouldn't do for him."

"What happened to Shilo?"

"She's in federal prison. I believe in a psych unit. We're all safer with her locked up." I stood. "Not sure what's in that, but I feel better. I'll need to get that recipe."

"Planning on an encore of last night?"

"No. Well, at least not the drinking part. That reminds me. I have that girl's purse." I lumbered to the desk and sat again. I opened the bag and pulled out her wallet and looked at her ID.

"Hmm. This is odd."

Lily looked at it too. She turned white and slumped onto the bed.

CHAPTER 7

---◆---

JUNO STARED AT the incoming storm. It was going to be a doozy by the time it hit landfall that night. She'd had hurricane impact windows installed on her condo. At least she was four floors up, so no flooding, unlike her neighbors on the first floor.

As she sipped her coffee, her phone rang.

"Update," a husky-voiced Agent H asked.

"I've not heard from my guy. I was getting ready to call him."

"I need it today. The heat is coming down fast and furious. I don't have to tell you what that means."

"Copy. I'll call the instant I know something." She disconnected and phoned Captain.

"Jess," he answered.

"Seriously, the accent again."

"Hey, in my line of work, never sure who's calling. Safer this way." He yawned.

"Long night? It better have to do with the job I hired you for." Hopefully her chagrined mood came clear through the phone. "What did you find out?"

"Nada. No computer, no documents. And where should I send my ER bill?"

"Your what?"

Captain proceeded to tell Juno all about his attack by a vicious Rottweiler. And two large dudes who'd jumped out of nowhere, coming to Foxy's aid.

Juno let out a heavy groan. "Go back to her apartment and check again. But I also have someone else in mind for the jo—"

"No!" Captain shouted. "I'll take care of your problem."

"You have until end of today. I expect results." She disconnected.

Captain awoke with body aches as if he'd just played a quarter on the field with the Miami Dolphins. He stood in the bathroom and categorized his injuries. He winced as he felt along his arm where that damn dog bit him. He was told to keep it covered and clean, staving off an infection. They updated his overdue tetanus shot, and it stung.

He continued checking himself in the mirror. His back and nose were sore from where that other woman—who came out of nowhere—gave him a fairly good butt whooping. For a dame. Obviously, she was attending one of the parties at the marina. There was no way someone like her owned one of those mega yachts.

But the worst injury was to his eye from where the shoe scratched his cornea. Had Foxy's heel impaled his eye socket, he could've lost his eyeball. It was bad enough he was told to wear a freakin' eye patch. The ER doctor told him to keep a low profile, or the pressure could cause more damage. Maybe even lose his eye.

Captain applied antibiotic drops and replaced the patch as his phone rang.

He squinted at the caller ID with his good eye. Unknown. He answered it with his fake accent.

Juno ragging at him about the job. Captain didn't go into detail, nor did he say he had his ass handed to him by a couple of women and a mutt. So, he made up a good, non-embarrassing story.

After he hung up, he stewed.

How could he have been so careless as to leave his gun in his Caddy? Because he didn't think someone so delicate looking would put up a fight. Captain was only planning to bring her down there for a private chat and maybe threaten to dump her into Biscayne Bay. The marina, where he was given access by a former client, would be a quiet, discreet location. Especially since he knew the marina's camera-free areas that ensured yacht owners' privacy.

Captain grabbed his laptop and powered it on. After a "special favor" he did for a high-ranking member in the local police department, Captain was granted access to programs unavailable to the public in exchange for his silence. After all, the guy owed him his life. Betting his paychecks at the races was a bad idea. But he'd learned his lesson. In return, Captain assured him he would seldomly use his access.

He opened the program and entered the passcode. Although Juno provided him with a description and the address of Francine, a.k.a., Foxy, it was not enough. And he wasn't about to ask her for more detailed information. That might make him appear inept. But this simple job was becoming more complicated. And it was now personal.

A search revealed more Francine Foxes than anticipated. So, he narrowed it down to her approximate age. Lo-and-behold, he hit pay dirt. Apparently, the Dancing Flamingo required their dancers to get fingerprinted. Go figure. And there she was. Everything, including family background. Her mother passed away. Unknown location of her father. And as Juno already told him, she had an uncle by the name of Gil Fox.

Captain pulled up another program and typed in that name. Gil's work must've been important because he held a Top-Secret security clearance. Beyond that, nothing. His record was inaccessible. No known address either.

"Back to Francine," he spoke to the screen. "She has Instagram and Facebook accounts under Foxy."

Captain knew a thing or two about nicknames. He served as an Army Captain, hence his moniker. Captain scrolled through Foxy's socials. No family pictures. But there was a gal named Stella who appeared frequently in her photos and posts.

He visited Stella's profile. She had long, dark silky hair, stunning green eyes, and olive skin. She was a hottie indeed. Stella worked as a bartender at the Dancing Flamingo. The wheels started spinning. He combed Stella's profile, looking through her photos.

"This can work to my advantage. And no better way to get to someone, than through their friend's loved ones."

Foxy would not get away again.

CHAPTER 8

"MAYBE IT'S JUST a coincidence, Lily." I sat next to her on the bed. "Fox is a common name."

Sue, who was lying on the bed, crawled over to nuzzle Lily.

"What if they *are* related?"

"Let's not jump to conclusions."

"It's my fault Gil's dead."

"It's not."

"If I wasn't looking for the truth about my parents, he'd still be alive." Lily rubbed her sternum. "Do you have any antacids?"

"In the bathroom."

Lily went to the medicine cabinet for a second time.

I returned to rummaging—okay, snooping as I've been accused—through Francine's purse. I dumped the contents onto my bed.

Lily returned and joined in my investigation.

"She's a college student at the local JC," I said. "It appears she's enrolled in summer classes. She's twenty-two, lives in Miami Beach."

Lily stared at her picture. "I think they look alike."

"How can you be certain?"

"I spent enough time with Gil." Lily drew a deep breath, her face white.

"Are you okay?"

"Uh … yeah. Just shocked. I keep seeing his dead body in my brain. Rose, what are the odds she would end up at the marina?"

"I'd say it was divine intervention."

"Yeah, and God knew you couldn't resist coming to her aid," Lily said. "We've got to help her."

"I say we take a field trip to her apartment. I'd also like to return her purse. But first I want to run her to make sure she's still living at this apartment in Miami Beach. Don't want to waste a trip."

I went to my desk, opened my laptop and entered her name. Then a thought hit. I would need to run Gil too. Boy, thank God for Gran's secret squirrel passcode I'd lifted the last time I was at her house.

"Yep, Francine still lives there." I turned to Lily.

She let out a heavy sigh and nodded. "Wait, the weather is going to start getting rough."

"Pfft. I've driven in snow blizzards. This is cake."

"Is Simon joining us?" She radiated, the color on her face returning.

"No, he and Tucker are getting supplies to help Saki board up her house later and move furniture off the dock."

"That's right. Your sis lives on Palm Island. They get slammed sometimes."

"They do. During the last hurricane, the storm surge came up to the house. The lawn furniture was in Biscayne Bay on its way to Cuba."

Lily chuckled. "Where is her husband?"

"James is up north on a call-out."

"Wow, this FBI SWAT team keeps him busy." Lily paused. "Have you seen your sister since they returned from their vacation?"

"No, Saki's still sore at me. But I invited her here for breakfast."

"Is she bringing her precious little girl, Violet?"

"No. My dad and Violet's nanny, Heidi, are taking the little nugget up to Tallahassee. The storm is supposed to miss that area completely."

The words were barely out of my mouth when Saki appeared in the doorway. Saki walked over to Lily and gave her a hug. My sister wore a flowing, baby blue cotton halter dress with pink and yellow flowers. Her golden locks were in a high ponytail that draped over her tan shoulders. She and our father shared the same athletic, lean body and contagious smile that lit up any room. Saki was the runt of the litter at five foot five inches, while Dad topped six feet by a couple of inches.

"It's wonderful to see you, Lily," Saki said. "The PT is working. No more crutches."

"Yes, luckily that bullet only grazed the soft tissue. Almost back to normal. I'm doing water therapy now."

Saki spun around, hands on hips. She stood, stoned face, staring at me. She didn't say a word.

"What, no hug for your big sister? I was shot too." I showed her my healed wound. Only a faint scar remained.

"Being shot is nothing new for you. And I'm still pissed!"

"I thought you stopped swearing for Violet," I said.

"It's not swearing if she's not around to hear it. And nice way to change the subject."

"What can I say, it's my superpower." I snorted.

This got a chuckle out of Lily, not Saki.

"Look, I'm sorry I missed her birthday," I said. "Come to think of it, I didn't miss it. I saw her the week before and gave her that life-sized doll house."

"You can't buy her love." Saki looked away and then back again. "You didn't call her on her birthday. We didn't hear from you."

"She's only one. She won't remember Auntie Rose didn't call her. She can't even carry on a conversation." I raised my voice.

"*Every* birthday is special! She was born a month early. That was after I had a gun held on me."

"Well, I'm sorry." I returned her sassy nod. "Actually, if you recall, Lily was kidnapped, and we couldn't locate her." I pointed to Lily, who was still looking through Francine's belongings. "Furthermore, I fell from the sky with a malfunctioning parachute. Thank God for Simon. And then after we found Lily, we had to clear her of murder charges. And *then* we were ambushed on our hike in Salmon. We all could've died. So, forgive me—" My volume was a bit over the top, I felt my blood pressure rise.

Lily jumped up and elbowed her way between us. "You two, stop!" She glared a hole at us. "I feel bad enough about Gil's death. The two of you should love one another. Instead of fighting. Life is too short."

Saki and I looked at our feet and spun with our backs to one another.

"You two even have the same pouty pose."

I drew a deep breath and turned. Apparently, Saki did the same thing.

"I'm truly sorry," I said slowly. "Do you forgive me, lil' sis?"

It appeared my sad puppy dog eyes worked. Saki stepped up and hugged me.

"I'm sorry, too. I guess I'm anxious about the incoming storm. I just packed up Violet and said goodbye to her. Now James is off on another call-out. With him being on the SWAT team, I get worried."

"Why didn't you take off with Dad and Heidi?"

"I've gotta hurricane-proof my fitness center. I'm heading over later," Saki replied more calmly. "Now where is my doggie niece?"

"Sue is hiding in the closet," Lily said. "Apparently, she doesn't like when you two fight either."

Saki and I shared a laugh.

"What's so funny?" Lily asked.

"You think this is fighting?" Saki asked.

Saki and I said, "I'm sorry" at once and embraced again.

"That's more like it." Lily plopped on the bed and dropped her head in her hands.

Saki and I rushed to her.

"A headache again?" I asked.

"And now dizziness," Lily added.

"That's it. I'm calling Doctor Ryan."

"Who's that?" Saki asked.

"She was Max's concierge doctor. I kept her on retainer. She's awesome."

"I'm fine, honest." Lily shot me what I knew was a fake smile. "What do you say we take some of our things to the storage unit after breakfast?"

I studied Lily. I didn't buy that she was fine and changing the subject so quickly. But I'd play along and keep an eye on her. "Sounds good," I said. "I'm going to shower first. That hangover remedy worked."

"Roosie. What did you do?" Saki asked in a singsong voice and a giggle.

I missed my baby sister's little girl laugh. It warmed me that we were okay.

Lily stood. "I'll tell you all about it while Rose showers."

I watched the two walk out, arm in arm. Something was off about Lily. Chest pains, dizziness, headaches. And then a gut-wrenching thought occurred. What if the serum injected by the hitman in Montana did permanent damage? I picked up my phone and called Dr. Ryan.

It's better to ask for forgiveness than permission.

CHAPTER 9

FOXY WOKE UP at 8 a.m. on Stella's couch. Stella was not only the bartender at the Dancing Flamingo, but she was a good friend. Despite their eleven-year age difference, they hit it off immediately. Like sisters.

Foxy considered the prior night's events. Did all that really happen or was it a nightmare?

Nope. It was real or why else would she have slept on a lumpy couch, rather than the comfort of her own bed? She deliberated some more. Foxy could not understand what the guy was looking for. He kept on at her about documents. What documents? The evil man could not be interested in her studies. Maybe he got the wrong person.

"Earth to Foxy." A soft voice spoke from behind her, accompanied by an aroma like lavender body wash.

With a jolt, Foxy whipped her head around.

"Boy, you're really shaken." Stella handed Foxy a mug of hot coffee and joined her on the sofa. "I've been standing there asking you about breakfast."

"I'm sorry, Stella." Foxy took a sip. "It feels like a bad dream and I'm ready to wake up anytime."

"And you don't know who this guy was or what he wanted?"

Foxy shook her head.

"You probably should call the police and report it."

"I don't have my phone. It's in my purse that creep took from me. And he threatened to kill me if I did." She rubbed her face. "I'll call from the club. But my car keys are in my purse. Do you mind driving me?"

"Sure thing. I just showered. You can hop in, if you want." Stella's phone rang. She grabbed it off the coffee table and answered. "Hel—yes, this is her—you what?!" She jumped to her feet and disappeared into her bedroom.

Foxy spun around to watch her friend as she slammed the door behind her. A few seconds later she emerged with her purse in hand and hopping on one foot as she put on a glittery tennis shoe.

"What was that about, Stella?"

"Um … oh … um, it's nothing. Harlee called. They need me to buy supplies on my way to the club to help board up the windows." She ran around the kitchen in a tizzy, stuttering and mumbling to herself. She reached into her wallet and threw a fifty at Foxy. "Sorry, can you take an Uber into work? I gotta go." She darted out the door and slammed it so hard the windows shook.

Foxy sat, mouth agape. "What the heck just happened?" she mumbled, staring off at nothing.

Harlee must've said something to upset Stella. She was usually calm and collected; she wouldn't let anything get under her skin. Not to mention Harlee and her sister, Nala, the club's owners, never insisted people jump when they asked. They were like overprotective aunts to their girls and took an immediate liking to Foxy. The feelings were mutual.

After her mother's passing, Foxy was lost. She'd received a small inheritance from her mom and put it into her college education. But that was insufficient; Foxy had to seek out a flexible, good-paying job. So, she found work as a dancer in a cheesy club in Miami. That was until she realized they were required to provide lap dances. And that's when she met Stella.

Stella, a bartender at the same club, informed Foxy that she'd accepted a position at a classier venue—the Dancing Flamingo. No back-room lap dances. Foxy followed suit and had worked there six months.

After a few minutes pondering her next move, Foxy used Stella's landline to make a few calls. Stella was one of the few left that had the old school princess phone. First, Foxy called to cancel all her credit and bank cards. She also called her cell phone carrier and reported it stolen. She had an extra key to her car, but it was in her apartment. No way was she going there alone.

After Foxy showered and changed, she called an Uber and headed to work to help prepare for the hurricane. It would keep her mind occupied. Despite being abducted from the club's alley, the tight security ensured that creep wouldn't gain entry.

After all, she knew what he looked like.

After Stella dashed out of her apartment, she drove to her uncle's place in South Beach, ran in and grabbed a bag off his kitchen table. She then drove another few miles back to the beach. She skidded her Mazda to a halt, jumped out of her car, zipped her raincoat, and threw her hood up.

The man she assumed was Captain sat at a bench. Upon seeing Stella, he stood. "You're late. Don't let it happen again."

"Screw you. Who the hell are you and where's my uncle? I swear if you harm him, I will personally cut you into little pieces and feed you to the gators." Stella's speech was pressured. In his mirrored sunglasses, she saw her jaw clenched.

With a hard wrench to her elbow, Captain practically yanked Stella off her feet, causing his sunglasses to fall. Though he stood two inches taller, his tanned and muscular build made him appear larger. He was Latino heritage with shoulder-length curly dark brown hair and a chiseled jaw, full lips. He looked like a body builder. Although it had begun to rain, he still wore a tank top, obviously wanting to showcase his muscular biceps. The eye patch and bandage to his left forearm didn't exactly improve his looks. He resembled Captain Hook. The only thing missing was the hook.

Stella pulled away, glaring into his hazel eye. She saw pure evil.

"I don't take threats!" He snarled. "You do what I say. When I say. No questions. You'll get your uncle back." Captain removed a cell phone from his linen shorts pocket and gave it to her. "Answer when I call."

Stella shoved a white bag at Captain. "My uncle has a heart condition and needs these meds."

"We'll see." He snatched the bag and scanned her up and down.

"What is it exactly you want from me?" Stella crossed her arms.

"In due time." He jutted his chin and spun on his heels.

"What the freak does that mean?" She ran after him. "Don't

forget the meds. If he dies, you'll be looking at murder charges."

Captain stopped and turned. He jabbed his finger in her sternum. "Is that a *threat*, sweet cheeks? No cops or you won't find him in one piece. If at all. As a matter of fact, you can't tell anyone about our little deal. And answer that cell when it rings. Now move on." He waved his hand dismissively.

She swallowed hard, sucked her teeth, and stomped away.

"Make sure Foxy doesn't call the cops neither," he called out.

Stella grunted. So much she wanted to say to that ass but she kept her thoughts to herself. For now.

CHAPTER 10

◆

ESSIE QUINLAN BOARDED Rose's superyacht. She called out for Rose or anyone else. No reply. So, she took herself on a mini tour.

Essie was no stranger to super and mega yachts. But never one belonging to a relative. She found what she assumed was the sky lounge and looked around. She immediately spotted a grand piano and glided onto the bench. She ran her hands over the exotic wood finish. As much as she wanted to tickle the ivories, it was frowned upon without permission. Not to mention it would surely bring in the crew.

Essie rose and continued scanning the lounge, admiring the ornate ceiling, bar, exotic stone, and power double doors leading to the aft. She then spotted a card table with a Sudoku and smiled. Essie picked up the book, settled into a soft leather recliner with her feet up. While the number puzzles were not much of a challenge to her, she was impressed with whomever was working this Sudoku as it was one of the more difficult ones.

A few moments later, a six foot, 170-pound man stood in front of her. His hands behind his back at attention. She scanned him. His uniform was crisp, clean, not a bit of dirt. He appeared to be in his late forties, with brown eyes and short, dark brown hair that was slightly graying. He was debonair with a twinkle in his eyes, dimpled chin. Given his age, he wasn't hard to look at, she thought.

"Excuse me, madam," he said with a Mid-Atlantic accent. "Could you please identify yourself."

Essie lowered the footrest and hopped to her feet. She craned her neck as she looked up. With her small stature, he had about a foot on her.

"Hello, Jeeves." Essie firmly and quickly shook his hand. "I take it you are the Purser."

"You are correct. My name is Kahn. Kahn Fullerton, madam. But you did not answer my question."

"My name is Essie Lee Quinlan. My friends call me Essie Q. Reporting for duty, sir." Essie saluted him and clicked the heels of her tennis shoes together, her skort swaying.

"I don't recall a new crew member reporting." Khan scanned her. "And I would certainly hope you would never report to an employer in your attire."

Essie chuckled and nudged him playfully. "I'm just messing with you. I'm Rose's cousin."

"I was not informed Ms. Rose was expecting family. And may I ask, how did you board the yacht? The head security officer was ordered to have one of his men stand guard."

"No one was out there."

Khan keyed his radio. "Mr. Hooker report to the sky lounge at once. Mr. Hooker to the sky lounge."

"Hey, has anyone told you, that you resemble that late actor. Um … Grant."

"Yes, madam, Cary Grant." He rolled his eyes. "Quite often. But aren't you a bit young to be familiar with him?"

"My nana loved his movies." Essie nodded. "And not to state the obvious, but you were born in England."

"Yes, madam."

"Please call me, Essie."

"Very well, m—Essie."

"Hey, can you fetch me an iced tea?"

"I am not a dog, and do not fetch. But I can have a steward bring you a beverage."

Just then a giant of a man walked through the double power doors. "Yes, Mr. Khan," he said. "And how many times have I asked you to call me TJ? Mr. Hooker was my father."

Khan cleared his throat. "Okay … *TJ*. It appears we have a situation." He looked at her with narrowed eyes.

"My name is Essie, and I am *not* a situation. I told you I'm related to Rose." Essie stood with a scrunched nose, shaking her head, fists on hips.

"I definitely see a resemblance," TJ said with a chuckle.

Essie turned to the giant who stood an easy seven feet. And put her hand out for a shake.

He lifted Essie as if she were a doll, raising her to eye level.

"Unhand me, you ogre." She kicked his groin.

TJ dropped Essie to the floor with a pained "Ugh," and she landed on her buttocks. Springing up, she delivered a swift kick to his shin.

"Ouch, you little shit!" TJ hopped back.

Khan looked at TJ with an open mouth.

"Okay, that's enough." A woman's voice came out of nowhere. She walked up to Essie. "You're going to hurt him, Essie Lee."

Cousin Rose.

CHAPTER 11

I STOOD THERE a spell, chuckling at what my little cousin had done to poor TJ. I remembered how cute she was. Essie stood five feet, one inch, with natural platinum blonde hair that fell in silky short waves to just above her collar bone. She had icy blue eyes with long lashes. Fair complexion with a sprinkling of freckles across the bridge of her nose and on her cheek bones. Her shade of blonde hair was natural as it came from both her parents. It was extremely rare as 1-2% of the world's population had it. It was caused by a mutation in the MC1R gene.

She was lean with an athletic frame. Good muscle tone. I admired that. And unlike last time, she got permanent eye liner and must've tinted her lashes, as they were normally light. I noticed it because that's what I do, being a fair skinned red head. Our lashes would disappear into our face.

Sue greeted Essie with kisses. Lots of them. Even though she'd never met Essie, she sensed instinctively she was family.

"So, Ess. It's been a while." I hugged her. "You were what, eleven, twelve?"

"Thirteen, to be exact," she said, wiping off dog smouches.

"That's right. You'd just graduated from high school and enrolled in college," I said. "I assumed you'd have a doctorate or be president by now."

"I have two PhDs. But I'd rather not talk about that. And no thanks on the president thing."

"Wow, time flies. You haven't grown much."

Essie shook her head. "Gee, I've never heard that before, cuz!"

"Sorry, madam, I wasn't aware you were expecting visitors." Khan interrupted our little family reunion.

"I wasn't," I said to Khan and turned back to Essie. "Was I?"

"Nope," she said with a cheeky grin, standing with her shoulders back. Just like Grandma Lil.

"Oh, correction. Mr. Khan, the concierge doctor will be here at ten to visit with Lily."

"Very well, madam. I will inform security. If you will all excuse me. I have work to do." Khan turned on his heels and left.

TJ stood with his arms crossed, glaring at Essie.

"Essie, can you please apologize to TJ?"

"He goes first." She pointed. "He picked me up like a figurine."

I looked at TJ who just shrugged.

"Please apologize to one another."

They shook hands, but neither appeared to mean it. TJ turned to exit and then spun. "I really am sorry, Essie. I like your spunk." He smiled. "I can see the family resemblance. You're a cross between Rose and Saki. All of you beauties have blue eyes, different shades too." He smiled and left the room.

Just then Lily walked in followed by Saki.

"What's the ogre laughing about?" Saki inquired.

"See, I called him that and he tossed me on the ground."

"Cousin!" Saki picked up Essie, giving her one-hundred-pound cousin a hug. She set her down. "What are you doing here?"

"Well, if it isn't Saki O'Brien," Essie said.

"Saki O'Brien-*Powers*." She put her hand out and flashed her wedding ring.

"I heard. Congrats!" Essie said. "Sorry I didn't have a chance to call and formally congratulate you. I was traveling Europe, visiting my folks."

"Sounds like a blast," Saki said. "I've been wanting to go there."

Lily stepped up. "Your aunt Lillian told me all about you. I'm Rose's friend, Lily."

Essie and Lily shook hands.

"Your aunt had been trying to reach you to help with the ranch while I was on the mend," Lily said.

"I heard. After visiting my parents in Ireland, I set off on a backpacking trip and by the time I got hold of Aunt Lil, it was too late. She'd found some—"

"Yeah. She did," Lily snapped. "She could've really used your help."

"Lily, she didn't know." I replied. Lily was never cruel or snippy. Good thing Dr. Ryan was going to examine her.

Lily slumped into the chair, shoulders drooping. "I'm sorry."

Essie walked over and put her hand on Lily's shoulder. "It's okay."

I picked up the Sudoku. "I don't remember finishing this."

"It took a couple minutes," Essie said.

"I'd been working on it for a month," I said. "That's right, you're the family genius."

"Nah, just good with numbers." Essie smiled.

"And good with people." Saki leaned into me. "She really is a genius."

"Yep," I said in a hushed tone watching Essie and Lily have a quiet conversation and then hug.

I studied her. Why did Essie show up out of the blue and why now?

My phone rang with a FaceTime call from Grandma Lil. I excused myself and returned to my room. Sue stayed behind, visiting.

I set the phone on my desk. "Hi, Gran." I updated her on my fun evening, leaving out my possible encounter with a relative of Gil Fox.

All she could do was shake her head and laugh. I could see she was also at her desk, looking out at her ranch in Darby, Montana.

"Question, Gran," I said in a serious tone. "Did you send any babysitters out here?"

Grandma furrowed her brows and shook her head. "Nope." Then typed at her keys.

"Lily thinks she's being followed. It's happened a couple of times now. She just told me about a second incident at breakfast. And last night, I could've sworn someone was watching me. But whoever it was, took off in a hurry."

"I would've taken off too had I been witness to your monkeyshines."

I heard Grandma's laptop ding.

"You're busy. Should we talk later?"

"No … just ordering supplies." Gran spun around in her chair. Her back was to the computer. There wasn't any order on the screen.

I knew my grandma enough now to discern when she was telling a tall story. Her fib was as large as the Grand Canyon.

"Oh, guess who just arrived? Essie Lee."

"I'd been trying to get a hold of her. My niece said Essie was visiting them. They traveled to Cork for a few days for some mother-daughter bonding. And then Essie took off on another adventure." Grandma laughed but it sounded more like a nervous chuckle.

Suddenly, Grandma's computer chimed again. My eyes were drawn to a chat message that appeared. It wasn't my intention to invade her privacy, but what I read puzzled me.

"Gran, who is M?"

Grandma dropped her phone and picked it up. "Um … no one … w—why?"

The second lie.

"I didn't mean to see your private message. But you asked someone you referred to as M if they were in Florida?" I stood and paced.

"It's nothing. Leave it alone." Her tone was strong and clear through the phone.

I knocked over my papers. When I bent to pick them up, Grandma disconnected. I tried to call back, but she didn't answer.

My gran was swimming in a sea of deceit. And the last time I was in Montana, she tried to throw me off track by telling me I should be a bodyguard and not take over her secret squirrel operations.

CHAPTER 12

FOXY RETURNED TO the Dancing Flamingo. Or as the locals called it, the Flamingo. She hesitated walking through the doors as her shift was cut short last night. She held her breath and stepped inside. Her eyes needed a moment to adapt to the darkness of the club.

"Well, it's 'bout damn time you show up," Harlee exclaimed, leaning against the bar, foot tapping. Her Northern Florida drawl came through loud and clear. Especially when she was mad. And pissed she was. Foxy had seen the ornery side of her. "We had to have one of the other dancers cover your set. This is a business, not a day care!"

"I ... I'm sorry, Harlee." Foxy wrung her hands. Her eyes filled with tears.

"Never mind my baby sister. She can be cantankerous for someone so young." Nala elbowed in front of Harlee. "Sheesh, you'd think she was eighty, not in her forties. "*I*," she squinted at her sister, "was worried. It's not like you to leave in the middle of work. Bless your heart. Come sit. You look plumb tired." Nala motioned to the bar and poured a cup of coffee.

"I had a situation." Foxy proceeded to tell the owners of the Flamingo what had happened last night. She kept staring at Nala until she had to ask. "What is going on with your face?"

"Damned lip filler. Had some work done yesterday." Nala looked back at Harlee, again. "You said it wasn't noticeable. But never mind me. What do you need?"

Harlee shrugged as her facial features softened. She plopped on a bar stool next to Foxy, tying her cream blonde hair in a ponytail. Nala sat on Foxy's other side, rubbing her back.

"Wait! We have the security cameras back there," Harlee said, pulling up the feed on her phone. "Doggonit. That jerk disabled them."

"Did you call the cops?" Nala asked.

"I … I'm not certain what I'd tell them. I only have a description of the man. My credit card company advised me to file a police report because my cards were stolen. But that man said he'd kill me if I did."

"Now that's a pickle. But you said a woman at the marina came to your rescue. Maybe you can track her down. You know, as a witness." Harlee's tone was more concerned.

"I agree with my sister for once," Nala said.

"What did this man want?" Harlee asked.

"Something I don't have. A document or USB drive that was supposedly mailed to me." Foxy dropped her head on the bar. A thought occurred; she sat up again and looked around. "Where's Stella? She said you all called her into work early to buy supplies and help board up."

"No. I didn't," Harlee said.

"Me neither," Nala concurred.

"Hmm, that's odd." Foxy wiped her tears. She was not an emotionally driven person, but this rattled her to the core. She sat tall. "I don't know what to do. I can't go back to my apartment." She paused. "He has my purse. Good thing I had my laptop here. And a couple of my college books. I was working on a paper between sets. And studying for an upcoming exam."

"I think you need to re-consider filing a report. This jerk can't get away with it." Nala looked at one of her bouncers who had just arrived. "We can have our guys protect you. Take the day off. Clear your head. Besides, we may close the doors early."

"I don't feel safe at home."

"I agree. You can't go home until he's caught," Nala said. "We have that room upstairs."

Foxy rubbed her face and yawned.

"You didn't sleep well, did ya?" Harlee asked.

"No, I slept on Stella's couch."

"Crash upstairs for a few," Nala offered. "I'll have the cook whip up something for ya."

"I think I'll take you up on that. Maybe I'll wake up with a clearer mind. Thank you."

Then Stella walked into the Flamingo.

All three turned their heads toward Stella. Foxy lifted a hand to her brow as the light from the outside blinded her.

"Hey, Stella. I thought you'd beat me here," she said.

"It's starting to pour out there." Stella shimmied out of her raincoat. "And … uh … I had an errand to run before coming in."

"I think there was some confusion," Nala said. "Your shift doesn't start 'till eleven. Neither of us called you in an hour early."

"Oh … it must've been a misunderstanding."

Foxy noted her friend's nervous behavior, then dismissed it. She had bigger problems.

"We're probably going to close early before the storm hits." Harlee walked toward the back. "I'm going to look at the schedule to see who's on tonight."

"And I've got some last-minute preparation to do for the lunch crowd." Nala walked away too.

"I've decided to call the police and make a report. Shoot. My phone. Can I borrow yours, Stella? I need to get a replacement one today." Foxy slid off the barstool.

"Um, cops? I thought you said that man threatened to kill you if you do. I … I wouldn't if I were you." Stella poured pretzels from a large container into small bowls.

"Stella, I have no money. No ID. That was all in my purse. What choice do I have?" Foxy leaned on the bar.

"You can borrow money, my car, whatever you need. And at least you have your computer, right? I think you said you left it here. That's something."

"Yeah. But my credit card company and my bank urged me to make a report."

"Well, it's your ass!" Stella snapped.

"Stella! I was a victim. He was going to kill me last night. I think the police should be aware of that. I can't get my life back without that report." Foxy paused.

"You're right. Maybe you should go back to my apartment and um, take a nap. Then when you wake, you can call the police." Stella reached into her purse and pulled out her car keys. "Take my car."

"I'm too tired to drive. I'm going to crash upstairs. Nala and Harlee offered it to me."

As Foxy walked away, she heard a cell phone ring. She watched Stella look around as she answered. A few moments later Stella grabbed her jacket and bolted outside.

What was going on with her friend?

CHAPTER 13

❖

AFTER ESSIE AND I caught up, I glanced at my watch; the concierge doctor was going to arrive soon. Lily was spitting fire that I called Dr. Ryan, but calmed a bit after she admitted I was right. Not to mention I only had Ryan another day. Once I was no longer a billionaire, I wouldn't be able to afford her.

I took Essie and Saki, along with Sue, and we left the yacht.

Francine weighed heavily on me, so we made our way to her apartment to return her purse and check on her. Simon and Tucker would have joined us, but after they finished with Saki's house, they were helping a friend of Tucker's.

While we made the fifteen-minute drive to Francine's apartment in Miami Beach, I told Essie about my escapades last night. Although my sis had already heard it from Lily, Saki said it was funnier coming from the horse's mouth. As we pulled up to Francine's place, I was shocked. You'd think being this close to the beach it wouldn't be so run down.

"Her apartment is upstairs." I put my Range Rover in Park as I contemplated the neighborhood.

Before I got out of the vehicle, I opened my fanny pack and considered taking out my Springfield Hellcat 9mm and carrying it. Since I was still in my yoga pants from earlier, I had no choice but to use my pack to carry my gun. Plus, after everything that happened last night, I wanted it nearby. Just as I opened my door, the rain started so I strapped the fanny pack around my waist, put on my coat and handed the gals theirs.

As we climbed the stairs, I scanned the complex with my hand ready to draw my pistol. As a parole agent, I used to frequent these types of neighborhoods. Cruising for felons. So, I was ever vigilant. Head on a swivel.

"I see you're packing," Essie nodded to my pack.

"Yeah, there isn't a time where she's not," Saki said. "Hey Sis, now that you're no longer in law enforcement, was it hard to get a concealed carry out here?"

"Didn't have to, but I did. And no. I sailed through the process with flying colors."

Essie stopped. "You're not on leave? I guess we have more to catch up on."

"That we do." I pointed to Francine's apartment.

I was about to draw my pistol and then remembered that I needed to act like a civilian now. Not to mention, I had un-armed back-up. I looked at my two companions and Sue and considered. In a 'hood like this, I kind of wished Simon and Tucker were with us.

When we made it to her apartment, I rapped on the door—okay, pounded. I couldn't shake my cop knock I'd been accused of having. Another thing I'd have to re-learn. Sheesh. But it was already open. The door had been splintered and the lock busted.

"Do you see what I see?" Essie pointed to the window.

We all saw as the shades were open too. This time I drew my gun and entered with it pointed out. I pushed the gals back and made a hand gesture to Sue. We'd been training in nonverbal communication.

I cleared her studio apartment in one full sweep. Because there was only a kitchenette and bathroom, it was fast. Not to mention the closet had no doors. But Francine's apartment had been trashed. It appeared someone was looking for a specific object. I'd seen this type of handiwork before.

"Close the door, shut the shades." I barked orders.

Without asking, Saki did it. While Essie turned on the overhead light.

"What has she gotten herself into?" I scanned the studio.

I had no clue if Francine was a tidy person. Her textbooks were tossed off the small table that was obviously also used to apply her make-up. Her mirror, make-up, brushes etc. were all over the floor. Her place had been searched with a fine-tooth comb. Perhaps looking for something small. And the pages of her books were thumbed through.

"We need to make this fast, ladies. Divide and conquer. Whoever did this, and my hunch is it was the creep from last night, may return."

"What are we looking for?" Saki asked.

"Anything that could tell us something about this poor girl," I said.

"Why are you so interested in her?" Essie asked.

"Your cousin rescues strays, both dogs and people." Saki looked at Sue.

"Sue wasn't a stray. A dirtbag was abusing her. So, I hit him with my car and took her."

Essie and Saki fell silent, staring at me.

"You said that as if you were just ordering a pizza." Saki laughed.

"Cuz," Essie interjected. "I like your style."

I started looking through Francine's chest of drawers; it was easy as the contents were dumped on the floor. I methodically searched her clothes looking for anything that might lead us to where she may have gone. And then I remembered seeing her phone in her purse. I was so messed up this morning, it didn't occur to me to turn it on.

"Saki, can you grab her cell out of her purse and power it on?"

Saki obliged. "Sorry, Rose. It appears it's dead."

"There's a wall charger." Essie pointed to the cord on the other side of her bed.

While my accomplices continued their search, I hit pay dirt. "Found a recent paycheck stub. Our girl works at a place called the Dancing Flamingo. And that's also what I discovered earlier during my internet search."

"Of course you did, Rose. James would be proud." Saki snickered. "You said the Dancing Flamingo? That's a strip club." She continued messing with Francine's phone.

Essie and I stopped our search and gave one another a quizzical look.

"Ookay. Do I want to know?" I asked.

"One of my staff moonlights as a dancer there."

I raised my brows.

"Hey, living out here can be expensive."

"True, but a stripper? Aren't there better paying gigs where you can keep your clothes on?" I asked.

"Hey, they're not drug addicted hookers. There are classy clubs, too," Saki said in a defensive tone. "Some dancers are working their way through college, single mothers, or even moonlighting, like my friend. I happen to know the Dancing Flamingo is a classy joint."

"Okay ... okay." I held up my hand in protest. "I misjudged. My apologies. Stand down, tiger. But it doesn't sound classy when you say 'joint.'" I laughed.

"Good point, sis," Saki said, raising the phone. "No service. She probably had it shut off."

"That was smart," I said.

"That she is." Essie held up an organic chemistry book. She sat and thumbed through it, then held up a small square. "I wonder who is this man in the photo. It was between the pages."

I walked over. "She looks happy. It was obviously taken at her high school graduation."

"Looks like she graduated four years ago," Essie said.

"Yes, she did. But what makes you say that, Ess?" Saki asked looking at it. "Did you cheat and look at her driver's license, too?"

"No, I didn't. But look at their clothing, hair style, and the cell phone she's holding."

"You're very observant," Saki said.

"Nah," Essie replied. "And some notes here have the name Foxy on them."

"When I combed her socials earlier, her friends call her Foxy." I stared at my cousin for a second.

I knew Essie was a genius, even though she refused to be tested. But she was a keen observer, too. I brushed it off and took the picture from her. My heart sank. I slumped on her bed and studied the man in the photo. It was Gil Fox. The last time I saw him, I was examining his body in a cold room just last month.

"Does he look familiar, Rose?" Saki asked.

"Um ... no. Uh, not at all."

I texted Simon: **Need Gil's prints. Stat please.**

After Gil's murder last month, Simon and I inspected his body. We drew blood and Simon took his fingerprints with his app. I vowed to find his people. But it appeared I didn't have to search far.

"Looks like an only child too," Essie said interrupting my thoughts.

"Why do you say that?" Saki asked.

"There's another framed graduation photo of the three of them, on the floor here." Essie picked it up. "An important milestone. You'd think if she had other siblings, they'd all be there." She cocked her head to the side. "And this man is not her father."

I spun my head. Now how did she know that? I had assumed as much.

"It's obvious the woman is her mother. They could be twins. The man and the woman share the same nose and smile. And look at their cheek bones."

We were all silent, examining the picture.

"Rosie, you're quiet. What are you thinking?" Saki asked.

I couldn't tell my baby sister the truth. She didn't need to get dragged into my tangled web and mad CIA experimentation theory. It was too dangerous.

"Um … nothing," I said. "We just need to help Francine. She's obviously in serious trouble."

I reflected on what Lily told me yesterday. Could she be right? Did someone find her? Find us? And Grandma was most definitely hiding something. I looked up, considering, tapping my chin.

That's when I noticed it. I squinted to be sure. Yep. A listening device up in Francine's overhead light fixture.

"Well, I think we're done here," I said.

"I'm not done," Saki said.

"No, there's nothing more to look at. And I think we should just forget going to her work."

Essie and Saki spun their heads in my direction with their heads tilted as if I'd lost my mind.

I put my finger to my lips and pointed up to the light. "This girl's got more problems than I want to deal with."

I nodded to my team, and we left.

CHAPTER 14

CAPTAIN SAT IN his Cadillac Escalade outside the Flamingo. He'd just called Stella asking for an update on Foxy. She told him Foxy was sleeping upstairs. He had to plan his next move carefully. The Dancing Flamingo was known for hiring retired cops as bouncers. He was already physically compromised and didn't need any more injuries.

Stella also informed him the Flamingo was closing early due to the incoming storm. Being raised in Florida, Captain wasn't afraid of hurricanes; he'd been through plenty. So, he'd wait it out. A thought occurred. If the girl left, he'd need a way of tracking her.

Captain remembered an AirTag he'd used in his last job was in his duffel bag. He retrieved it and paired the device together with one of his many burner phones. He then remembered a previous glitch with the tag. He wanted to be sure it was working, particularly indoors. So, he ordered Stella outside.

A few seconds later, Stella marched across the street. This time her raincoat was open. Her work attire left nothing to the imagination; skimpy shorts and a matching hot pink tank with "Dancing Flamingo" in neon green print across her chest, she could easily be one of the dancers.

He took off his shades.

"What do you have?" She must've seen him looking at her breasts, because she zipped up. "And when are you going to release my uncle? Did you give him his meds?"

"I've got that covered. Don't worry your sexy little head off."

She glared at him. "Nice eye patch. Is that for show?"

"Drop this in her purse." Captain handed her the AirTag as he told her that two big guys and a Rottie attacked him.

"She doesn't have her purse," Stella hissed. "She thinks you took it."

"I didn't. She obviously lost it."

And then Captain recalled overhearing some women in her apartment stating they would leave it. Come to think of it, who were they? Cops? No, she hadn't called them yet. Or had she? He pondered.

"Then what the hell am I supposed to put it in?" She kept looking back at the Flamingo like someone doing a drug deal, hiding from the police.

"Not my problem."

"You're an asshole."

He shrugged. "Not the first time I've been called an assoholic. Let me know when the bouncers have gone home. Unless she leaves before then." He showed her the app. "Make sure this is paired before you leave. There was a malfunction the last time I used it. Tap this here—" he pointed— "and bring it back when you're done."

"You're a malfunction. I know how this works, jerk off." She snatched the phone, spun on her wet glittery tennis shoes and ran across the street.

Stella returned to the club, leaving her coat on.

"Where the hell have you been?" Harlee barked. "You had a customer. Nala had to cover for you." She stood with hands on hips.

"I'm sorry. I ... I had to take an important call."

"More important than work!"

"Harlee, that's enough." Nala slapped her sister upside her head. "What in tarnation is wrong with you, woman?"

Harlee heaved a deep sigh. "I'm just stressed that we've gotta close early. Gonna lose a lot of money. And we have that expansion to pay for." She turned back to Stella. "Just get to work."

"O ... Okay. Um. But I have to use the bathroom. You know, that time of the month."

Harlee groaned.

Stella ran back to the employee lounge and dressing rooms. She tried Foxy's locker and found it unlocked. She kept peeking over her shoulder and delicately opened it. Just then one of the dancers came in and made her way to her locker, pulling out her costume. Stella smiled and nodded and watched the gal go to the dressing room.

Nala and Harlee valued the girls' privacy when they changed. Not to mention, the male staff had access to the lockers as well.

Stella began to sweat under the raincoat and swiftly opened Foxy's locker. She scanned it for the ideal place. She could put it in her backpack … no, that wouldn't work. What if Foxy left it there again? Stella thought for a beat and that's when she saw it hanging on a hook: Foxy's raincoat.

If Foxy left, she would for sure wear it. Stella closed the locker door and with her mind's eye vigilant, verified the AirTag and cell were paired before dropping the tag deep into the inner pocket. She spun around and almost stumbled.

Foxy stood there.

"What are you doing with my coat?" Foxy glared, arms crossed.

"I … I was going to put cash in there, to surprise you." She wiped the sweat from her forehead and gave a nervous chuckle as she discreetly dropped Captain's cell in her pocket and pulled out a wad of cash. "I thought you were sleeping upstairs."

"I couldn't rest. I've got a big exam on Monday. And keep your money, I don't need charity. But thank you. Also, may I use your cell to call the police?"

"Oh sure, let me go get it. It's behind the bar."

"I just saw you put it in your pocket."

"No, this was left on the bar … um, I'm going to turn it into lost and found." Stella shoved past her friend and made a bee line for the rear exit.

"Where are you going? The bar's the other way."

"A quick smoke break."

"When did you start back up?"

"What is this the Spanish Inquisition? Get off my back."

Stella slipped out the door and leaned against the building. She felt sick to her stomach. Not only was Foxy her friend, but she didn't deserve to be treated that way. Especially after all she'd gone through last night. Stella stood tall and pulled the phone out of her pocket and checked the device was still paired. She looked over her shoulder and ran back to the jerk wad waiting across the street.

CHAPTER 15

◆

IT WAS ELEVEN thirty when Essie, Sue and I returned to the yacht. Saki drove to her fitness center in downtown Miami to make sure all her employees were gone. But not before they boarded the windows. The perks of being the owner/boss.

I parked at the marina, and we headed straight for the yacht. I was eager to hear the results of Lily's appointment; plus, we needed a serious chat. I wasn't going to keep her out of my findings. This involved her, too.

Before we left, the crew had been preparing to get the Max One moved into dry dock storage ahead of the weather.

Ideally it would have been done already, but last night's fundraiser had been planned for months. And since it drew big money donors, it could not be changed. Even though I was walking away from it all, I still cared what happened to the crew members and about the foundation.

We boarded and instead of the cleared decks and silent rooms I expected, the crew were running around like school children who'd had too much sugar. But in a methodical manner. No one appeared to panic, just moving swiftly and efficiently. They were literally battening down the hatches, securing anything that couldn't be removed. I stood with my mouth agape. This was not how a yacht was prepared for dry dock.

And then I noticed my bags were already on the lower deck. Ready for my departure.

"Mr. Khan, am I being evicted already?" I snickered.

"Madam." Khan stood at attention, hands behind his back,

straight faced. "There's been a slight problem. The last dry dock storage gave the Max One's reservation away. They assumed we had journeyed out to sea. We are securing everything to the best of our ability, including tillers and wheels. We've arranged the dock lines to keep the yacht supported as there is great anticipation for the rise in water surges. We are going to power down any electronic devices, except for the bilge pumps."

"We have adequate batteries for the pump. They are fully charged to outlast the storm. With backups, of course. We have impact resistant tires, as they can offer the yacht extra protection. The captain is preparing as well. We've encountered this problem previously. Usually, Mr. Max had us head out to sea. But time does not allow as the hurricane is headed this way. It is a Category Two but could be upgraded." He gestured to my bags. "And I had the purser bring your suitcases. You need to go somewhere safe."

"Thank you, Khan," I said. "The Max One is in stellar hands with you."

"If you need any assistance," Essie said. "I've spent my fair share of time on a yacht or two."

"I appreciate the offer, Ms. Essie, but it's unnecessary," Khan responded. "We have it as you all say, dialed in." He smiled.

"Again, I'm grateful." I looked around the deck. "Where's Lily?"

"She is packing as well."

"The minute everything is handled, please send everyone home," I said.

"Madam, some live as far as Orlando. No time. They were going to stay at the Mo—"

"Absolutely not. As long as I still have the money, I will pay for the W Hotel in Miami."

"But that is the most exclu—"

I held out my palm. "They all deserve it. Is that understood? Everyone leaves before it hits."

"Very well ma'am." He stood tall, eyes shiny. "On behalf of the crew of the Max One, it has been an honor to serve you."

I felt tears forming as well. I cleared my throat. "You've all welcomed me with open arms. It's *I* that should be thanking you." I pulled Khan in for a hug.

His rigid body gave him away; he was clearly uncomfortable. Khan gave me a cursory pat on the back but then succumbed to my charm and returned my embrace.

"Ahem." We turned around, and there was TJ holding a phone receiver out to me. "I don't mean to interrupt, Ms. Rose. Doctor Ryan is on the phone. She would like a word with you."

"Thank you." I took the phone, stepped away from my crew and Essie, and listened to the doctor's information. "Unh, huh I see. Okay. How quickly can you get the blood panel? Can we put a rush on it? Unh, huh. Thank you." I disconnected.

"Is Ms. Lily, okay?" TJ asked.

"Yeah, is she?" Simon's voice boomed from behind me.

I spun and Simon and Tucker were now standing with TJ, Essie, and Khan. All of them staring at me. Probably waiting for me to give away Lily's secrets.

"Uh, the doctor didn't say. Patient confidentiality."

A white lie since Dr. Ryan had Lily's permission to tell me. She was concerned about Lily's symptoms. Lily was complaining about chest tightness, nausea, and trouble sleeping. Even blurry vision. She kept it vague about the drug, nor did she mention our CIA experimentation theory. She only told Dr. Ryan she was poisoned by an unknown substance.

That was the partial truth. We knew the source.

CHAPTER 16

I ASKED ESSIE and Tucker to take Sue for a walk around the marina and check the area where I found Francine's purse, while Simon and I chatted with Lily. Tucker grunted in his usual fashion and left with Essie, while Simon wore a concerned look on his face. But he also gave a nod of understanding. Other than Lily, Simon was the only one privy to what occurred in Montana last month.

The minute Simon and I entered Lily's cabin, she stopped packing and sat on her bed.

"You spoke to Doctor Ryan?"

"*I* didn't. I'd like to hear what's going on." Simon sat next to Lily, rubbing her back.

She put her head on his shoulder. "I'm okay."

I sighed and pulled up a chair and joined them. "I hope so. The doctor is putting a rush on the lab tests. But with the storm, there may be a delay."

"So?" Simon urged.

"I'm more curious about what you found at the apartment," Lily said.

"Simon first." I glanced at Lily, ready to let her share her health problems if she wanted.

"A couple weeks after I was … drugged by Mac." Lily growled. "I started having headaches. I thought it was from the trauma of being kidnapped and shot."

"But you were shot in the thigh," Simon said.

"Exactly. And then I assumed it was a reaction to the pain meds the hospital gave me. But they continued long after I stopped the medication. And then I began getting dizzy spells and not sleeping. And this morning chest pains started." She drew a deep breath.

Simon leaped to his feet. "I'd like to find that dirtbag, Mac, and beat the crap out of him." Simon hit his palm with his fist as he paced.

"You and me both," I said. "But don't forget he was just a hired hitman."

"Yeah," Lily said. "Hired by the CIA."

"Speaking of." I looked over my shoulder to make sure we didn't have ears on our conversation. "Lily, I don't mean to alarm you, but our suspicion of Francine being related to Gil is true."

Lily's face turned white. "How do you know?" She too jumped to her feet.

I raised my hand and asked her to sit.

She obliged.

"Essie found a picture of Gil, Francine, and a woman we suspect was her mother. It was tucked between the pages of a textbook in her apartment."

"What are the odds? Was Gil her father?" Lily asked.

"No, we think he was Francine's uncle. When I did an internet search and combed Francine's socials, I didn't find any mention or picture of Gil. No family pics. Only friends. He was almost identical to the woman in the picture. Essie pointed out the similarities between them."

"Observant young woman," Simon said.

"She's a smarty pants, too." I stood. "But back to Francine. She's in serious trouble. We need to find her and help her. I know where she works. I say we pay her a visit."

"Wait, Rose. Do you think that whoever has been following us is linked to all this?"

"What?" A crease formed on Simon's forehead. "You're both being followed, and *neither* of you thought to mention it?"

"Down, boy," I said. "It's uncertain if we're being followed." I told him about Lily and my encounters.

"Maybe with what happened to Lily in Montana, you're both being paranoid?" Simon asked.

"Doesn't mean someone *isn't* following us," I said.

Lily rolled her neck and started to hyperventilate.

"Lily, do you have a paper sack in here?" Simon looked around her cabin.

"Yes," I said. "I purchased some toiletries and put them in her bathroom." I walked over and dumped the contents and gave the bag to Lily.

"Breath into this," Simon said to Lily.

Lily took a few breaths as Simon and I monitored.

"I need to go to my stateroom and get my laptop and gather some papers." I headed to the door.

Lily took the bag away from her face. "And finish your resume?"

"Yeah ... how'd you know?"

"I saw you turn it over," Lily said. "What skill set are you putting on it?"

"Still working on that part."

"How about punching jerks in the face or surviving leaps from a moving vehicle minutes before it crashed into a mountain side." Lily smiled.

"Hmm ... maybe?"

"Kidding, Rose, wow," Lily said.

"I got it," Simon said. "Shooting a bazillion people."

"Like I said a *bazillion* times before, it was only five."

"And an alligator," Lily snarked, obviously feeling better. "Don't forget that."

"It was a crocodile," I said. "Remember, it was planted by some mafia guys in the Keys."

Lily and Simon simultaneously nodded with scrunched faces. Both most likely reflecting on Saki's husband, James', recollection of watching his enemy being chomped by a croc and his own attack and how I saved him from it.

"Hey, I'm well spoken," I said.

"More like smart-assed," Simon said with a raised brow.

"At times," I said. "But I can diffuse situations. And have in the past."

"Yeah, with your charming, persuasive personality," Simon said. "Oh, and your need to control everything, too."

I gave him a half-raspberry.

He walked over, gave me a big bro hug. "You know I love you."

"Me too." I smiled.

"So, what do you want to do when you grow up?" Lily asked with a serious tone.

Simon pushed away from our hug. It was getting too sappy for him. "That implies she plans on growing up."

"What is this, my roast? Any hoo. I've got time before the storm hits. I want to run Gil Fox. Now that I know he has family down here. And a sister someplace."

"Dare I ask how you're going to do that?" Simon asked.

I looked at him and shrugged.

"That answered my question," Simon said. "I'm going to see if Essie and Tucker found anything. Tucker was also going to check with the marina's security office. Maybe he was able to get a plate or description of the attacker. Tucker is connected down here. Someone will talk." He walked out.

"Sounds good." My voice dropped as I scanned Lily's stateroom.

"Are you trying to avoid the elephant in the room?" Lily asked.

"No. I'm at peace with giving all this up." I waved my hand around. "The money was never mine to begin with. I only want to—"

"Save Francine Fox?" Lily stood. "It's just like you to come to another's rescue. Sometimes you've got to look out for yourself. And in this case, you do. You're going to be homeless soon."

"That's midnight tomorrow. I want to find Francine *today*."

"I'd like to meet her too, after I finish packing. I ... I feel responsible for her uncle's death." Seriousness returned to Lily's face as she rubbed her chest again and removed a roll of antacid from her pocket and popped a couple.

I considered her symptoms. What if the drug Mac gave Lily was making her sick or even causing a heart attack like we assumed it did to Gil?

That thought I'd keep to myself until the test results came back.

CHAPTER 17

"SOMEONE'S SHOWN INTEREST in Gil." Agent H spoke quietly into his cell from his go to spot at the memorial garden. With it being Saturday, there weren't many people working. "What's going on down there?"

A pause fell on the line.

"Juno, I'm waiting."

"I haven't a clue what to say," Juno said. "I know better than to search his name. What's the IP address?"

"You know I'm not at liberty to reveal that information." Agent H took a long sip from his bottled water.

"What do you mean? If you entrusted me with this task, how am I expected to track who's been investigating Gil!" she snapped.

"On a need to know. And what's the status?"

"A delay."

"What kind of *delay*?"

"It's nothing to be concerned about. But we have a hurricane brewing down here. It's due to hit landfall by the end of today. I might need an extension."

"This is unacceptable. It was a simple job your guy should've dealt with last night."

"Well, he was injured."

"By whom? A little college student?"

"Apparently, she had two large men, and a vicious dog come to her aid."

Agent H loosened his tie. "Not my problem. It must be done tonight! I want everything this girl has."

"It will be. Now back to the search. You must understand it wasn't me. I'll check with my guy, but I doubt it's him. Do you have anyone else down here?"

"No, I don't." Agent H's phone dinged with an alert. Then a second one came through. "I need to go." He disconnected and dialed his trusted computer whiz analyst on his disposable phone. "It's me. Yes, this is a burner. Listen and don't say a word. I need you to get the location of two IP addresses. Stand by, I'm forwarding them." He texted the information. "I need it stat. I'll wait. Use this phone to text the addresses."

Agent H drew in a deep breath as he listened to the water coming off the rock outcropping, while on the other line his computer genius was typing away at lightning speed.

"Sir," the man said. "Both addresses are in Miami. Both laptops."

"And? Are they in the same location."

"No, sir. I sent you the addresses. One was from an apartment. Whoever it was used a local law enforcement database. And the second—I'm uncertain about the accuracy of this."

"Go on."

"The other was from a yacht. And well ..."

"I don't have all day!"

"The password was secured, and I traced who it belongs to." He paused. "Agent H. It's one of yours, sir."

"What!" Agent H's voice was so loud it caused the other CIA employees on their break to stop their conversations and stare.

"I triple checked."

"Keep this under your hat, am I clear? And delete everything you just ran. No records."

He disconnected and drew a note pad from his inside pocket and wrote down the information. Then Agent H dropped his phone and crushed it under the heel of his black loafer. He picked up the pieces and stuffed them into his pocket. Instead of returning to his office, Agent H headed directly for his vehicle. Blowing off an important meeting.

H sat in his car thinking. Who would have access to his passwords? Who would be interested in Gil Fox? After his death, Agent H just told the Agency Gil went off the rails and died of a heart attack in a seedy motel in a small nowhere town in Montana.

He neglected to reveal the exact location, and that Gil also had a postmortem gunshot wound. H had the details of his death covered up and his body quickly cremated upon his arrival back to D.C. He also covered up any involvement with Lily Cazier. He couldn't risk tying her to Gil. He even had his analyst erase any electronic correspondence between Gil and Lily.

He almost felt bad for her. After all, Lily's parents were killed in a plane crash. Another tragic accident. He was good friends with Lily's father, Gerald. They served together in the Air Force. And then it hit him. Who would still have their hands in unquestionable affairs? Agent H pulled out another burner phone and powered it on. He thumbed through his phone book and found her number and dialed.

"I get the hit called off your family, and this is how you repay me?" he snapped.

"What the hell are you talking about, Hansel?"

"Don't play coy, Lillian. You know damned well what I'm talking about. And don't call me that."

"I'd say your job is getting to you. You paranoid fool."

"Where are you right now?"

"None of your damned business."

"Just answer this, are you in Florida?"

"No, why?"

"And you didn't just conduct a search for Gil Fox, fingerprints and all? Using *my* code?"

"Heavens no! As far as I'm concerned that matter is closed. For good."

"Well, someone doesn't. And this is bad, Lillian."

"Will you tell me what this is about?"

"I apologize." He drew a deep breath and proceeded to tell her.

"Oh, this is bad. I … I have not used that password in a very long time. I promised you if I ever needed to use it, I would let you know first. Besides, I now have my own … don't ask."

"I apologize for accusing you. But who in Florida would be interested in Gil? There were two separate IP addresses used. One at an apartment in Miami. The user must be a local LE. And the other, on a yacht at a marina in Miami, just off the causeway."

"Did you say yacht?" Lillian asked.

"Yes. Do you know anyone there?"

Silence fell on the line.

"Lillian?"

"Um … no. But I've got to go. I promise I'll help you get to the bottom of it."

"No! Don't. The fewer people looking into this the better. I have someone down there working on a project for me."

"Oh … okay, then."

"Promise me, Lillian."

"I promise. Goodbye."

After Agent H disconnected, something was off. He knew Lillian enough to recognize when she was frazzled. And frayed she was. And he didn't buy what she was selling.

He picked up his phone and texted Juno.

It's H. New number. Call me now!

CHAPTER 18

IT WAS 1 P.M. when Saki, Sue and I were dropped off at the Dancing Flamingo while Essie and Lily shopped for supplies and checked into our hotel.

Lily had wanted to go with me. She said it was important to meet and apologize to Francine. Given her recent health scare, I didn't think that was a good idea, so I insisted she go with Essie. Since Essie was new to Florida, she could use someone who knew their way around. Lily finally agreed and they took off shopping.

The Dancing Flamingo was off the strip, no pun intended. Since I'd only been a full-time resident of Florida a few short weeks, I wasn't used to the updated Art Déco District in Miami Beach, known for its vibrant historic buildings.

I gazed in awe at the architecture. With pastel colors, neon lights, and geometric shapes, Miami Beach was not what I remembered growing up. It was now, let's just say, colorful. And that included the buildings. I suppose I didn't give it much thought as a child.

Simon and Tucker were itching to join us and found it ironic that we would go to a strip club without them, but this was *business*. They decided to follow up on a lead from what Tucker and Essie discovered when they talked to the head of security at the marina. The guy informed Tucker that one of his, now former, guards was paid off last night. He allowed a black Cadillac Escalade to drive onto the marina, no questions. The security footage was erased. But a second guard on duty heard the commotion and remembered hearing shouts coming from the docks and saw the vehicle. He was called away to the baby billionaire's out-of-control party. As was the Coast Guard.

It started raining harder when we exited my vehicle, and we practically sprinted to the front door. The instant I opened the door, I stood still for a second, allowing my eyes to adjust as most of these clubs were dimly lit. Although it wasn't a sunny day, it was still brighter outside. Once my vision regulated, I spotted a sign that said women were free and no cover for men during the day.

My eyes were then immediately drawn to the horseshoe-shaped stage. There were three poles strategically placed and two dancers moving rhythmically. The stage had a line of chairs; ten in all. There were five guys sitting front and center. For lunch hour, the club had few patrons. I then observed a few round tables behind the chairs. Men in business suits were in what appeared to be a serious conversation.

From what I gathered about strip clubs, they're the perfect location to carry on nefarious business meetings as the patrons are discreet and the music is loud. They're open during the day and provide a dark lunchtime meeting place with a multitude of distractions. Plus, the lack of windows and cameras makes videotaping nearly impossible. Unless done on someone's cell phone. A delicate operation, to be sure.

A strip club is surprisingly useful for gathering intelligence; the women are great sources of information as men have loose lips around beautiful women.

I continued scanning the place and noticed flat black paint with florescent dancing flamingos everywhere. Mirrors lined the walls.

One thing I didn't see were private rooms where lap dances were offered. This was the classiest strip club I'd ever been in. Not that I've frequented these places. It's all what I've heard about or seen on television.

The best part was the music was not deafening with that pounding and pulsating like most places. It was low enough that I heard the hum of the AC. It felt refreshing and cool. I hesitated to take off my raincoat, but I did and shook off the excess water.

A blonde woman in her forties greeted us. "What can I do for ya?" she asked with a southern drawl and looked at Sue. "No pets allowed."

"Oh shoot. I left her service vest in my car. We were just

dropped off. I promise she's a good girl."

Sue scampered to the woman and stared with her big brown puppy eyes, tail wagging.

"I'm a sucker for cuties." She gave Sue a scratch behind her ears. "What's her name?"

"Sue," I replied.

Right as she started to ask the usual "why Sue?" question, I cut her off.

"Long story. I named her after a friend." I reserved the unabridged version for people who planned on being in my life longer than a minute. Telling strangers she was named after my murdered friend, Sue Sullivan, was too much. So I'd been told.

The woman nodded, stepped back and scanned Saki and I from head to toe. She walked around us like we were a new vehicle. She all but kicked our tires.

"Not bad," she said.

"Huh?" I spun around to face her.

"Hold on." She walked behind the bar and presented Saki and I with two sheets of paper.

I held it under the leg lamp that sat on the bar. It was an application. "What's this for?"

"Ain't ya here for a job? I mean we take all ages and cup sizes." The woman looked at my breasts.

I peered at my B cups and pulled my raincoat toward my chest.

"Nice muscle tone in your arms and legs. Looks like ya workout." She continued scanning me. "But you need to do something about that awful bruise on your leg. Men don't find that attractive."

I perused my wardrobe. I was still wearing my yoga shorts and tank top from earlier. In my haste to pack and move boxes into storage, I'd neglected to change. And the injury on my thigh from where Simon shot me with the Simunition bullets was spreading and turning a pretty shade of purple. I was used to having bruises and didn't think anything of it.

"We're *not* here for a job," I finally said. "We're looking for a woman."

"Ooh, *that* club is across the street." She nodded to the door.

"We're not like that!" Saki snarked. "We prefer sausage."

"Saki!" I elbowed my baby sister. "We're looking for Francine

Fox. We came to return this." I held up her black purse.

"Hmm." The woman motioned for us to have a seat at the bar. She continued to study us a spell.

Just then, a woman with long, dark silky hair and a larger cup size than me emerged and moved behind the bar. "What can I get for you ladies?"

"They're here for *Francine*." She emphasized her name.

"Umm ... you cops?" The gal asked.

"No, do we look like cops?" Saki sniped again.

"No. But we get undercovers in here all the time," the blonde said. "My name is Harlee. I'm co-owner of the club. My sister, Nala, owns the other half." She returned her attention to the dark-haired lady. "This is Stella, she's the bartender and a friend of Fox—um Francine's. We can return her purse." She held out her hand.

"I'd prefer to give it to her in person. I need to ask her a couple of questions." I stood with my arms crossed, most likely wearing the cop face I've been told I pull out occasionally.

Harlee and Stella exchanged glances and fell silent. "And?" I asked, probably sounding pissed.

"She's uh ... not here." Stella glanced at Harlee.

"How did you come across her purse again?" Harlee asked.

"I'd rather not say," I replied. "It's a personal matter."

"What are your names and numbers?" Stella asked. "I can pass it along to her."

I looked at my feet and drew my right leg back, hand on hip and let out a heavy sigh. "You said you're friends of hers? I think she's in serious trouble." I returned my gaze to the other women.

"Wh—why do you say that?" Stella stammered.

I disregarded her question, grabbed a notepad and pen from the bar, scribbled my name, and handed it to Harlee.

"Rose O'Brien," Harlee read from the paper. "What makes you think she's in trouble?"

"My sister kicked a man's ass last night when he was attacking your friend. And Sue bit him." Saki pointed to Sue. "That's how."

My sister did not mince words or beat around the bush. She had no filter and swore like a sailor. I assumed she quit after having her baby. Saki said she knew when to turn off her potty mouth.

"Oh. I heard about that. That was you!" Harlee pulled me in for

71

a hug. "Thank you. We owe you a debt of gratitude." She turned to Stella and handed her the piece of paper with my name. "Their drinks are on the house. Hold tight." Harlee made her way to the back.

Saki and I asked for iced tea and spun around in our barstools. We watched more men pour into the club and check us out as they walked by. I felt like a piece of meat. How did these dancers handle it? But these guys were average dudes, looking for entertainment with their lunch. No mafia-looking guys. So much for my theory.

"Here ya go ladies." Stella put our tea on the bar.

I turned back and took a sip and immediately spit it out in my glass. "Oh, crap. This is a long island. Sorry, I meant virgin." I scrunched my nose.

"Virgin, huh?" A man's guttural laugh sounded from behind me. "I'll have hers." He said and nodded to a barstool. "May I?"

"Free country," I replied.

I looked down, to see Sue's hackles raise and she growled. I placed my hand on her back to quell her. I could tell she didn't like the guy. He was a bit creepy for my taste too and not because he was in a T&A club.

Saki sat to my left and the dude on my right. I felt him staring a hole through me as if he were trying to figure out the color of my underwear.

The bartender put down fresh beverages. Just as I drank, the creep said, "Mm, you smell *good*."

I put my glass down, stretched my neck, and sucked my teeth.

"Uh oh. If she cracks her knuckles, the chum's going down," Saki said to Stella and snickered.

He dragged his stool closer, his breath hot on my neck.

Sue growled at him again. This time I allowed her.

The guy then made another perverted "Mmm" sound.

That did it. I slowly turned my head, glaring at him. But he was now drooling over Saki. I cracked my knuckles.

"You got a problem, pal?" I growled through gritted teeth. "The dancers are that way." I pointed to the stage and pushed his stool away from me.

"Easy lady." He put his hands up in surrender. "Just makin' convo. Damn. You know you *are* in a bar."

I looked at Saki and we shared a WTF look. She narrowed her azure blue eyes. I knew my sister and we were probably thinking the same thing. As if being in a bar gave permission for us to be hit on. I was about to hop off my stool, but Saki beat me to it. She skipped around to the other side like a cheerleader, her high ponytail flapping around.

I turned to grab my tea, and the bartender was just about to say something, but I put my hand up and mouthed. *We got this*. I spun my stool back, crossed my legs and waited for the show. Popcorn would've been nice.

"You like what you see?" Saki pulled her shoulders back.

He nodded. "What I'd like are your digits, sweet cheeks." He licked his lips.

"You got it." Saki took a pen out of a plastic cup on the bar. "What's your name?"

"Joe … Joe Daddy." He let out a guttural belly laugh.

"Okay, *Joe*," Saki said with a mocking head shake. "Give me your hand." She wrote on his palm.

He grinned like he'd just won the lottery and put his hand to his eyes. "Fuck. Off!" The man kicked his barstool out from behind him.

Just as Saki headed for her stool, the dirt bag grabbed her by the ponytail and threw her on the floor.

I leaped off my seat. As Sue lunged at the man, I ordered her to stand down. I turned and palmed the jerk in the face with my left hand and thrust my right elbow, giving him a swift upper jab to his nose.

"Listen ass wipe!" I growled as he fell backward. He immediately jumped right back up and swung at me. My reflexes were quicker; I ducked, sprang up, and prepared for a fight with my fists up, ready to whip his perverted ass.

Before I could get another swing at him, two large men emerged from the back room along with Harlee. The two patrons that sat at a table closest to us also jumped to their feet. Obviously, gentlemen looking to come to the aid of two "helpless" women.

"Get him outta here boys," Harlee ordered. "He was eighty-sixed from here last week. If you ever return, Joe, I'll call the cops!"

Her two bouncers escorted the dude out the front door. One on either side.

"We've got rules," Harlee said. "Don't be an asshole and bring money. No pervs welcome here. Joe's broken all those rules. Last week he groped one of the girls. And it got him kicked out. Stella should've never served him." Harlee looked around, fists on her hips. "Where's Stella?"

CHAPTER 19

◆

AFTER STELLA POURED the non-alcoholic iced teas, she received a text message from Captain. She grabbed her coat and slipped out the front while Rose put the beat down on that shmuck, Joe. Served him right. She never liked the depraved drunk. The second she stepped out, vehicle lights flashed. And that's when she spotted Captain's Caddy parked curbside two doors down in front of a liquor store. He motioned for her to come inside. Since it was now starting to pour, she obliged.

"Damn it, I just had this detailed too." He handed her a towel. "Don't get it dirty."

"Thanks for your concern, Captain *Asshat*."

He shrugged. "I got your text. What'd you find out?"

"First, you release my uncle and then I'll tell you."

Captain reached into his waist band and pulled out a gun. He held it down low and aimed it at her. "How 'bout you tell me what's so important and I won't blow a hole in ya."

Stella growled and glared at him. "So. Two dudes and a Rottie put the beat down on you, huh?"

"You came out here to ask me that?" He sucked his teeth.

"How about *I* spread the word that a chick and her mutt did this to you?" She waved at Captain's bandaged arm and face. "And I heard Foxy nailed you in the eye with her shoe, too."

"You can spread whatever you want. No one will believe a dead woman and her deader uncle. What the freak do you have?"

"The woman's name is Rose O'Brien." Stella handed him the piece of paper with Rose's number. "She and her dog, along with a blonde are in there now asking a lot of questions about Foxy. She returned Foxy's purse."

Captain snatched the paper and crumbled it into his tight fist. "What does she look like? Is she tall?"

"She's kinda tall, about five-eight. Legs to her ears, red hair, blue eyes. Pretty hot."

"Are they cops?"

"Don't know. Rose asked for Francine. No one calls her that. And Rose said she wasn't a cop. She acts like it though. But she certainly didn't dress like one. She was wearing yoga clothes."

"You sure don't know a hell of a lot. I couldn't care less what she's wearing. And why are you out here? I need eyes and ears in there."

"Screw you! I figured you'd want to know the chick that took your ass out is right in front of you."

As Stella put her hand on the door handle, two of the Flamingo's bouncers tossed Joe out the club's door and on his backside. One gave him a boot to the rib and yelled for him to stay away.

"Shit." Stella ducked down. "Tell me when they go back inside."

"Not my problem."

"It will be when I get canned for dereliction of duty. Then you won't have anyone on the inside."

"They're back in."

She sat up. "I need a pack of cigarettes."

"What for?"

"I need them to think I bought some at the store."

Captain reached in his back seat. "I don't smoke. But I found a pack back there. It must've dropped out of the last guy's pockets that I wacked."

"Prince freakin' Charming." She snatched the pack, stuffing them into her bra.

"Oh, that's classy."

Stella flipped the bird and exited the Escalade.

Captain waited for Stella to return to the club and uncrumpled the note with Rose's number. He had nothing to go on but a phone number. So, he reached into his backseat once more and pulled out his laptop. Again, he accessed the law enforcement database and entered Rose O'Brien's phone number.

"Dammit. A prepaid." He typed her name into a search engine. There were a ton of Rose O' Briens. He narrowed his search to her approximate age, mid-thirties. Nothing. She must not be a local.

He closed his laptop and contemplated. Should he call Juno and ask for her help? Nah, he could handle this on his own. Not to mention, she would want to know why he was inquiring about another person not Foxy.

The longer he thought about Rose, the angrier he got. He couldn't admit to anyone a girl beat his ass. And then a thought occurred. She must've been at a party at the marina last night. He picked up his cell and phoned the security guard from last night, Dave.

"Yo, I need some info—hey, not my problem you got canned. If you'd pay your gambling debts, you wouldn't have to take care of things like last night. I can make your racetrack debt disappear … Yeah, I thought you'd see it my way. A chick named Rose O'Brien. She was at one of the parties last night." Captain proceeded to provide her description that Stella gave him. Her dog, too. "Seriously? She's a yacht owner. Which one? … Consider yourself in the black. I'll make the call."

After Captain disconnected, he contemplated his next move. Rose and her dog were going down. But not until after his job was finished. Eliminating her would be icing on the cake.

CHAPTER 20

I PICKED UP the barstool that Joe had tossed.

"Hey, if you ever want a job," Harlee said.

"I made it clear I wasn't applying as a dancer," I said.

"No. Bouncer. We don't have a female. My girls would feel at ease with you. You can hang out in the dressing rooms."

"Hey, Rose. Not a bad idea. You're gonna need a job at the end of the week." Saki turned to Harlee. "How much does it pay?"

"Thank you, little sister. I'm going to do freelance work for a while."

"That bodyguard thing?"

I shrugged.

A woman with golden blonde hair walked up.

"You missed all the excitement," Harlee said to her. She turned back to me. "Rose, this is my sister and co-owner of the club, Nala."

We shook hands. "I hear we owe you a big thank you," Nala said.

"Huh? Oh, that d-bag started it," I said.

"No, I'm referring to what you did for our gal last night."

Just then a girl, in her early twenties, who I thought might be Francine came from the back.

"This is Foxy." Harlee made the introductions.

Foxy approached me with tears in her eyes and gave me a big hug.

I stepped away from our embrace. "I take it you're Francine Fox?"

"Everyone calls me Foxy." She wiped her tears. "It was a nickname since I was a kid and not because of my current job."

Foxy stood five feet, three inches, slim build. She was dressed in capris and a tank. Since she wasn't wearing a costume, I assumed she took the day off, given what happened last night. Francine had hypnotic reddish-orange hair with blonde streaks. Beautiful cool undertone skin. Light green eyes. From the picture we found, she had her mother's eyes. I stared for a spell.

She also looked like her uncle Gil. Heavy sigh. I never knew him alive but was up close and personal with his body.

I shook it off and handed Foxy her purse.

Just then, Stella came storming through the front door.

We all stopped and stared.

"Where the hell did you disappear to … again?" Harlee snapped.

"Uh, pack of smokes." She pulled them from her bra.

"I thought you quit?" Nala asked.

I saw her jaws tighten. "I picked it back up. What's it to you?" Stella resumed her duties and began wiping off glasses.

"Don't be so defensive." Harlee scrunched her face. "What's gotten into you?"

"No—nothing. Just family stuff. I've got to restock the pretzels." Stella proceeded to the back.

"Don't bring out too many. We're closing at four, maybe earlier," Harlee called out. She turned back to us. "Come on Nala, let's have a come to Jesus meeting with Stella. Not like her to act—"

"Like you," Nala said.

"Come on now," Harlee retorted.

"You know I'm right." Nala and her sister continued to banter to the back. They reminded me of Saki and myself.

"This seems like a fun place to work." Saki sat back on the barstool.

"It is." Foxy sat next to Saki.

I sat on the other side. "Can we chat in private?"

"I don't see why not." Foxy looked around. "Given there's only the three of us here at the bar. I don't think we're going to get much more business today. Not to mention, Harlee put a note on the door saying we're closing early."

She rummaged through her purse. "Oh my God! Thank you." She pulled out her car keys and cell phone and held them to her chest like she just struck gold. "You wouldn't believe what a life saver you are." She hugged me again. "And your dog too." She petted Sue.

Sue wore a grin as if she knew she was the goodest girl.

"Sue is my wing dog." I smiled.

"Sue?" Foxy tilted her head.

"Long story."

Foxy nodded. "So, what did you want to talk about?"

I briefed Foxy on only what Saki could overhear. That I was the one who found her at the marina. And we cruised to her apartment, looking for her. I kept out the rest. But asked her if she received anything in the mail that would cause someone to do harm to her. I couldn't really grill her on anything else with Saki sitting there.

"That man kept asking me about documents Uncle Gil sent me. I didn't receive anything. The last correspondence I received was a death notification. My uncle died of a heart attack. He didn't tell many people he had a heart condition. But one thing was puzzling. He was cremated before I learned of his death."

"Who sent the notification?" I asked.

"The State Department."

I scanned the room as dread formed in my gut. She said State Department. I most definitely had to stop questioning her. Saki was not privy to everything that transpired in Montana. My sister needed to be shielded from my mad CIA theory.

Think, Rose.

"Hey, Sak. Can you call Lily and Essie and see how far out they are?"

"Sure thing." She hopped off the barstool and stepped away from us. Fortunately, she didn't catch on that I was hiding something. This was too dangerous for her. She had a baby to think about now. When the time was right, I'd let her in on it. Although even I didn't know what *it* was.

"Keep the thing about the State Department to yourself, for now," I mumbled to Foxy. "We need to have a serious talk."

Foxy looked at me quizzically. Then she must've then caught on I didn't want Saki in this conversation because she looked at my sister and nodded as if she understood.

Saki returned. "They're stuck in traffic across town. People are evacuating Miami Beach right now. I need to return to the club. There's an emergency." She shook her head. "The perks of owning a fitness center."

"I can have Lily drop you off to get your car," I said. "It's at the marina."

"No, I have to get there now. I'll call an Uber."

"That's okay, I have my car in the back lot. Now that I have my keys, I'd love to drive you. Besides, Nala and Harlee gave me the day off. And I'd rather not be here." She turned to me. "Rose, you can wait here for your friends."

"No! Um … if it's all the same, Sue and I will join you. That's if you don't mind my dog in your car."

"I'd be honored. You guys are my heroes. Let me grab my raincoat out of the back and we'll be on our way."

Phew, she didn't question the reason I wanted to stick by her. She didn't need to know that she was now my charge. That creep from last night was probably not the only person interested in those documents her uncle sent.

I'd keep that a secret for now. Like Grandma always says, some secrets are best kept.

CHAPTER 21

CAPTAIN RECEIVED A text message from Stella telling him Foxy and the other two women, along with the dog, were leaving the Flamingo. He pulled up the AirTag location, but it didn't change. It was still at the club. Perhaps it wasn't working or with the storm, it wasn't updating. Stupid technology.

So, he'd have to do this the old-fashioned way. He'd put a tail on them. He just wasn't sure of the make of her vehicle, so he texted Stella back.

Just as Stella responded, he watched Foxy pull out of the back parking lot. He saw her orange hair before the car registered in his consciousness. An early model white Toyota Corolla hatchback, with one red door. He put his Cadillac in Drive and followed the women out of Miami Beach, over the MacArthur Causeway.

The traffic leaving Miami Beach was a bear as those not accustomed to hurricanes were evacuating.

Foxy was obviously impatient as she kept switching lanes. But seeing how they were down to two lanes, it was futile. The fifteen-minute drive over the causeway turned into a half hour. Captain had to stay back a couple cars to not alert them. Just as they exited the causeway, they took the turn off to Miami. With traffic worsening, Captain fell back three cars. He repeatedly attempted to refresh the AirTag's location. No luck.

The car made a quick left and a quicker right. Was this chick doing countersurveillance? Or was she just a crazy driver?

As he watched them pull into a strip mall, his phone rang.

"Yo," Captain answered as he parked.

"Why have you been running Gil Fox?"

Stillness came over the connection.

"I'm waiting," Juno snapped. "I'm aware of your law enforcement connections and were recently at the marina. Perhaps on a yacht?"

Captain straightened in his seat. "Yes, I ran him. Since you didn't tell me anything about my mark, I had a right to know. Don't like being in the dark. But no. I wasn't on a yacht. Only the marina. And I certainly didn't have my computer with me at the time." He rubbed his forearm. A reminder of that stupid dog.

He thought about that for a second. It must be Rose. His source told him she lived on the yacht. He would keep that to himself for now. Since this chick was loaded, he may be able to work both sides. She'd probably pay handsomely for her dog. And he knew just the person to help him with his plan.

"Captain, are you there?"

"Yeah, yeah."

"You need to forget about Gil and focus on the Fox girl. You've got to cover your tracks. Erase the digital trail."

"Now you've got my curiosity up. Who was this guy? He had a Top-Secret clearance. And I know you used to be a spook for the CI—"

"This conversation is over! You've got one simple job. Am I clear?" She disconnected.

Just then a blue Range Rover pulled up next to Foxy's car. He took his binoculars from his backseat and focused on the occupants. A short gal with platinum blonde hair and the driver, another dame with long black hair. Four hotties. They all entered the SP Fitness Center.

"What are they doing? They seriously can't be working out." Captain pulled out his smart phone and conducted a search of the fitness center. The owner was that blonde who was at the club. "Saki O'Brien-Powers. Huh. She's somehow related to Rose." He set down the phone. "What are they doing with Foxy?"

While he waited for something to happen, Captain called his buddy. "Easy. I'm not calling about the money you owe. I need a favor. I need to borrow that tranq gun. Not for a person this time. For a vicious dog. Yeah, I'll need some of that stuff too. I need it today ... I'm aware we're under a hurricane watch. Don't care.

Can you get it or not? ... Fine. I need you to meet me ... Can't. Doing surveillance ... Can't tell you. High-profile case."

Foxy, Rose, along with her mutt, and that long-haired beauty exited the gym. They jumped back into the Toyota and tore out of the parking lot. Captain waited for two cars to pass and followed.

"I'm on the move. I'll text you my next local." He hung up and followed for two blocks. He let off the gas pedal. "What the hell now? Why did they pull into an empty parking lot?"

CHAPTER 22

◆

"ESSIE, THANKS FOR agreeing to help out Saki," I said. "We can meet up at the W Hotel when you're done." I gave my baby sister and Essie hugs goodbye before they disappeared into the fitness center.

Foxy and I hopped into the front seat of her Toyota, while Sue jumped in the back with Lily. Foxy sped out of the parking lot and two blocks later I spotted an empty lot. "Foxy, pull over here." I motioned.

"Why?" Foxy asked. "I thought we were going back to the club. I forgot my backpack. If I'm going to stay at the hotel with you, I need my books to study. And clothes." Foxy yanked the wheel sharp and put her car in Park.

I turned in my seat. "Let's have that talk."

Foxy looked in her rearview mirror at Lily.

"It's okay. She's privy to what I'm about to tell you. But you must keep this under your hat."

"O—kay," Foxy said.

I paused and exhaled. "Foxy, what exactly did your uncle do for a living?"

"He was a scientist for the government."

"What branch?" Lily leaned forward. "Did he tell you anything else?"

"That's all he was able to tell me. He had some kind of high-level security clearance."

"Top-Secret," I said.

"When did you find this out, Rose?" Lily asked. "Were you

going to share with me?"

I looked back, and she furrowed her brows at me.

"I couldn't tell you what I found. Essie and Saki didn't need to hear this. It's bad enough Foxy will know."

"Will you please tell me what the hell's going on?" Foxy slammed the steering wheel.

"What I found out just *today*." I looked at Lily. "When we were in Montana last month, I kind of found my grandma's passcodes."

"You mean you were snooping," Lily said.

"No. Just looking for a note pad in her drawer. And it was her fault. She should've kept them hidden better. Anyway," I said. "I discovered this morning that your uncle had a Top-Secret clearance issued by the State Department."

Foxy sat with her mouth opened and stared straight ahead for a second. "If you were in Montana, did you see him?" She urged. "Do you know what happened to him? All I was told was that he had a heart attack. I guess he went out there to do some fly-fishing."

Lily's face turned white, and she sat back. I watched as tears welled in her eyes. I patted her knee. She nodded and sucked in her sob.

Foxy spun. "Are you okay, Lily?"

I nodded to Lily so she could tell her story.

After a few minutes, Foxy stared straight ahead. And what Lily said must've been a shocker. Hearing it re-told by Lily was almost unbelievable. It sounded fabricated—more like a thriller movie.

"So, you're telling me, Uncle Gil probably worked for the CIA?"

"It appears so," I said.

"But first he told you he was a PI? And he was going to tell you the truth about what happened to your parents." She nodded to Lily. "And then you, Rose." She returned her gaze to me. "Examined his corpse. But, not after Lily was kidnapped, drugged and framed for his murder because her hand was on the gun that shot him. But Rose proved it was postmortem." She paused. "Only it was the CIA who actually ordered the hit on him?"

I nodded in agreement. So far, so good. I thought we had her on our team. Next, to ask her about any correspondence he may have sent her. Just as I opened my mouth to speak, she slammed the hammer.

"*But* … Rose and Simon found suspicious looking marks like the smallpox vaccine. That doesn't leave a scar? And the body absorbs it? So, you drew blood, Rose, but your grandma Lil, who used to be in the CIA, took it from you?" I saw her temple pulsating. "And you expect me to believe this … *crap*." She snarled. "How can I be certain this wasn't planned from the start? I don't find it coincidental that … that man brought me to the marina where you were." She raised her voice with every other word. "Both of you, out of my car … now! I never want to see either of you again."

Okay. So, this wasn't the reaction I'd hoped for. But Lily was already in my crazy espionage world. I guess I should've eased Foxy into it.

"Look." I sighed. "I realize this is hard to believe. Sometimes I find it bizarre too. But I have pictures to prove it and audio recording on my phone."

"It's the truth. Bizarre things happen to Rose—or do they find her? Either way it—"

"Out! Or so help me, I'll call the police."

Lily and I hopped out, just as the rain started hammering down. I looked up and saw eerie storm clouds forming from the south. Sue popped out after me. We watched Foxy burn rubber out of the parking lot, leaving us stranded.

Yeah, not completely, since my sister's place was two blocks away. And then something out of the corner of my eye struck me wrong. A black Cadillac Escalade, that was parked across the street came to life and abruptly flipped a U-turn and followed Foxy.

Something was way off.

Then a white SUV headed straight toward us.

Talk about bizarre. "Rose!" Lily gripped my arm. "It's the same car that's been following me."

The windows were completely blacked out. The driver purposely sped up. We ran toward my sister's gym as fast as our feet would carry us. I had no time to pull out my gun, nor did I have a clear shot behind us. Too many bystanders. No one stopped to help. This was downtown Miami, and people were in hurricane mode. Looking out for themselves. Stocking up supplies.

I was more concerned about Sue, so I swooped her and kept

running.

The white SUV jumped the curb and drove onto the sidewalk. Hitting anything in their way. Stop signs, bus stop benches. Pedestrians screamed and jumped out of the deranged driver's path.

Who was in the vehicle? CIA? Cora Alvarez? Nah, she was in the wind, and she was CIA too. They don't usually work domestically, nor do they operate that messy. Not to mention, they generally get their targets.

Foxy appeared in my peripheral vision. She screeched to a halt at the curb, with the windows rolled down. "Jump in," she hollered.

Without questioning, we obliged. I hopped in front with Sue, Lily in the back. "There was a Caddy following you. Where is it?" I asked.

"I don't know. After I took off, I saw that white SUV go after you guys. I'm so sorry, I should've listened to you."

"It's all right." I turned in my seat. Both Lily and I had our heads on a swivel. "I don't see either vehicle."

"Me either," Lily said. "What are the odds? Do you think they're working together?"

"Don't know." It was obvious, one was after us and the other Foxy. I pondered.

That's when I spotted an unoccupied drive-through car wash. "Foxy, hurry, in there." I pointed.

Foxy didn't question and swung into the carwash, practically driving on two wheels. Impressive.

We waited and watched every vehicle as they passed. The black Caddy was the first and a few moments later, the white SUV. I sat silently for what felt like an eternity. The last person to charge me like that was crazy Shilo. She almost ran me down on the tarmac in Montana. She was wacked and would kill anyone in her way. But … it was impossible. She was locked up in a federal loony bin.

"Rose, Rose. Did you hear what I said?" Lily patted my shoulder.

"Uh … no, sorry. I was thinking of something else."

"I asked Foxy if she received anything from her uncle."

"Oh, wait." Foxy spoke up. "I have a post office box I haven't checked in a month. It's in Hialeah."

I turned to face her. "Do you mind driving there?"

"Not at all. I want to get to the bottom of this." Foxy pulled out of the car wash.

"Rose, should we tell Simon what just happened?" Lily asked. "You can imagine how he'd get his underwear in a bunch if we didn't."

"Later. I think we're out of danger for the moment."

"If you say so," Lily said. "It's your funeral."

I chuckled and opened my fanny pack. I checked to see how many magazines I put in there this morning. I pulled out two. That wasn't enough.

"Whoa, I didn't know you were packing." Foxy's eyes widened.

"She's got guns hidden all over her yacht, too." Lily laughed. "You have to be careful where you sit."

I turned to Lily. "It's not that bad. You should've seen my house in California. I had a safe room."

Foxy stared at me like I was a space alien coming to take her. I guess it was all too much. It wouldn't be the first time I overwhelmed someone.

Thanks to traffic, we arrived in Hialeah twenty-five minutes later. Just as we pulled up to the post office, I received a text from Grandma:

Rosie. Back off! Don't become a statistic to your own curiosity.

"What the?!" I yelled at my phone.

CHAPTER 23

◆

I QUICKLY DIALED Grandma. But straight to voicemail. She obviously didn't want to chat with me about her message. So, I texted back.

What??

I saw the conversation bubbles appear and then disappear. No reply.

"How does she know what we're up to?" I mumbled.

"Rose, what is it?" Lily asked.

I sat sideways in my seat and showed Lily my phone.

Lily stared with an open mouth.

"I know, right?" I shook my head.

"What's going on?" Foxy turned off her car.

"Not certain. My gran has always been cryptic," I said, petting Sue.

"I'll go check my mail." Foxy exited the car.

"What does this text mean?" Lily asked.

"I haven't told her what we've been doing or that we've made contact with Gil's niece. But I suspect she knows something because I used her passcode … oops."

"Oh my gosh, Rose." Lily gasped. "You don't think whoever has been following us was sent by her."

"No, she'd never harm us. Like I told you earlier, during our FaceTime call, Grandma had been messaging a person with the initial M. She asked if M was in Florida."

"Who's M?" Lily asked.

"Haven't a clue. She appeared nervous when I asked."

"We need to have a heart to heart with Lillian. She's hiding something. First telling you to forget those marks you found on me and Gil and then she took the vials of blood from you."

"That we do. In Montana when I told her it all reeked of a CIA experiment, she told me to leave it alone. And that it was dangerous, and she would tell me when it was safer. She said it was bigger than us." I drew a deep breath. "Lily, she sounded, well … scared. And you know Grandma doesn't frighten easily."

"Scared for who?"

"Good question." I glanced at my watch. "Foxy's been in there too long. Let's go inside."

As the three of us exited the vehicle, I heard sirens wailing in the distance. I looked at Lily and she wore a concerned expression on her face as I'm sure I did. We bolted for the door and that's when I saw employees and customers huddling in a corner, talking to one another.

To my surprise, the post office was quite large, with two separate entrances. That meant two exit doors.

"Crap, Lily. You take the right. Sue and I will go left. She's got to be here."

I scanned every inch of the post office as did Lily. When we met up, both of us shook our heads. Lily and I walked over to a postal employee. She told us a muscular man with a patch over his eye grabbed a woman with bright orange hair. That had to be Foxy. The man dragged her out the back door.

"Come on Lily," I said as we ran out the back. "I should've never let her go in there alone. I didn't realize there were two entrances."

"Me too, Rose. But we saw him drive past. How did he find us?"

The second we exited, we spotted Foxy crouching down at the side of the building, shaking.

"Foxy." I ran to her. "Are you okay?"

"I think so." She let out a sob.

I grabbed Foxy's hand and helped her to her feet. She wept so hard in my arms; I felt her body tremble. Sue was at her side in a millisecond.

"Foxy, I'm so sorry. I shouldn't have let you out of my sight."

"*We* shouldn't have, Rose." Lily walked over.

Foxy pulled away and wiped her face.

"Was it the same man?" I asked.

She nodded. "Since our last encounter, he has a patch over his eye. And his left arm is bandaged. Same vehicle and all."

"That rat!" I seethed. "How did you get away?"

"I gave him a swift sidekick to his thigh. I was aiming for his junk. But he jumped back in time. He obviously didn't want me bad enough and only took my package."

"He must've followed us. How did I miss him? I kept a look out. I guess not hard enough." I paused. "My skills of observation are getting rusty."

"Well, we were talking," Lily said to me. She turned to Foxy. "Wait—package? Was it by chance from your uncle?"

"No, it was a blouse I ordered. With school, it slipped my mind."

"I don't suppose you were able to get a good description of his vehicle. Or plate?" I inquired.

"All I know is it was the same vehicle."

"I got a picture of his license plate," a woman's voice came from behind.

I spun.

An elderly, white-haired woman stood behind me, smiling. "Dang kids these days. With their loud music, sagging pants. We aren't safe anymore. It's a good thing I carry this." She waved around her cane. "I can really whack 'em hard. And have done so."

"Thank you, ma'am. But you should be careful. Some of them carry weapons."

"Me too." She winked and patted the side of her hip. "This cane is just for show. I still run in the senior marathon." She laughed.

"That's good to know." I looked back at Lily with wide eyes.

The woman showed me her cell phone with a clear picture of the Escalade.

"Ma'am, you're a life saver." I snapped a shot with my iPhone.

"My name's Ruth. And is your friend, okay? She managed to get in her licks too. She kicked him square in the nuts."

I laughed so hard, my face hurt.

Foxy did too as she was now beside me, standing tall. "I was aiming for them." Foxy shook Ruth's hand. "Thank you for getting his plate."

"Yes. We appreciate your help," I said. "But you have to be safe."

"I think it's the little thugs who need to be worried," Foxy said.

"You're lucky he didn't take you with him," Lily said.

"Too many people around," Ruth said. "Well, gotta run. Gotta finish shopping. I'm hosting a hurricane party at my house. It's something we do every time there's a tropical storm brewing. Food and margaritas. I have my gals over and we kick up our heels. Play games. I live in an evacuation area. Sometimes we get so hammered, we pass out and miss the show." She spun on her heels and turned back. "You should join us."

"Ruth, that sounds like fun." I looked at the picture on my phone. "But we have a fish to catch."

"You mean an eel," Lily said.

I nodded and watched Ruth stroll away with a pep in her step. I liked that lady.

"Does she remind you of someone?" Lily shoulder bumped me.

"Me, in about forty years." I laughed.

I turned back to Foxy and returned to business. "I don't suppose you have any other mail."

Foxy put her hand in her coat pocket and pulled out a post office key. "Maybe. There were two keys in my box. I was only able to get one before that jerk took the package."

I looked at Lily and we probably had the same thought.

"Let's go look. This time, I'm coming with you. But first you have the cops to talk to." I watched two police cruisers pull up.

Foxy turned to face me. "Rose, I can't. There's nothing I can say to them."

"Sure, you can. We have his plate now."

"No, you don't understand. The last thing he said is if I go to the cops he will come back and finish the job. He knows *everything* about me. Where I go to school, where I live and work." Foxy had a death grip on my arm. I saw fear in her green eyes.

"Okay, okay. We'll find the patch man ourselves. But we turn him over to the police when we do."

"Gee, Rose. When did you start handing over bad guys?" Lily asked.

"I no longer wear a badge," I replied to Lily and turned back to

Foxy. "Lily can go check the box and Sue and I will take you back to the car."

"Sounds good to me." Foxy handed Lily the key with number five on it. "Thank you, ladies."

Since I did not have law enforcement connections here, other than Saki's husband, I needed to run this plate. And it was obvious that Grandma was monitoring the passcodes I took from her desk. *Think, Rose.* And then it hit me.

Simon and Tucker. I dialed.

CHAPTER 24

◆

CAPTAIN DROVE LESS than two miles from the post office and turned into the first parking garage. He couldn't risk being caught. He jerked his wheel sharply as his tires squealed with every turn. Captain drove to the top level. He had a bird's-eye view as he watched two patrol vehicles fly by. Most likely looking for the man who tried to kidnap a woman, stealing her mail.

Captain rubbed his inner thigh. That girl was going to be the death of him.

He looked at the package on the seat next to him. Fortunately, the AirTag updated.

Just as Captain picked up the burner phone to see if they were still at the post office, his other cell dinged with a text from his guy, Bo. Captain almost forgot he'd asked for a favor.

Bo: **Got the tranq. Am heading out of Miami ASAP.**

Captain: **Meet me. Top level. Parking garage on E. 25ᵗʰ. Hialeah.**

He was about to set the phone down to pick up the package when he got a call.

"Jess," Captain answered with his fake accent.

"Cut the crap," Juno said. "It's getting old. Did you get anything?"

"Yes." Captain put the call on speaker and set it on the seat, then picked up the parcel. He opened it. "Shit."

"What?"

He flung it in the backseat. As much as he didn't want to admit it, the cat was out of the bag. "It's not the right one."

"What do you mean, not the right one?"

"Maybe Gil didn't send her anything. She had a gun at her head and insisted she knew nothing. I tossed her room. No signs of correspondence from her uncle."

"My intel says he penned a letter to his niece and mailed it prior to his death."

"Your *intel* is obviously wrong."

"Negative," Juno said. "My intel knows all. Hell, he most likely knows what color underwear you're wearing."

"Commando." Captain let out a guttural laugh.

"Jeez, you're crass. Save that for your bar skanks." Juno groaned. "I want that information. *Now*! Am I clear?"

"Yeah, yeah." Captain disconnected.

After they hung up, Captain pulled up the AirTag again. It was still at the post office. This long? Maybe the app stopped functioning again. He called Stella.

"Yeah," she answered harshly.

"Is that how you answer all your unknown numbers."

"Whatever. What the hell do you want now? And where's my uncle? You promised!"

"I didn't promise shit. I didn't get what I want."

"What is that exactly?"

"Has Foxy returned to the club?"

"No."

"Does she have any other friends or family she could have gone to?"

"How the heck am I supposed to know? She's a college student and as far as I know, was an only child. Her parents are dead. And her uncle just died."

Captain thought. "Who are the dames with her?"

"What do I look like, Siri?" Stella hissed.

"You're kinda smart-mouthed for someone who should be kissing my ass. Have you ever seen them before today?"

"Again. I. Don't. Know," she said slowly and deliberately.

"I need Foxy's cell number."

Stella growled and was silent for a beat before speaking. "Just sent it. And what about the AirTag?"

"Don't think it's working." Captain's phone dinged with a text. "Tell me if she shows."

"Fine! But I want my uncle."

"Not yet. Not until I get what I want."

"Again … I don't even know what that is?"

"You don't need to."

"Then I want assurances that my uncle is alive and unharmed. Did he get his heart meds? If he dies, I swear on my aunt's grave I will hunt you down and personally kill you," Stella said without coming up for air.

"He's fine. And yes, my people gave him his meds. If you threaten me again, you both will be dumped into the Everglades."

"How the hell do you sleep at night?"

"On my back, with my eyes closed."

Stella ended the call.

Captain stared at the phone. "Bitch," he snarled. No one hung up on him. His neck and face felt hot.

As he was about to call her back, Bo pulled up in his white Humvee. Blacked-out windows. Captain stared at it for a second. Perfect, he thought. The cops would be looking for Captain's Cadillac. Not to mention, Foxy and her friends knew what his vehicle looked like. He needed new wheels.

Bo argued with Captain and repeatedly asked why. Captain advised him it was none of his business and that all of Bo's debts would be forgiven. And assured they'd meet up later to switch vehicles back.

Captain neglected to let Bo know about his escapades at the post office. He brushed it off. So what if they stopped Bo? They simply got the wrong guy.

After removing their personal items from their respective vehicles and switching, the two men drove in opposite directions.

CHAPTER 25

◆

I PACED OUTSIDE the car and listened while Simon scolded me for not calling sooner.

"Furthermore, Rose. What do you *mean*, you're going after the guy that tried to off Foxy? You'll be next."

I pulled the phone away from my ear. "Look Simon, I've been chasing bad guys ... alone since before I met you!" I snapped back. "And he wouldn't be the first guy to try to whack me."

"So, I've heard."

"You can't believe everything my brother-in-law tells you." Mostly. "So, you gonna run the plate for me or not?"

Simon groaned. "Yeah. But you better make sure Lily is safe."

"Can you locate a cell number too?"

"Anything else ... perhaps his blood type?"

"Don't get smart with me."

"Sorry, we've been tied up at Tucker's um ... girly friend's. There's a hurricane coming, or have you forgotten?"

I rolled my shoulders. "No! I would run these myself, but I don't have access anymore." I told him about Grandma's text and that her code was no longer a viable option.

"Rose, if your gran is telling you to stand down, don't ya think you should heed her warning?"

"Since when did that ever stop us? And no!" I sighed. "Disregard. I'll get the information some other way."

I disconnected and jammed the phone in my pack. I didn't appreciate being lectured. Simon called back, but I ignored it. A few minutes later, Lily returned with a priority mail small box in hand and hopped in the back. Sue joined her. She was on the phone.

"Yes, I'm safe." She looked at me with a quizzical look and handed me the phone.

I pushed it away. "No, thanks. I'd rather have a root canal than another lecture," I said loudly into the phone's receiver.

"Did you catch that … uh huh. Okay. I'll tell her." Lily ended the call. "I can't believe you hung up on him." She chuckled. "He's working on your request." Lily air quoted the last word and handed Foxy her package.

I leaned into the window too mad to do anything other than sulk.

I asked Foxy if I could drive. That always helped calm me and since I was a control freak at times, it was better for my sanity. Along with everyone else's.

Foxy obliged and ran over to the passenger side. I jumped behind the wheel.

"Hmm, no return address." Foxy opened it and a large manila envelope dropped into her hands. She turned the box upside down and shook it. "That's odd."

Lily leaned forward. "What?"

"Nothing else was in here, but this." She proceeded to open the envelope.

"Wait!" I put my hand to stop her.

Foxy drew her head back. "Why?"

"Never open anything from an unfamiliar source. Especially if you weren't expecting a package." I took the box and looked at the return postage. "It was postage marked from Missoula, Montana. It was sent a month ago." I glanced at Lily and her face turned white.

"What's the date, Rose?" Lily rubbed her sternum. She sat back and popped some antacid.

I handed her the box.

What I didn't want to say out loud was that it was mailed the day Lily was kidnapped and Gil murdered.

Even though I suspected the correspondence was from Gil, I shook the envelope. Can't be too careful. But I didn't feel anything suspicious. I took my phone out of my fanny pack and shone it behind the envelope. Nothing but a few sheets of paper. I stepped out of the car. With my head turned and arms far away from me, I opened the manila envelope.

Phew. We didn't go kaboom. Just a three-page letter, with a smaller envelope. I returned inside and handed it back to Foxy.

Since the cops were questioning people in the post office, we wanted to create distance.

So, I headed back to Miami Beach as Foxy read the letter in silence.

After what appeared to be an eternity, Foxy finally put down the letter and sobbed.

I glanced at Lily in the rearview mirror, and we shared a wide-eyed expression.

"Are you okay?" I asked.

Foxy wiped her face and shook her head. She cleared her throat and finally said, "Lily is your last name Cazier?"

"Yes. Why?"

Foxy handed Lily the small envelope, along with the three-page written letter.

"I'd rather not read your personal mail," Lily said.

"It's okay," Foxy said. "It's for you."

"What?" Lily looked at it with furrowed brows. She opened the envelope addressed to her. "How would he know you'd be able to find me?" She stared at a small piece of paper and scratched her head with a twist to her lip. "It's a Sudoku. I don't get it."

She dropped it and leaned her head against the seat. "And Foxy, I … I can't read your letter." She returned it to Foxy.

"I get it. But I'd like for you ladies to hear what it says." She grabbed it back and cleared her throat. "My dearest Foxy Loxie. That was his nickname for me."

I looked back at Lily, and she looked like she was going to cry. She was caressing the locket around her neck. Sue plopped on her lap, giving her kisses.

"To start off, always remember I love you to the moon and back. My purpose in writing is twofold. Firstly, I need to tell you a confidential matter pertaining to my employment. As you know, I am a scientist. But I neglected to mention my position is with the Central Intelligence Agency. I wish to state that if anything should happen to me, do not believe what my Agency tells you as they are the cause of my demise.

"Secondly, another confession. During my time with the CIA, I was on a sensitive project's unit. I was recruited by a team of scientists to develop a groundbreaking new truth serum. In the post-911 era we were told everything we were going to be doing was all about protecting the American people. For the greater good. I will address this later in the letter. Upon discovering the true nature of our work, I began trolling underground government conspiracy chatrooms. I flagged anyone interested in covert mind control experiments.

"After weeks of monitoring, I encountered a woman known as Lily C. She was seeking the truth about her parents' deaths. After weeks of correspondence, I vetted her to ensure she was legit and not with any government agency. Email correspondence replaced chatroom conversations. As things progressed, I told her I was a PI and would investigate her parents' deaths. I didn't want to alarm her by telling her the truth. At our initial meeting, she shared with me information regarding her parents' occupations and that she had suspicions about their plane crash.

"Her honesty prompted me to send her a microchip detailing my discoveries. The enclosed envelope addressed to her is a passcode for the chip. It is in the form of a number puzzle. Lily's contact information is also included at the conclusion of this letter. I will be meeting with her again in two days to tell her the truth and to give her your information as well."

Foxy eyed Lily. "I assume your meeting went well and you know what all this means."

Lily rolled down the window and put her head out. The rain was steady, and her face was getting soaked.

"Stop the car, Rose!" Lily's voice was rattled, and she was hyperventilating.

"I can't, we're stuck in the number two lane."

The words were barely out, when Lily bounded from the car. Without her raincoat. She played leapfrog across three lanes of traffic. Thank God they were all slowing down. A few were rude and honked their horns at her. Some gave her a middle finger salute.

Sue had her front paws on the door panel and was ready to jump until I ordered her to stop. She listened like a good dog.

"Is Lily okay?" Foxy asked.

"I hope so," I mumbled, keeping an eye on her. I watched as she sat at a bus stop bench, face in her hands, and rocking. The light turned green, and we were slowly moving. I honked and yelled for Lily to stay put.

She waved a hand as if she understood.

My phone rang, but I ignored it. Something was wrong with Lily.

CHAPTER 26

◆

CAPTAIN MADE HIS way out of the parking garage and turned right. The moment he approached a bus stop, he noticed a woman sitting on the bench with her head between her knees. Had he seen her before?

After all Captain was a ladies' man. It was totally possible he'd bought her a drink somewhere, sometime.

He pulled over. "Hey lovely lady, are you okay?"

She picked her head up and waved her hand.

She certainly looked familiar. And then it hit him. This gal was the one with Rose and Foxy.

That meant one thing. They were nearby. He quickly raised his window and pulled up. Changing vehicles was the smartest thing to do. And with his blacked-out windows, they would never spot him. Captain put on his emergency flashers and waited. Someone would be picking her up or if she took the bus, he'd follow.

And just like that, Foxy's vehicle pulled up and the black-haired beauty hopped in the back seat. But the redhead, Rose, was driving.

Who needed the AirTag? Captain mused as he let two cars go by and trailed them. They appeared to be leaving Hialeah, possibly heading back to Miami.

Just then, his phone rang.

"Yo, Bo. What's up. Don't tell me you wrecked my vehicle. I swear if you did, you're dead meat."

"Easy, Cap'n. Not exactly. But I think I'm being followed. Two big guys in a GMC truck. You didn't sleep with Tony's wife again, did ya? Looks like his vehicle."

"I don't know … maybe. Where are you?"

"Headed northwest. Away from the storm. Where are you?"

"None of your concern. What do these guys look like?"

"Hard to tell with the glare. I just see two large dudes in the front seat."

"That ain't Tony. He's a short, fat schmuck. Can you lose them? But easy on my Caddy."

"Yeah." Bo hung up.

Captain thought about who'd want to put a tail on him. Nothing came to mind. And a thought occurred. He dialed Juno.

"Yes," Juno answered. "Tell me you have good news."

"Working on it. So, who'd you put on me? My replacements?" Captain growled.

"No. But I will if I don't see results by end of business today."

Rose turned onto the causeway headed back to Miami Beach. Traffic was light as most people were evacuating. And just a few short minutes later, Rose turned into Foxy's apartment complex.

This might work to his advantage.

Captain pondered as Juno continued to threaten him.

"Yeah, yeah, sure. Gotta go." Captain disconnected.

———

Bo knew he was being followed. Or was he? He had to be smart about his next move. Since the vehicle's windows were all dark, he had no clue if there were more people in the back. And Bo was not a big guy. Stocky, sure. Five feet, five inches. In his mind he stood six feet. A chick he dated told him he had short man syndrome. Especially driving a Humvee. He dumped her like a charred hot dog.

He turned onto the seventy-five, away from the coastal areas, toward Naples. He had to see his gal, Nevaeh, his angel. At least most of the time. But first he had to lose his tail, so he accelerated to ninety. They wouldn't be stupid enough to try anything at that speed, would they?

Suddenly, a thought occurred. Did Captain call off the dogs like he said? Of course he did, Bo was driving his vehicle. And then another thought occurred, were they after Captain? Captain was the biggest horn dog he knew.

"That's why that ass wanted to trade vehicles." Bo seethed. "Screw this!" He punched it to one hundred.

Bo kept looking in his rearview and side mirrors. Sweat dripped down his forehead. He wiped it off with the back of his hand. His knuckles were white as he had a death grip on the steering wheel.

Finally, after fifteen minutes of nothing in his rearview mirror, he slowed down to the posted speed limit of seventy. He couldn't afford another ticket.

The gas light came on.

"Thanks, ya mook. Give me less than half a tank," Bo grumbled as he spotted a gas station at the next exit.

Pulling into the station, Bo hopped out, paid at the pump, and put fifty bucks in. That should get him through until he got his Hummer back.

Just as he returned the nozzle and closed the gas tank door, massive arms circled his neck.

He swatted and clawed and flailed.

He tried speaking, but he was being choked. What the hell!?

Lights out, Bo.

An unknown amount of time had passed when Bo woke with something over his head. A cloth bag of sorts. He was able to peek through the bottom and saw his wrists zip tied in the front and his legs bound in the same manner. He was in the backseat of Captain's vehicle.

"What do you want from me?" Bo massaged his neck with his bound hands.

"Where is the owner of this vehicle?" a man asked.

"I ain't no snitch," Bo replied. "Screw yourself."

Another man spoke up. "We can do this the easy or hard way." The man's massive fingers grasped Bo's pinky and bent it until his finger was numb. His diamond pinky ring fell to the floor. "You have nine more to go. I can do this all day. Now, who owns this vehicle?"

"I told ya, I don't rat on my friends," Bo roared. "And ya betta not steal my ring. It cost a fortune."

The man grabbed his right ring and pinky fingers at the same time and broke them.

"Argh!" Bo let out a blood-curdling yell. "If I tell you, you're gonna kill me. So, get it over with."

"Hey, jack wagon. This wouldn't be a fair fight. All we want to know is where is ..." Bo heard the glove box open, and papers riffled through. "Um, Terrance Folley?"

Bo emitted a guttural laugh. "So that's his name?" He sniggered again, but it was mixed with a pained moaned. "Captain's never gonna hear the end of this."

"Captain?" One of the men asked. "Does he have a patch over his eye? And a bandaged arm?"

"Yeah, a recent injury."

"Who is he? And why is he after Francine Fox?"

"Who? Never heard of her. Is she your dame or sumtin'?"

"Or something. Where is he?"

"Don't know Captain's business. It's safer that way."

The man with the big hands grabbed Bo's other hand.

"I swear, I swear! Don't know his business. He's a local hit man. And crazy. You don't mess with him."

"That sounds like a challenge, Tucker. Whatya say?"

"Always up for a challenge, Simon."

"Look, whatever your name is, we don't want you." The guy he now knew was Tucker, twisted his whole hand, bending all four fingers back until Bo saw stars.

"Argh ... okay, okay. All I know is that we exchanged vehicles. I don't know where he is. Only that he's driving *my* Hummer."

The men chuckled.

"A Humvee? That makes sense," the man named Simon said.

"Screw you guys. If you're gonna kill me, just get it over with. Spare me with the insults."

"Nah, we got what we want," Tucker said. "I take it your vehicle has lo jack or other anti-theft device?"

"Yeah. But please don't hurt my baby. It ain't paid off."

"It's not your vehicle we want," Simon said. "And if you call Captain to let him know about our conversation, we'll know. And our next meeting won't go so well."

His sentence was barely finished when he felt the zip ties release his wrists and heard the car doors slam.

"Hey, ain't you guys gonna take the ones off my ankles ... guys, guys?" He removed his hood and breathed a sigh of relief.

They were gone.

Bo shook his hand, wincing. He looked around for something to cut the ties off his ankles, found a folding knife and freed himself.

Bo hopped in the driver's seat and considered ignoring the warning to call Captain. But then, his swollen, aching fingers prevented him from easily shifting gears as he tried to drive off.

"Screw him. He deserves what those guys are gonna give him."

CHAPTER 27

◆

AFTER COAXING LILY back into the car, she apologized profusely, overcome with embarrassment.

I'd never seen her so rattled. Until last month. Lily was a ranch hand who never buckled under pressure. I studied her as we returned to Foxy's place since she needed to pack a few more things. The plan was for us to check into the W Hotel and wait out the hurricane that was now headed straight for Miami Beach.

"Oh, shoot!" Foxy interrupted the silence that filled the air. "I forgot my backpack. I have an important exam to study for."

"Isn't it at your apartment?" I pulled into her complex.

"It's at the club ... wait, how do you know where I live?" Foxy turned sideways and stared.

"It wasn't hard to figure out," I said. "We needed to find you and return your purse. But there's something you should know. Your studio is trashed."

"I know. I came back last night."

I parked Foxy's car, and we headed up to her place. I kept my head on a swivel to make sure we didn't have a tail. I didn't spot Foxy's abductor's vehicle or the SUV from earlier. That one was still a mystery. But someone wanted us dead.

My mind drifted to Cora Alvarez. She was still in the wind, but I had ears and eyes out for her return. So far, none. Although I'd never met her, so she could be standing right in front of me, and I wouldn't be able to identify her.

We entered Foxy's apartment, and it hadn't changed. I locked the door and closed the blinds but kept a lookout, Sue by my side.

Before talking, I stood on Foxy's chair and removed the bug from the light fixture and crushed it beneath my tennis shoe.

Foxy shook her head, then fixed the mattress that was askew. "Who are these people that are after me?"

"I have a hunch," I said. "But we'll find the truth. You have my word."

"I know," Foxy said. "Thank you, again." She removed a duffel bag from under her bed and started packing some clothes. First, she picked up the ones on the floor.

As she entered the bathroom for toiletries, my phone rang. It was my attorney, Keith Fenner. I felt my blood pressure rise. I let that go to voicemail. My accountant called right after. I also let it go to voicemail. I'd call her later.

Then Lily's phone range. Her face turned ladybug red as she answered. It must be Simon. Those two were the perfect match. As I watched my friend blush, my phone dinged with two voicemails. I skipped the one from Keith. He was probably wanting my final answer which I hadn't given him yet. But I listened to my accountant's. My heart skipped a few beats, and my stomach churned. I felt the blood rush from my face. I dropped the phone and plopped onto the bed.

"I'll call you right back." Lily hung up and hurried to my side. "Rose, what happened?"

I caught my breath and exhaled slowly. Sue was on my lap in a heartbeat.

"I lost it all."

"What?" Foxy and Lily said at once.

I looked up. "The stock tanked."

"Everything?" Lily asked.

"I still have money socked away in my savings account. But everything from the sale of the house was dumped into this high yield stock. My accountant advised against it. I didn't listen." I stood and tried to compose myself. I scanned Foxy's apartment. "How much does your rent cost? And do they take pets?" I asked with a nervous chuckle.

I watched Lily and Foxy exchange wide-eyed glances.

"Rose, you will not be renting in a flea bag apartment complex." Lily looked back at Foxy. "No offense."

"None taken. It is." Foxy came over to me and put her hand on my shoulder. "Rose, I'm going to pay you for your services. And I can loan you some money."

"Um … Foxy, that's awfully sweet of you," I said. "But you're a starving college student."

"That all changed today."

"What?" I cocked my head.

"I didn't finish reading you ladies the letter. That's if you're up to it."

I sat back on the bed and Lily joined me. With my financial situation now critical, some good news couldn't hurt. I inhaled deeply, but it didn't help the inferno bubbling inside my gut.

Sue rested her head on my lap and remained still.

"You'll get through this." Lily put her arm around me. "And I'll help you."

I nodded but had a hard time believing it.

What was I going to do?

CHAPTER 28

◆

I SHOOK OFF my pending financial doom—nothing I could do about it anyway—and prepared to listen to Foxy read the remainder of the letter.

"Sorry ladies, this is kind of long, bear with me." Foxy removed the letter from her pocket. "I think I left off with Uncle Gil meeting with Lily." She perused it and cleared her throat.

"About six months ago, I knew something was wrong when a fellow scientist who was on my team, mysteriously fell to his death. He was known as the chief poison maker. That will make sense in a moment. Shortly after he died, another scientist, I will leave his name anonymous too, met me in secret to tell me he suspected our colleague was pushed. He further revealed the experiment we'd been working on, known as Project X, was not what we were originally told.

"You see, we were unknowingly building on a mind control experiment that was shut down years ago due to its inhumane treatment of its test subjects. These subjects, referred to as irrelevant, were given a combination of psychedelic drugs, hypnosis, and torture. In many of the test subjects, their minds were fried as were their consciences. This breaking point allowed the scientists to test their impulses whereby another personality could be embedded. The experiments determined whether a person could involuntarily be made to perform acts of attempted assassination, through hypnosis.

"Their goal was to brainwash the subjects, erase their memories. Some of the test subjects were detainees in foreign countries in

111

undisclosed safe houses who were literally interrogated to death. The experiments were out of control and pushed the envelope until it burst at the seams. I assure you, had we have known they were building on those wretched experiments, we never would've agreed to it.

"All the scientists on our teams were taken to a clandestine CIA lab, which I believe was on a closed military base in the Nevada desert. We were blind folded and transported in the back of a van with no windows. We were separated and told for this study to work we could not collaborate. I found that peculiar, but being it was the CIA, I let it go. Here's another part I could not understand. They were experimenting with Project X on our pilots, telling them it was standard testing, but only when they were put in simulators. They sought to determine whether their test subjects could and would do something against their will."

"You mean like fly a plane into the side of a mountain!?" Lily said with a tight jaw.

I knew where she was going with this and that her father's accident was no accident. And then a thought occurred.

"Lily, do you remember much of anything else about that night you were drugged?"

Foxy looked in horror. "What?"

"Bits and pieces are coming back to me. I remember now that I did everything Mac told me to do." She ran her hands through her scalp. I could tell she was getting a headache again.

"Lily, I'm going to ask a painful question for both of you to hear." I shot glances between Foxy and Lily. "Did Mac tell you to shoot Gil?"

Foxy's face turned white. She eased on the bed, letter still in her hands and remained quiet.

Lily sighed. "I remember now, after he gave me the, you know ... heroin. He put the gun in my hand and pulled the trigger." She rose and paced.

"Do you think you remember this because of Mac's confession?" I asked.

Lily shook her head. "I recall his hand over mine."

Foxy leaned forward with her hands on her knees.

"I'm sorry, Foxy, that you had to hear all this," I said.

She sat straight and drew a deep breath. "It's okay. I need to know the truth."

"And I'm sorry I got Gil into this," Lily added.

"It's not your fault and by what the letter says, it appears my uncle contacted you first." She held up the paper. "May I?"

"Yes, please," I replied.

"Okay, where was I?" She scanned the sheet.

Lily stared off. No emotions this time. Just an empty gaze.

"I know this is hard to hear, Lily. It is for me too. It's almost finished," Foxy said. "Here we go. I apologize for the interruption as this letter has taken me almost three days to finish. But back to our experiment. Subsequent investigation by my colleagues and myself revealed Project X's side effects to be lethal, including sudden cardiac arrest, unpredictable mood swings, and amnesiac trance states. Had we worked collaboratively, these critical outcomes would have been expected.

"Upon meeting Lily, I discovered that her father, Gerald, was one of those pilots with such reactions. Following his decision to withdraw from the testing, he and his wife, Maisy, were tragically killed in a plane crash. I suspect they too were murdered. Further investigation revealed that our actions were not authorized by the CIA. Rather, a rogue team of CIA scientists, headed by Dr. Pierre. (He failed to offer his last name; no one questioned it.)

"I have arranged a meeting with Lily today to provide her with two USB flash drives. As I mentioned at the start of this letter, I sent her a microchip, a third source. All of my work has been destroyed. But I fear my co-scientists' work is still out there and most likely in the wrong hands. The laboratory and its operations must be located and permanently dismantled. That's why the data is in separate locations. In my line of work, the professional paranoia is necessary. Lily mentioned her employer was an Agency alum.

"I have complete confidence in Lily and those she vouches for. I don't want you in harm's way, so meet with her and provide all significant information. One undeniable fact; I am being followed. My phones and home bugged. The Agency considers me a whistleblower and a traitor. It is only a question of time before they find and eliminate me. After meeting with Lily, I will be going underground. If they don't reach me first.

"In closing, I love you more than words can describe. You are like a daughter to me. As I have no children, you are my sole heir, and I leave all my possessions to you. My investments proved prudent. You will have enough to finish college and more. But I implore you, do not work for the government. Use your degree for the real greater good and not what they want you to believe. PS. I sent you a key via certified mail. It goes to a safe deposit box at your bank."

The three of us sat silently, drinking it all in like sour lemonade.

CHAPTER 29

FOXY LOOKED AROUND the room. "I remember that, but I was in the middle of midterms and a wreck." She opened all her drawers, turning them upside down. She threw everything on the floor and ran to the open closet and tossed the boxes. "That's right! I stuffed it in my backpack so I wouldn't forget."

"At the club." I stood.

"Yes."

"Alrighty then," I said. "Finish packing and we'll head out."

Lily's phone rang. She gazed straight ahead.

"Lily are you okay?" I asked.

"Uh … yeah." She continued to stare off. "But I don't recall two flash drives. I remember Gil trying to say something to me in the hotel room." She shook her head. "I'm in shock hearing all this."

Lily wasn't the only one. I had no money, no home, and no real job. And now, hearing the letter, I had to add this mystery to my list of things to figure out.

"Rose." Lily interrupted my thoughts. "We need to get to the bottom of it."

"I was just thinking the same thing. But do you remember getting anything in the mail, Lily?"

"No. No letter, chip or otherwise. Maybe Lillian got it by mistake. And—" She glanced downward. "Gil was murdered before we had a chance to talk. The USB drive was also taken by that creep." Lily clenched her hands into tight fists. Lily's phone rang again. "It's Simon. You take it Rose." She passed it to me.

"Hi, we're kinda in the mi—oh. I see. Alrighty then. We'll be on the lookout. And we need to meet up. But first we're returning to the Flamingo. Foxy needs to get something. Let's rendezvous at the W in Miami. There's a room for you and Tucker in case you guys don't make it up north."

After I disconnected, I informed the gals we may have been tailed. Simon gave me the description of the Hummer, including license plate.

I turned to Foxy. "Do you know a man by the name of Terrance Folley, street name, Captain?"

She drew her head back and shook her head. "Never heard of him. Why?"

"He was your abductor." I peeked out the window and saw the Hummer. It stood out like a sore thumb in this neighborhood. "I assume you don't have any kind of weapon, rope, or anything that we could tie someone up with?"

"Didn't you say earlier you were going to call the police if we found him?" Lily asked.

I shrugged. "Old habits die hard. I'm kind of in the mood to bust someone's head. Losing more money makes me ornery." I groaned.

Foxy stood amidst the messy room with wide eyes. While Lily grinned. She was used to my ways.

"Just kidding about busting someone's head—kinda." I said the last word almost under my breath.

Foxy shook her head and laughed as she walked into the bathroom. She opened a drawer from a plastic rolling cart. She drew a stun gun and pressed a button. It made a zapping noise.

"Ahh, music to my ears," I said.

"It's high voltage. I bought it for protection. I'm not comfortable with guns. I'm not against them, just never used one."

"I can help with that." I winked at Foxy.

She ignored my comment. "I also have duct tape. I had to fix a leaky pipe, and that was all I had. The super is a loser." Foxy pulled a roll out from the same drawer.

"That'll work." I walked back to the curtain. This Terrance, a.k.a., Captain guy, was still in his vehicle. I pondered. "I don't suppose you have anything to knock someone out?" I snorted.

"Too bad we don't have your grandma's special sauce." Lily air quoted the last two words and chuckled.

"What did I miss?" Foxy asked.

"You *really* don't want to know," Lily and I said at the same time.

"You're correct, I don't." She opened the cabinet under her sink and pulled out a red plastic bag with cross bones on it. "Oh boy! I forgot about this." She showed us. "But please, please don't let anyone know I have it."

I walked over and inspected the bag. "What is trichloromethane?" I struggled to pronounce it.

"TCM, formula $CHCl_3$."

"Huh? I was never good with chemistry." I rubbed my forehead.

"This is an organic compound known as chloroform," Foxy said matter-of-factly.

"Um … do I want to know why you have chloroform?" I asked.

"No," Foxy replied.

Lily and I stared at one another with dropped mouths. "And I thought *you* colored outside the lines, Rose." Lily chuckled.

"No, not like that. It was for my molecular biology class. I meant to return it to the supply closet, but I absent-mindedly put it in my backpack with my books. I hid it here a few days ago, until I can return it."

We must've had dumfounded looks.

"It's used as a laboratory reagent for the detection of primary amines, bromides, and iodides. It's used in analytical chemistry to isolate these compounds. You'd be surprised at its many purposes. Which include DNA extraction from cells, using an extra—"

"Okay, okay. I get it, Madame Curie. We don't have time for a science lesson," I said. "We need a couple of rags and large baggies." I stood hands on hips. "Is there a back way out?"

"The bathroom window leads to a fire escape and the back lot." Foxy jutted her chin to the bathroom as she put together what I requested.

How was this going to play out? I didn't have Grandma's Sprinter van with her bag of tricks. My thoughts drifted to Grandma. I was certain she was keeping dark secrets. Did she know what happened to Lily's parents? Was she aware of these rogue experiments? When I confronted her in Montana, I saw pure fear in her eyes.

All this was linked somehow.

Without a doubt, we were treading in dangerous CIA waters and Grandma knew. Hence her warning.

CHAPTER 30

CAPTAIN SAT IN Bo's Hummer watching Foxy's upstairs apartment, considering his next move. Three of them and that dog. He was outnumbered and didn't want to gun them all down in daylight. Not to mention Rose was loaded and would pay handsomely for her pooch's safe return. So, he'd continue to follow them.

Ten minutes went by and nothing until he received a phone call. Blocked number again. Probably Juno. He had nothing new to report, and she was getting antsy. He ignored the call. Then a text came through.

J: Answer your damned phone.

Captain: Busy

J: STATUS!

Captain: Working on it.

J: You have two hours. Then I'm sending in someone else.

Sweat rolled down his neck. He knew Juno wasn't bluffing and he would be toes up in the everglades, because that's how it was done. After all, Captain fed gators with those schmucks who failed to come through.

He needed help on this case, so he dialed Bo. It went straight to voicemail.

"If he did something to my car, I swear I'm gonna kill him," Captain growled and called again. It was obvious his phone was off.

Next, Captain called Bo's gal, Nevaeh.

"Yo," Nevaeh answered in a heavy Bronx accent.

"Where the hell is Bo?"

"Hello to you too, asshat."

Captain cleared his throat. Nevaeh was a non-nonsense kinda person. She wasn't going to tell him anything unless he was nice. He'd have to put on his give-a-damn voice. He needed help.

"Yeah, yeah. Hello, doll."

"That's betta. What do you need?"

"Bo's phone is off. I need his assistance."

"Well, uh … I haven't heard from that no good for nutin' land shark. He was supposed to meet me in Naples at my aunt's. When you find him, tell him it's ova. When I get back to Miami, he can find his shit on the front lawn."

Captain contemplated her initial hesitation. She knew where Bo was and didn't want to tell him. But, why … unless he wrecked his vehicle.

"He better not have put so much as a scratch on my Caddy."

"Wait, where's his Humma?"

"We switched cars. So, you really haven't heard from him?"

"I may be many things, but I ain't no liar. No. I haven't seen the short troll today. We was gonna cuddle and watch movies." She paused. "Does he have a skank on the side?"

"Oh, Nevaeh. He's too scared of you to do that."

"Aww … ya think so? Well, okay then. If I hear from my snookum', I'll have him call ya."

Captain looked at the phone. The dame was unhinged. A real whack job. He'd seen her cut off a gal's pinky who looked at her last boyfriend wrong. Come to think of it, that poor bastard hadn't been seen in a year. He wondered for a second but shook it off.

"Alright, doll. I gotta go."

As he disconnected, his phone rang. Probably Juno, again. He ignored it and peered at his watch. It'd been a half hour. Something didn't feel right.

Better check out the apartment.

He got out of the car, then remembered he'd put his gun in the back seat. No way he was leaving it behind this time.

As he turned to open the rear door, Foxy's Toyota skidded to a halt next to him.

Out jumped the black-haired hottie from the bus stop. He scrambled to open the door and grab his gun, but he felt a hot zap to his neck.

He'd been stunned before and knew he'd be fine. But this was different. It was a high-voltage electric charge. Captain's body stiffened and then his muscles rapidly contracted. He couldn't move. What the hell was this? Intense pain followed. And then something unexpected happened. One of the crazy dames covered his mouth with a cloth.

Lights out.

When Captain woke, he was lying in the backseat of the Toyota. His wrists and ankles were bound in duct tape and that damned dog was sitting on his stomach, growling at him. After the vision in his good eye came into focus, he heard a gal's voice that sounded like Foxy.

"Dirtbag is waking up." It was the dark-haired one.

She was behind him in the back of the hatchback. Rose, the redhead, was driving, with Foxy beside her.

"Hit him again, Lily," Rose said to the gal behind him. "And given his size, you need to increase the dose."

"Wha?" Captain slurred. He shook out of it and was ready to take them on, including the mutt. He pushed the dog off him onto the floorboard, but she jumped back on him, snarling.

"Sue, come," Rose said. "I don't want you getting hit."

"That ain't gonna happn'." Captain sat up, but the backseat was spinning.

What in the hell did they give him? He yanked his wrists so that the duct tape loosened, and he turned his head to the left to find something—anything. And then he heard zapping again, followed by the familiar searing pain. Rose rolled down the window and Foxy pulled out a cloth from a plastic baggie and put it over his nose and mouth. Now he remembered that pungent smell like ether—chloroform.

Those bitc—lights out, again.

———

Captain opened his eyes, but the room was blurry.

"Wakey, wakey, shit head!" A female's voice boomed and his head pounded.

"Wha—" He was sitting in a chair that felt like it was swaying.

Or was it from the crap they gave him? He tried to move, but he couldn't.

His ankles were still bound together, but this time tighter—with rope. His wrists were bound in the back in a similar manner. He felt plastic cuffs. Rope tethered his waist to the chair.

With a shake of his head, his good eye focused better. Captain saw four large men standing over him. The Dancing Flamingo's bouncers wearing their resting bitch faces. The room looked familiar. He'd been back there before. It was the private room of the club. There were no windows. That he remembered.

"Where are those crazy women?"

"If you're referring to me," a female's voice echoed from behind him. "I'm right here." It was Rose along with that mutt. It was her voice that woke him, and she gave the chair another kick. Her dog was growling, too.

"Get it away from me!"

"Sue's not an *it*."

"Don't care. I hate dogs."

"Believe me, the feelings are mutual."

"What do you want?" Captain spit his words.

"It's not you we want. But information." Rose looked at the bouncers. "Thanks for bringing the big lug inside. He's a bit heavy. Lily and I will take it from here." She nodded, and they left the room.

He glanced left and saw Lily scowling, arms crossed.

Lily and Rose each pulled up a chair and sat in front of him. The dog, Sue, sat next to Rose, staring at him.

"Who are you?"

"You don't ask the questions." Lily sat back.

"Not telling ya shit."

"Very well," Rose said. "But I have someone on speed-dial who might be interested in knowing your whereabouts. I believe you owe him a lot of money."

"Are you threatening me?"

"I don't make threats."

"Humpf." He paused. "Two can play that game, hot stuff. If I don't make a phone call—" He looked around the room for a clock. The time read ten after four. "In a half hour, a certain old man will be pecker up in the everglades."

Rose and Lily looked at one another and shrugged.

"Who?" Rose asked.

Captain smirked. "It seems I have some leverage. I ain't tellin' you jack unless you release me."

"How do we know you're not lying?" Lily inquired.

"Go ask the bartender."

"On it." Lily left the room.

While Lily was out of the room, Rose pulled her chair closer to him and got in his face.

"You might intimidate some people, but you don't scare me. You have no idea what I'm capable of doing. And right now, I *really* have nothing to lose." Her dog put her paw on Rose's leg and whimpered. "Okay, sweet girl. Maybe you. But that's it." Rose yanked his head back. She pulled out a knife from her fanny pack and put it to his throat.

Captain chuckled bitterly. "Same goes for me ... sweet cheeks."

"So, who hired you?"

Captain turned away and said nothing.

"I get it. You really don't know, do you?"

"It's above my pay grade. I don't ask. I just do a job."

"Foxy. Why are you after her?"

Captain snapped his gaze back to Rose. "You seem like a smart gal, you tell me."

"Okay." Rose bent over and got in his face, staring a hole through Captain. "By the frightened look in your eyes ... CIA."

Rose stood and paced in front of him. "But you don't appear to have that CIA operative look. So, I'd say you were hired by someone you haven't met." She bent down and was in his face again. "This is not my first go round with this kind of situation. But you see last couple of times, I had a bag of tricks and all kinds of tools at my disposal. I'm really becoming quite proficient at enhanced interrogation."

"You really going to torture me ... in here? You don't have the equipment. Or better yet, taze me again? I can take that all day. And not the first time I've been chloroformed, either. I kinda like the smell."

Rose opened her fanny pack and pulled out a gun. "That's getting boring. You see, I can cut you loose and shoot you. After all, it would be self-defense. While I'm not sure if this is your first job doing contract work for the Agency, I know they seek out people who have nothing to lose. No one will miss you."

"You're nuts."

"You have no idea. I've seen her do some crazy stuff." Lily's voice sounded from the doorway. "And right now, she's a donkey on the edge. She's losing her fortune because she won't carry Satan's spawn." She walked up to Captain and leaned over him. "Not to mention, she's survived five gunshot wounds. I think it's made her loonier." Lily made little circles near her head with her index finger. And stood up tall.

"Six." Rose smirked at Lily.

"See? Crazy." Lily pulled Rose away and whispered something in her ear.

Rose put her gun back in her fanny pack and peeked over her shoulder at Captain and returned to her huddle. She spun back and Lily left the room again.

"It appears you *do* have something to lose," Rose said.

"What?"

"Listen, Terrance Folley. You have a great aunt in Boca."

Captain drew his head back. She'd done her homework. He lunged forward, but the chair toppled over, crashed to the floor, and he took a header.

"So help me, if you touch her, I'll hunt you down," he raged from the floor.

That dog came over and growled in his face again.

"Get your fukin' dog away from me." Captain attempted to kick her but couldn't get his legs to work well enough.

"Sue, come." Rose called and she retreated.

"Who the hell names a dog, 'Sue'?"

"It was my murdered friend's name."

"You are nuts!"

"Meh." Rose grunted as she picked up his chair and returned him upright. "I go to great lengths for my family and friends. So, here's the deal. You cut Stella's uncle loose, and we call the dogs off your aunt." She pulled out her phone. "What's the number of the thug who's holding him?"

Captain turned away and thought for a spell. Juno didn't pay him enough for this BS. He gave her the number.

"Now wasn't that easy." Rose dialed. "And you should know,

after you gave the Agency what they wanted, you would've disappeared for good. My suggestion to you is to never work for them again. Stick with breaking kneecaps." She put the phone on speaker.

"Yo!" A man with a Latin accent answered.

"Cut the old man loose."

"You got what you needed?"

"Yeah."

Rose covered the phone. "He needs to bring him here."

"Drop him off at the Flamingo."

"Can't do that. Power lines are down. The hurricane hit landfall. Ain't you watching the news? It's a Cat Two."

"I'm a little tied up."

"Sorry, bro." He disconnected.

Captain shrugged. "I tried."

Rose squeezed his bicep where her dog bit him. "Where's he being held?" She dug in deep with her nails.

"Shiiit!" Captain shouted. "You heard him, the storm's here. And listen to that wind."

"We're safe here. I've been told they had this addition built to withstand a hurricane. Now where is he?"

After Captain gave Rose Stella's uncle's location, she walked over and called someone.

"Simon, I'm going to text you an address, please pick this man up—unh huh. Okay, thanks."

"So, you gonna cut me loose?"

"After I get confirmation he's alive and well. But first we have unfinished business." Rose and her mutt left the room.

CHAPTER 31

◆

SUE AND I walked out of the back room and joined Lily, Foxy, and Stella in the lounge area. The bouncers had just finished boarding up the windows and were sent home. Through the hurricane-impact glass, I saw palm trees whipping violently in the strengthening wind. A torrential downpour had begun. This was a Category Two? I hoped everyone made it off the yacht and were headed for safety.

I'd just pulled my phone out of my yoga shorts when it rang. It was Saki. She said she and Cousin Essie returned to Miami Beach because they dropped off one of her staff. But they were stuck as the causeway heading toward Miami was blocked with downed lines and fallen trees. They couldn't meet us at the hotel in Miami until later. I informed her that we were at the club, riding out the hurricane, and she and Essie should join us.

Foxy came out of the employee area; her face white as a sheet. She held up an AirTag. "I found this in my raincoat pocket." She threw it on the table. "Who would be tracking me?"

"Captain," Lily and I said at once.

Stella walked over with her head down. "I'm sorry, I had to." She plopped at a table and dropped her head in her hands. "I'm so worried about my un—cle." She sobbed.

"I know. But not for long." I put my hand on her shoulder.

"You should've let our bouncers handle him," Harlee said as she walked up with freshly made coffee. Her sister, Nala, followed with mugs and set them at the table.

I sat at the table, Sue on my feet. I watched the palm branches sway by the door. The lights flickered on and off. "How is your electricity still on?"

"We have a generator," Nala said, looking up. "It just kicked on. And this is the safest place for us to be. But I suggest we head to the back room where your man is being held and get away from any potential flying glass."

I texted Simon regarding the status of Stella's uncle. "Shoot. No cell service." I went to the door and peered out.

It was getting worse. The streets were flooding, and a huge palm tree that was in the front was ripped out of the ground and crashed down. I jumped. As soon as my heartbeat returned to normal, I looked at my phone again hoping by some miracle that standing next to the door, I'd get service. Nada.

"Saki and Essie should've been here by now. They were only a block away." I turned to Lily. "I need to find my sister and little cousin." I put on my raincoat.

"Rose, that's not a good idea," Lily said, walking over to join me. "It's not safe out there."

"I can't let anything happen to them."

"At least put on these." Harlee handed me bright yellow rain pants, jacket, and boots.

Sue did her tippy tap dance like we were going on an adventure.

"Sweet baby, you stay here. Not unless you need to go potty. Which would be ill advised."

Sue looked at me with her big brown eyes. I could tell her excitement was not a pee break, but to go with me. Just as I donned the rain suit and boots, Saki and Essie pounded on the door. Two drowned rats.

I flinched as I didn't see them pull up.

I tried the door, but it was locked, and the key wasn't in the door. "Hurry, I need to unlock it."

The wind was whipping the gals around, and they were hanging on tight to the door handles.

Nala ran over, unlocked the doors, and quickly opened them. It was a joint effort since the wind practically sucked us outside.

"Holy shit balls." Saki shook out of her coat.

"Nice to see you too, little sis." I hugged her tightly. I turned to Essie and embraced her too.

"We had to walk," Essie said. "The roads are flooding. Downed power lines. Some are even surfing."

"Happens all the time," Harlee said.

Saki stepped back from me and giggled. "What the hell, Rose, you look like the Morton sailor. Where were you going?"

"To find you, Ms. Potty mouth."

"Like I told you, I only swear when my daughter's not around."

"Yes, she's said things I'd not heard since … forever." Essie laughed.

"Sorry about that. My staff pisses me off sometimes. You ask them to do a simple f'n job. If you want something done right, you've got to do it yourself." Her face scrunched. It was the same angry face she'd made as a child.

"You got that right," Harlee agreed.

My phone chimed with a text message and two missed calls. Thank God the cell was working again.

"You're a popular woman, Rose." Essie walked over and peeked at my phone.

I pulled away. Why was she so interested in who called me? I pondered for a second.

The text was from Simon. A picture of Stella's uncle, safe in the back seat of Tucker's truck. They were headed to the hospital to get him checked out. I showed it to Stella.

"Thank you so much. How can I repay you all?" Stella asked. "And will you forgive me?" She directed the last question to Foxy.

"Of course, you're my best friend." Foxy gave her pal a hug.

Essie's phone vibrated with a call, and she excused herself to take it.

"What do we do with the creep in the back?" Nala asked as she placed water bottles on the table.

"I say we toss his ass in the hurricane," Stella said with tight fists. "Better yet, let me at him."

"Get in line," Foxy said.

Harlee emerged from the back room. "Neither. He broke out of the plastic cuffs. The bonehead bled all over my floor before hightailing it out the back door."

Great. One more tied up loose end again. Of course, odds were good he'd be taken out by a falling tree or branch. I decided to worry about Captain's whereabouts later.

Harlee, Nala, Foxy, and Stella walked to the back. Lily, Saki and I stayed in the lounge area where I had privacy to finish playing my messages. I grabbed a bottle of water and listened.

My jaw dropped. I already knew I was losing Max's money and all my own money I'd invested, but what my attorney, Keith, said left me gobsmacked.

"What is it Rose?" Lily asked.

"Shilo escaped from federal custody."

Saki had just taken a sip of water and spit it out. "I thought she was in *state* prison."

"Apparently she had unrelated federal charges here in Florida," I said.

"Wait! She's here? In Florida?" Saki's voice rose with every question.

"Yep. It came as a shock to me, too," I said. "Anyway, when they searched her cell, there were notes and drawings depicting me dead in various ways. She had written crazy letters to Max, even though he's dead. She said something about having something that was rightfully hers and that Max always loved her. Blah, blah, blah."

"How did she escape?" Lily asked.

"She was on a medical transport to an outside hospital as she was complaining of chest pains. Keith further warned me that they found another note with my yacht location. Shilo apparently hired a private investigator to find me. And since she had a lot of money socked away from when she milked Max for all her private therapy sessions, Shilo could afford it.

"Even worse, Keith informed me that my deadline was midnight tomorrow to give him my final answer. If I chose to be inseminated, he'd need to schedule it for the day after tomorrow." I covered my face with my hands.

In a daze, I wandered behind the bar and helped myself to a whiskey shot. I mean, isn't that what you're supposed to do in a hurricane? I was on automatic and was about to pour a second and then remembered that I wasn't on my yacht. I mean the yacht that used to be mine.

Saki and Lily plopped at the bar, staring at me.

"So much for not drinking after last night," Saki said.

I toasted with my shot glass. "It's that kind of day."

Sue hopped up on a stool too and put her paws on the bar. A

silly thing I allowed her to do on the yacht.

"Little doggo, you can't do that here," I said.

"All good, it wouldn't be the worst thing that's been up there." Foxy walked out from the back room and joined us. She sat next to Sue and chuckled.

"I don't want to know." I picked up the whiskey bottle, pulled out three shot glasses, and poured. "Put this on my tab," I said to Foxy.

"It's on me. It's the least I can do." Foxy shook her head. "But none for me. I need my brain cells. Gotta study."

Saki threw back her shot. "What the hell. Why not. Hit me again, barmaid."

"I'm game." Lily grinned and drank too.

Sue gave me that "what about me" look, so I searched for a bowl. I found one with pretzels, tossed them out, and poured Sue water. She was always up for a party.

"So, this is where the festivities are." Essie bounced in and joined us at the bar.

"I take it your call was successful." Saki smirked.

Essie nodded.

What was that about?

I waved it off; I had too much on my plate. "Where are the sisters and Stella?" I asked and poured Essie a shot.

She drank it and tapped her glass for another. "They're in the upstairs loft cleaning broken glass. Apparently, someone neglected to board up a window." Essie threw back her second.

"I think they're putting Stella to work for betraying me," Foxy said. "I don't fault her."

"Stella felt bad and offered to help." Essie ambled to the table and brought us all back more bottled water. "Oh, Rose. Your guy escaped from the downstairs back room."

"I heard. Oh well, I didn't need him anymore."

"You know how to find him, huh?" Essie asked.

I gave Essie a cheeky grin. "Boy for someone who hasn't been here long, you sure know a lot about what's going on."

"It's a curse. People spill their souls to me," Essie said. "I just watch and listen."

"Yeah, I noticed that, Essie," Saki said. "You're crazy observant. It's that cute little brain of yours, always thinking and watching. If I didn't know any better, I'd say you were sent to spy on us." Saki snorted.

"Saki!" I slapped her hand.

"What? Sheesh, just kidding." Saki pulled her hand away and rubbed it. "Essie knows I'm joking."

I studied Essie; she wasn't smiling. Could Shilo have hired her? Infiltrate the enemy and report back? She certainly took several phone calls. Nah, I shouldn't be drinking if that's what my brain came up with.

Lily and Saki cocked their heads at me.

"What's going on upstairs in your brain?" Lily asked.

"Do you really have to ask?" Saki rolled her hair in a bun. "Whatever it is, it's frightening."

I walked around the bar and sat. Sue hopped onto my lap. "Shilo escaped." I rubbed behind Sue's ears.

"Who's Shilo?" Essie asked.

"Only some whack doodle nut job obsessed with Max," Saki said.

"Oh, I remember hearing about Max," Essie said. "He believed Uncle Teddy was responsible for his father's death."

"Don't blame Max," Saki said. "I mean, dear ole' dad did shoot him."

"True. Dad served time in federal prison," I added.

"Not the whole sentence." Saki took a swig of water. "He turned on some bad guys."

"But what does this Shilo have to do with it?" Foxy asked.

"As you know, Max was Richie Rich loaded. And seeing me after all these years … well he couldn't shake his obsession, so he hired a therapist."

"Which personality hired her?" Saki asked. "Thomas or Max?"

I tilted my head at my sister. "Don't speak ill of the deceased."

"It's true." Saki shrugged. "I guess I shouldn't be too hard on him. He left you his entire fortune … until tomorrow. But he did have two personalities."

"Yes, he did. But remember, he took a bullet meant for me and Dad. And Thomas eventually disappeared. Anyhow, his therapist, Shilo, quickly became infatuated with Max and would do anything for him. She started to follow me around, I believe to report back to Max. Long story short, since I was involved in too many shootings, my department ordered me to seek counseling. Unbeknownst to me, Shilo killed *my* therapist and took her identity."

"Not before she changed her hair color and had colored contacts to look like you, sister." Saki interjected.

"She did what?" Foxy asked.

"And to prove her loyalty to Max, she wacked off her own finger, after abducting Heidi." Saki looked at Essie. "You see, Heidi worked as Max's nanny when he was a child, practically raised him. And then I hired her to help me with Violet. We knew her when we were kids."

"That's right. You guys played with Max when you were children," Lily said. "Didn't all your parents hang out?"

I nodded. "Shilo was sentenced to serve life in California for murder and Montana for kidnapping. She also had unrelated federal charges. After she served fed time, she was going to be transferred to the state pen. And now she's in the wind." I shrugged.

"Is that all you got? A shrug, Rose," Lily said.

"What else can I say? Just giving Essie the condensed version." I took a sip of water.

Lily turned to face me. "Wait a minute, what day did she escape?"

"Five days ago," I replied.

"And they're just now telling you this? She tried to kill you, Rose!" Lily said. "Don't they have a duty to warn you?"

"They do. However, they had a hard time tracking me down."

"Let me get this straight," Saki said. "A crazy woman had no problem locating you, but the Feds took their sweet time?"

Essie, Foxy, Lily, and I laughed.

"Okay, point well taken." Saki chuckled too.

"Wait a minute," Foxy said, "remember today when a blacked-out SUV tried to run you guys over. Do—"

I bit my lower lip.

"What?" Saki hopped off her barstool. "Why wasn't I told about this?"

"Sorry, little sister. It slipped my mind. With the hurricane and all."

"It slipped your mind, Rose?" Saki put her hands on her hips and shook her head like a bobble head. "You promised no more secrets."

I exchanged glances with Foxy and Lily. Saki will flip a lid when she finds out we were keeping one big CIA Project X secret from her. I felt an ulcer developing.

CHAPTER 32

AS I CONTEMPLATED Project X and what to do next, my phone rang.

I put Simon on speaker.

"It's crazy out here. The hurricane has uprooted trees, power lines are down, the rise of water." He said it all in one breath.

"I know, alligators in the sewer," I said.

"Funny. But I swear I saw one surfing down Ocean Avenue."

"Welcome to Florida," Foxy said.

"Where are you?" I asked.

"Stuck in traffic."

"Why didn't you go to the W?"

"Remember, we had to take Stella's uncle to the hospital," Simon said. "They ended up admitting him ... and Rose, when have you ever known me to run and hide?"

"Point well taken, Simon. I would've done the same."

"Trust me," Simon said. "I know."

"I thought the causeway was blocked coming into Miami Beach."

"It's clear—hey. Did you release your Captain Hook?"

"Um ... he escaped. Why?" I asked.

"Because he's running like a bat out of hell down the street. And only guilty parties run in street clothes. Do you want me to pick him up?"

I pondered that for a second. "Nah. He's not worth it. He's just a pawn and doesn't know who the players are. He's irrelevant."

Saki gave me a furrowed brow. She knew I wasn't telling her

the truth. And Essie, well she's a human lie detector and just looked at me with a raised forehead.

"Crap, Rose," Simon said. "The police are turning everyone around. We can't get to you."

"All good. We are fi—" Just then, a crashing sound came from upstairs, followed by screaming. "Hey, Simon. Gotta go."

"Wait! Is everyone o—"

I disconnected. We all jumped off our barstools and headed upstairs.

Simon was going to kill me; I'd hung up on him twice in one day. But that wasn't the current concern. The moment our feet hit the first step, the shouting intensified.

"Help us, the roof caved in on Stella," Harlee hollered. "Call 9-1-1."

"On it," Foxy said and stayed downstairs.

The stairwell was narrow and from what Foxy told us, the upstairs had just one tiny room. I turned and Sue was on my heels.

"Saki and Essie, please stay downstairs with Sue."

They obliged me. Lily and I raced upstairs where we saw a tree had partially collapsed the roof.

Stella was under it, sobbing and flailing. "I can't move. Something's stuck in my leg!"

The four of us scrambled to remove plaster and roof tiles off Stella. After the last bit of insulation and sheet rock were gone, we all let out a collective gasp. A tree branch, connected to the tree, was sticking through her upper thigh.

Stella looked down and her face turned as white as well … the sheet rock.

"Shouldn't we take that out of her leg?" Harlee asked.

"No!" Nala and I replied at once.

"That could worsen her condition. She could go into shock and bleed to death." I shot my eyes around the room. But it was more like a loft with a bed. "I need something to secure the branch. And a first aid kit."

Harlee stood with a gaping mouth, running her hands through her hair.

"Harlee," I shook her shoulders. "Look at me. I need your help. Do you have a first aid kit?" I asked slower.

She nodded.

"Go downstairs and get it for me," I calmly said. I looked at Lily. "Can you help her?"

Lily knew the various "looks" I've been told I have. She knew I wasn't trying to get rid of her, and that it was meant to keep Harlee busy.

Lily gave a nod of understanding and bolted downstairs. The last thing Stella needed was for us to panic.

I returned to Stella. "Okay, Stella. Look at me."

Her eyes were starting to close as water pounded her face.

"Stella, can you hear me?"

She opened her eyes. And said nothing.

"Get me an umbrella. And a raincoat." I called out and turned back to Stella. "Stay with me, okay." I kept my voice even. "Help is on the way."

I looked at Nala and she shook her head with a worried look. The tree wasn't going anywhere.

Foxy's head appeared above the stairs. She gasped. I held my palm to her like a traffic cop slowing cars. Stella did not need to see the frightened look on Foxy's face, so I walked to the steps.

Foxy handed me the coat, umbrella, and the first aid kit and whispered in my ear that the roads were blocked, and emergency personnel were busy handling other calls. They would get to us as soon as possible. For now, we were on our own. I asked Foxy to return downstairs since there wasn't much space.

Nala walked over and heard part of the conversation. She took the raincoat and draped it over Stella and opened the umbrella.

I returned to Stella and went to work. Her leg was now gushing blood. Quickly, I removed a wad of gauze from the kit. I would've also liked to have used quick clot, but there wasn't any. I placed the gauze around the protruding branch to support it, trying my best to keep it in place until it was surgically removed.

Rain continued to pound our faces from the gaping hole in the ceiling. But keeping Stella as dry as possible was a priority. By now the wind was blowing so hard as the hurricane hammered landfall, they were expected to exceed ninety miles per hour.

Category Two? It felt more like a three, or even a four.

We were all tossed about by the strengthening winds. The umbrella was blown inside out, and Nala was thrown back and hit her head against the wall.

"Dagnabbit!" Nala bellowed.

I dropped to my knees. "Are you okay?"

"Good thing I've got a hard noggin." She rubbed her head. "I'm so mad. We called to have that doggone tree removed. Now look at her."

Nala and I sat on the floor, looking at one another. For the first time, I had no idea how we were going to get out of this or keep Stella safe. She started wailing and saying things that didn't make sense.

I continued to monitor her, as I was worried about her going into shock. All the signs were there.

CHAPTER 33

◆

AFTER CAPTAIN BROKE free of the plastic cuffs, his wrists were bloody. He slipped out the back door and made a run for it. The hurricane was now in full swing, but he didn't care. He ran as fast as his feet would carry him. The water was rising, and he watched as the waves slammed against the docks. Miami Beach streets were empty, and the causeway must be blocked off as there wasn't much traffic.

He thought he saw an alligator float by but shook it off. Probably side effects from the chloroform. Downed power lines blocked the streets, sparking like crazy. No one dared cross them, especially with police blocking the roads. A sudden gust of wind almost knocked Captain off his feet.

A black Chevy truck crept by. Were they watching him? Nah, those bold enough to be on the streets were inching their way through the high water. He stared at the truck just to be certain. He only saw two large shadows; he couldn't make out their faces. Captain ignored it and bolted the five blocks to Foxy's apartment complex.

The moment he arrived, he was shocked. "Oh shit, shit, shit." Bo's vehicle was on blocks and all four tires were missing. The Hummer's emblem was stripped too. Bo was going to kill him. But first, Nevaeh would chop off his nuts. She loved that Hummer. He walked around the vehicle. None of the windows were broken.

Other than missing wheels, the Hummer didn't have a scratch on it. Most likely the fools that did it, thought it belonged to one of the many drug dealers who frequented the 'hood.

They saw him get abducted, they had to have. He tried the door handle, but it was locked. At least those crazy dames locked it. He patted his shorts pocket for the key fob. Small favor, but he still had it.

Captain unlocked the Hummer and hopped in to get out of the storm. He scanned the backseat. Relief fell over him, again. His gun, wallet, and cell phone were still on the floorboard. Go figure.

He called Bo, but his call went to voicemail once more.

What happened to Bo? Captain drew a breath. He'd call the girlfriend again, and brace for an ass chewing.

He scrolled through the phone ignoring the five missed calls. All unknown numbers. Probably Juno. He'd deal with her later.

Nevaeh's phone rang.

"Yo," Bo said.

"What the hell, Bo. Where've you been?"

"Excuse me? The same applies to you."

"Hey you, mook," Nevaeh roared into the phone. "You got my shnookums hurt. Wait until I get my hands on ya'. My size six stiletto is gonna be so far up ya ass, it'll give you a tonsillectomy."

Captain shuddered at the thought. She'd do it, too. "Look Nevaeh, I don't know what you're talking about."

"I'll tell you what I'm talking about." It was Bo again. "Two thugs kidnapped me, thinking I was you. They broke my fukin' fingers. Ya ass wipe. I'll send you the ER bill."

"Well, I was abducted too. Tazed, drugged, and worked over." Yeah, he made up the last one. He didn't dare tell Bo those nutso gals took him.

"Ahh, geezo, sorry, buddy. You okay? Was it those two big dudes with the Rottie?"

"Oh, yeah. I barely escaped." Captain needed to milk this for when he told Bo about his wheels.

"Are you callin' to exchange cars?"

"Um … kinda. Um … there's a slight problem."

"You didn't wreck my baby, did ya?"

"No, nothing like that. But, you know, when they abducted me, um … your Hummer was left at that apartment complex in Miami Beach."

"No! The Gardens? That shit bag place?"

"Yeah. Well, they took your wheels and the hood ornament."

"Is that all?"

"As far as I can tell. So, I kinda need a ride."

"You're tits outta luck. Miami Beach is isolated. Serves ya right for leaving my baby."

"Where the hell am I supposed to stay?" And that's when he looked up and saw Foxy's apartment. He had to take a leak in the worst way.

"Ya betta stay in the Hummer and watch her," Nevaeh growled in the phone. "Ya ass."

"Yeah, yeah." Captain disconnected. With his wallet, phone, and gun in hand, he locked the doors and ran to the apartment.

When Captain stepped into Foxy's studio, he discovered the roof had partially caved in under the weight of the water. And what remained of her belongings was damaged.

Not his problem. He stepped over debris to the bathroom and relieved himself. His wrists were still bleeding and now throbbed. He had to avoid an infection. He rummaged through her medicine cabinet and found antibiotic spray and dressing.

While he was there, Captain checked his other injuries. The arm bandage was soaked with blood, so he removed it and discovered puss. Great. And he'd forgotten the ointment the hospital prescribed, so he cleaned it the best he could, applied antibiotic spray, and re-wrapped it. He retrieved trash bags from under the sink and used them as a rain shield for his arm. At this rate, he'd need a full body suit.

During his wound check, he looked under the patch. The eye was still swollen shut and hurt like no one's business, so he retrieved the eye drops from his pocket, administered them, and reapplied the patch. Thankfully he didn't forget that medication.

"How'd you let these dames do this to you?" Captain continued to curse himself in the mirror. And who the hell was this Rose chick? Did she work for the CIA? She knew too much about how they operated. Captain pondered as he turned his head sideways and noticed his neck was red with welts from the taser. Anger brewed. These ladies were going down. That was a promise.

Forty-five minutes later, Captain emerged from the bathroom. His phone rang. Unknown number. Must be Juno.

"I don't get paid enough to be tazed, drugged and kidnapped."

"Let me guess, two big guys and a Rottweiler?" Juno laughed.

"I'm glad you think it's funny."

"What's funny is that I know it was Rose and her crew that you're up against. Did you get your ass kicked by Charlie's Angels and Scooby-Doo?"

"More like the Dirty Dozen and Cujo."

"I'll tell you what's not funny, you still haven't produced anything," Juno snapped.

"I. Was. Kidnapped." Captain spoke slowly and deliberately through gnashed teeth. "And who the hell hired you?"

"Need to know only. You don't."

"I do know. I'm going to go right out and say it. The CIA."

Juno became silent.

"I'll take that as a yes." Captain ran down the steps, back to the Hummer and hopped in the backseat. "I need a way out of Miami Beach. I'm stranded."

"Can't. I heard it's inaccessible."

Captain punched the back of the headrest.

"Tell me where you are, and I'll see what I can do," Juno said.

Captain contemplated. "Hell, no. I don't trust that you won't send in someone to whack me."

"I wouldn't do any such thing." Her voice gentled and he wished he could believe her.

"The hell you wouldn't." His head was on a swivel. He turned in his seat. And looked up. "How do I know you don't have access to a drone and have been tracking me?"

"You watch too many spy movies."

"Bull shit. I've seen what the government can do. And what information is *so* important that you're this desperate?"

"End of business today. Or else."

"Or else what? You're in no position to make demands. It seems to me that you would've already sent in someone else since I have failed to produce."

"What do you have so far?"

"She didn't get anything in the mail. No USB. And her laptop is inaccessible. Again, she was held at gun point and insisted there was just college crap on it. I believe her."

"If she has nothing, then why does she have protection around her? I need that data."

"True. But I'm one person."

"Hire a second."

"I'm seriously not getting paid enough for this crap."

"Fine. I'll double your f—"

"Triple. If I'm going to bring someone else on board."

The line went quiet. Captain checked the phone to make sure the call didn't drop.

"Fine," Juno finally said.

"I'm seriously stuck in Miami Beach."

"Wait out the hurricane. It's only a Cat Two. You've been through worse."

"I've got no wheels."

"Not my problem. Figure it out."

"This is bull cra—"

Juno disconnected.

"What the hell?" Captain sat back thinking about his options.

He snapped his fingers. That guy who worked for Miami Beach PD. Another cop who owed him. Then, another thought struck him. What did Foxy have that had Juno so frazzled?

Or better yet, the CIA.

CHAPTER 34

AGENT H SAT outside a D.C. restaurant. He had dinner reservations with his wife at 5:30 p.m., but eating was the last thing on his mind. H looked at his burner phone. Surely, he should've heard something—anything—from Juno by now.

He dialed.

"Yes," she answered curtly.

"Where are we?"

"*We* are nowhere."

Agent H loosened the tie that was choking him, and his chest tightened. This situation was going to give him a heart attack. "Do I need to remind you how detrimental that information is?"

"Since I don't know specifically what it is we're looking for, it's a challenge."

"I can't divulge that to you. And besides, you don't want to know."

"Is that why you didn't have your own people handle this?"

H ignored her question. "How can one girl be a problem? She's a college student for crying out loud."

"She has help. A woman by the name of Rose O'Brien and her friends. Have you heard of her?"

"I'm afraid I have."

"Rose has become an obstacle," Juno said.

"You don't need me to tell you what to do with obstacles."

H's wife stepped out of the restaurant and looked around. She spotted him and pointed at her watch. This was an important date as his marriage was on the rocks from his long hours at the CIA.

He put his finger up to her and mouthed, *one more minute.*

"Juno, I have to go." He disconnected and rolled down his window. "Sweetheart, I'll meet you inside. One more phone call. I promise and then I'm all yours."

His wife, Katrina, shook her head in disgust. H watched as she turned on her heels and stormed back into the restaurant.

He dialed.

"Yes," a woman answered.

"Lillian, your granddaughter has been sticking her nose into places they shouldn't be. This situation is critical, to say the least. I will not be held responsible for what happens to her. She needs to stand down at once."

"I've told you how stubborn she can be. I have as much control over that girl as I do the weather."

"Handle Rose. I wouldn't want to see any harm come to her. I'm only giving you a warning as a courtesy. If it were anyone else … well, there would be no phone calls, no warnings, no mercy."

H hung up, wiped the sweat from his forehead, straightened his tie. Before exiting his vehicle, he grabbed the dozen roses and went inside the restaurant, putting on his doting husband's face. He needed to save his marriage. His life changed for the better when he met Katrina.

Simon and Tucker made their way through Miami Beach to the Dancing Flamingo. While Rose didn't ask for his help, as per the norm, Simon had a gut feeling. And given that crashing noise he heard before she hung up on him … again.

He was glad Tucker had a lift to his Chevy, Simon thought, or he wouldn't have been able to drive through the flood waters.

Tucker dodged sparking power lines as they slowly cruised. They drove in silence as they passed partially caved in roofs from where uprooted trees fell. Sirens wailed in the distance.

"Looks like a war zone," Tucker finally said.

"No kidding and we've seen plenty of that." Simon reflected on their multiple tours in Afghanistan.

Simon's satellite phone rang. With the cell towers down, he'd been using his backup.

"Yes," Simon answered.

"What in the Sam Hill has my granddaughter gotten herself into? You need to get her to back down. She's in way over her head. I thought you were supposed to be keeping an eye on her."

"Good day to you too, Lillian."

"Sorry. I just received a phone call from someone giving me or should I say, Rose, a not so gentle warning." Lillian exhaled. "That girl just frustrates me sometimes. I've been trying to reach you both for a while. It's going straight to voice mail. Then I remembered your sat phone."

"First, we've had spotty cell service and have been trudging through high waters. And second, you know what an impossible task that is. She's stubborn and frustrates me, too. When she sets her mind to something, she's a dog with a bone and won't let go. And to answer your question. I have no idea what she's gotten herself into. Tucker and I have been dealing with other pressing issues." Lillian was hiding something and didn't want to show all her cards. So, he played naïve. "Would you care to enlighten me?"

"She hasn't told you?"

"Told me what?"

A pause fell on the line. "Just keep an eye on her, please. She's in grave danger."

"Lillian, what are you not telling me?" Simon raised his voice.

Tucker gave him a wide-eyed look.

"All I can say is she needs to stand down. At once! She'll know. I've got to go." Lillian disconnected.

"What the hell was that about?" Tucker asked.

Simon didn't want to give away the farm to Tucker. He trusted his military bro, but the fewer people involved, the safer.

"This Foxy thing," Simon said. "It has Lillian thinking Rose is in danger."

"From whom? Cora Alvarez? I thought the hit was called off," Tucker said. "I also heard chatter that after Cora changed her name and fled to another country, that someone had her terminated. So, it's not her. And isn't this why you've been training Rose so hard?"

"Partly. But as you can see, she's always getting herself mixed up into some crazy business. She's got to save the world."

Tucker grunted. "That's why you two get along so well."

"Touche," Simon said.

"Crap!" Tucker said, pulling up to the Dancing Flamingo.

They sat in silence for a moment, staring at the building.

"It's worse than I thought," Simon said. "I'm pretty sure that tree doesn't belong there."

CHAPTER 35

IT WAS 6:15 P.M., and forty-five minutes had passed. Stella's lips were bluish, and she was shivering. Nala and I had layered on more blankets to keep her warm. The only saving grace was the rain had stopped, and even the wind was calming.

I heard a truck door slam. I looked out the window and saw Simon and Tucker make their way to the entrance. Thank God!

"Up here, hurry!" I called down through the massive hole in the wall and ceiling.

"What do you need?" Simon asked.

"You happen to have a chain saw?" I asked.

Simon gave me a cheeky grin. "We're the grown-up Scouts. We come prepared." Returning to Tucker's truck, he retrieved an orange, cordless chainsaw.

"And a first aid kit," I shouted

Moments later, Simon and Tucker were upstairs.

Since it was a tight fit, especially with a tree in the room, Nala left after brief introductions.

"How is the electricity on?" Tucker asked.

"Generator," I answered back.

Tucker nodded and grunted. He and Simon shared a look without saying a word. They didn't need any verbal communication to ... well, communicate.

Tucker went to work with the chain saw.

I stepped aside so Simon could tend to Stella. After all, he was a medic in the military, among other things.

After Tucker cut away part of the tree, I helped him toss it out the window. We didn't have to be choosy about where it went. Getting Stella free and to the hospital was the priority.

"She's in shock," Simon said calmly.

"I've been monitoring her. Her lips just started turning that color. We were trying to keep her warm and dry the best we could. She's losing more blood, too. I ran out of gauze." I eased to my knees and held her hand.

"You ladies did a great job." Simon applied QuitClot and more gauze around the protruding branch.

With a small folding saw, Tucker carefully severed the branch near Stella's leg.

Her face was contorted in a pained grimace as she moaned.

"You have anything for the pain in your kit?" I asked.

"You know I do," he said to me. "Stella." He gently touched her arm. "Do you have allergies to any pain medication?"

Stella shook her head and said she didn't.

Simon pulled out a syringe and vial. He drew it back. "This is going to help."

"Look at me, Stella." I wiped her forehead with a cloth.

"I ... I'm so sorry," she cried.

"Shh. It's okay," I said.

Simon gave me a sideways look.

"Long story. Tell you later."

Stella's furrowed brows softened.

"Let me guess, Ketamine?" I looked at Simon.

He gave me his Gomer Pyle grin. He looked at Tucker who was busy making a clear path to the door. Simon leaned over and whispered in my ear. "Your gran called. She said to back down."

"Yeah, okay," I said. "I'll get right on that."

"She sounded terrified. We need to chat later."

"All done," Tucker said. It was a good thing he didn't see or hear our interaction.

Simon looked around the room. "Is there a sheet we can use to carry her downstairs? The Ketamine should keep her comfortable for a while."

I approached the steps and called out for one. Moments later Nala threw a flamingo-patterned sheet up and we eased it under Stella. Next, I heard the clatter of tables and chairs being moved.

"Okay, ladies, we're coming down," I shouted. "Please have

someone open the front door and the back seat of Tucker's truck."

I turned back to Simon, and he gave me a nod. We certainly worked well together. I'd miss training with him. I shook it off as we hefted Stella and gingerly carried her downstairs. After we got Stella in the back, Simon gazed at me. I could see worry in his eyes. And it wasn't for Stella, she was going to be fine.

Harlee jumped at the chance to open the truck door as she told me she felt awful for coming down so hard on Stella. Before she'd bolted out the door, Harlee grabbed Stella's purse. She insisted on going to the hospital, too.

I watched the four of them take off for the ER. As I turned to go back inside, I paused for a moment. A warm breeze replaced the howling winds, and the hurricane had moved on to wreak havoc in another part of the state. Even the water levels were quickly receding. Except for downed power lines and no electricity, things were calming down.

Yet another unsettling brewed. This time in my gut as I pondered my next move.

CHAPTER 36

CAPTAIN SAT IN Bo's Hummer and looked at his watch. Quarter to seven. His law enforcement "friend" was busy doing his job and had canceled last minute.

So, Captain called Bo again to pick him up.

Bo answered this time and said they were already back in Miami as he wanted his Hummer. Since it had no wheels—literally—Nevaeh called her uncle Vincent who owned a tow truck company. Uncle Vinny, as she called him, would do anything for his niece.

While they were on the phone, Captain told Bo about a job he had for him. Bo jumped at the chance to make some extra dough. Twenty minutes later, Bo and Nevaeh arrived at the Gardens in Captain's Caddy.

Boy, were they a sight for his sore eyes. He hopped out of the Hummer and walked around his vehicle, inspecting it for damages.

Bo jumped out and did the same. The two scanned one another.

"You're lucky my baby ain't got no scratches or dings," Bo rumbled.

"Same here." Captain returned a snarl.

"I can't say the same thing for you two mooks. Ya both look like hell." Nevaeh hopped out. "Vinny's guy's right behind us."

Captain towered over the couple. He'd never seen Nevaeh without five-inch heels. Damn she was tiny. Bo stood five-five, while Nevaeh was barely four-eleven. Captain was five-nine but told everyone he was six feet.

Nevaeh might be small in stature but had a huge personality.

Big brown eyes, light-brown hair with blonde highlights. She was draped in gold necklaces, rings, earrings, and bangles. She was a cute dame, but a little on the whack doodle side. One thing was certain, she was well connected to the underground.

As for Bo, he was a mean, little SOB. He had hazel, close-set eyes and dark brown hair. If those two ever had kids, they'd come out the chute with angry scowls and would put the fear of God into the delivery nurses and doctors.

Captain shook it off as he slid behind the wheel of his Caddy while Nevaeh hopped in the backseat. Bo waited outside his vehicle for the tow.

"What's this job you got for us?" Nevaeh asked.

Captain turned to face her. "It's an easy gig now that there's three of us." He watched Bo's vehicle being raised on the flatbed. "Let's wait for Bo."

A few minutes later Bo jumped into the front seat.

"I'm getting hangry," Nevaeh said. "I need to eat."

"Yeah, we betta feed my gal. She turns into a gremlin if she don't." Bo shut the door.

Nevaeh slapped Bo upside the head.

Bo flinched. "See what I mean."

"What's open?" Captain asked.

"My uncle Tony's place in Miami," Nevaeh said. "Vinny said they're open for business. A hurricane afterparty."

Captain looked in the rearview mirror at Nevaeh. "How many uncles do you have?"

"Don't ask," Bo replied. "They aren't really her uncles. Business associates of her father's. All mafioso type."

Nevaeh wacked Bo again. "Have some respect for my departed fatha'." She made the sign of the cross.

"K. Tony's it is." Captain pulled out of the Gardens. "Hope to never see that shitbag complex again."

Twenty minutes later the three of them walked through the crowded Italian restaurant/bar. Standing room only.

"We'll never get a seat," Captain said. "I think all the Miami locals are here."

"She's got this." Bo nodded to his gal who walked up to a short, stocky, scarred-faced man. He looked to be straight out of *The Godfather*.

A couple moments later, Nevaeh waved to the guys.

"Told ya." Bo followed.

The stocky man seated them in a small room in the back, away from the crowds.

"Didn't know you had this much pull." Captain looked around. "Do we get menus?"

Nevaeh shot Captain a scowl. "You eat what they put in front of you. Don't ask. No substitutes."

"This is the chef's table." Bo sipped his water.

"Good to know." Captain did the same.

Ten minutes later, an Italian meal fit for the Godfather himself was served. Antipasto, seafood pasta, the best smelling garlic bread Captain had ever experienced. Chianti was poured.

The crew scarfed in silence. Captain had never seen a gal eat so much food. She wasn't a nickel over a hundred pounds. Where did she put it? Captain kept that thought to himself. You never ask a woman about her weight, especially this one.

Bo pushed his plate away and let out the loudest burp.

Nevaeh slowly looked at him and paused. "That was a good one, babe." She sat back and patted her stomach. "So, what's the gig?"

Captain laid out the plan to snatch Foxy. The icing on the cake, kidnap the dog, extort money from Rose.

"You said this chick, Rose, is uber loaded?" Bo asked.

"Yeah, she lives on a yacht at the marina," Captain replied. "Although since the hurricane, she's not staying there."

"How do we find her?" Bo asked. "And her mutt?"

"I got Rose's number. And Foxy has been hiding out at the Flamingo," Captain said.

"So, we get paid from your boss lady? *And* we extort money from Rose?" Nevaeh asked.

Captain nodded.

"How much we talkin' total?" Nevaeh asked.

"A couple mill," Captain replied. "And that's just for the dog."

"Damn, this chick *is* loaded," Bo said.

"Wait. You said she lives on a yacht?" Nevaeh stood. "Is she a tall, leggy, hot looking red head?"

Captain nodded again.

Nevaeh leaned on the table. "What's her last name?"

"O'Brien … why?" Captain replied.

"Be right back." Nevaeh grabbed her cell off the table and walked away.

Captain and Bo shared a shrug.

Shortly after, Nevaeh returned and plopped down. "I got us more money. And you get Rose outta the way."

"The dog?" Bo asked.

"Fuhgeddaboudit," she replied. "Not part of it."

"You're forgetting one thing." Captain crossed his massive arms and leaned back in his chair. "The lady I work for is tripling my fee. I've got to deliver Foxy and whatever info she's got or I'm pecker up in the glades and some gator's gonna have my nards for a snack."

"You said Foxy doesn't know anything," Bo said.

Nevaeh bounded to her feet again. "Got it. We deliver both and tell each interested party where they can pick up their merchandise. We get paid from both. It's up to them who gets their pound of flesh first."

"This one!" Bo grabbed Nevaeh by her waist and scooped her onto his lap. "Beauty and brains." He gave her a tonguey, wet kiss. The heavy gold chains around their necks tangled and clinked.

"Jeezo you two, get a room." Captain rolled his eyes.

Bo and Nevaeh turned their heads to Captain, each giving him the finger, untwisting their chains.

"Wait. Who else is interested in Rose?" Captain inquired.

"Don't know, don't care. It's third party." Nevaeh answered. "There's a hefty bounty. Served alive. All I know is we've got a job to do. You tell your boss lady we got her gal."

Captain shook his head. "Not until we have Rose." He threw back the rest of his wine. "Where are we taking them?"

"Tell you in the car," Nevaeh responded.

CHAPTER 37

IT WAS 8:45 P.M. by the time Lily and I finished helping Nala board the upstairs and tidied the best we could. Essie cleaned the bar area.

The high winds didn't touch the downstairs. Thank God for hurricane impact windows. They were a must in Florida.

While we were cleaning, Foxy warmed us wings and whatever food she could scrounge in the kitchen. That included a couple warmed frozen burgers for Sue.

As for Saki, she had a call from the Palm Island security office. Her alarms were going off and there was debris all over her front yard. I offered to help after we finished at the Flamingo, but she insisted she had it covered. So I called Simon and asked if he and Tucker could assist her. He obliged.

We'd just inhaled our snacks when Nala's phone rang.

"Harlee said Stella's still in surgery. Knowing my sister, she's pacing like a worried hen. They'll also be keeping her overnight for observation and for signs of infection. Not to mention further damage to that leg." Nala hefted her purse on her shoulder. "Thank you *all* for your hard work. I'm going to head to the hospital." She turned to Foxy. "Can you be a lamb and lock up for me?"

"Sure thing. I'll swing by and see her when I'm done here," Foxy replied.

"You mean *we*," I interjected. "I'm not letting you out of my sight."

Foxy heaved a sigh. "Rose, no offense to you, but how long will I need a babysitter? You can't follow me around forever."

Because I didn't know the answer, I carefully considered before responding. And then a thought occurred. How do you catch a rat? You set a trap. I smiled. "Not long."

"Roose …." Lily laughed. "I know that grin. Spill it."

"In due time. Let's wrap things up here, check on Stella, and head to the W. I think we all need a proper meal, shower, and sleep." I pushed in all the stools while the gals finished the final clean-up in the kitchen.

Another thought occurred. I called Khan to check on the yacht and crew members. Even though after midnight tomorrow they were no longer my responsibility, I cared about their well-being.

Khan advised me the yacht sustained major damage, but the crew were all safe. I informed him I would see him tomorrow to say goodbye and pick up the rest of my belongings.

While I was on the phone, Essie received another phone call and stepped outside. She wore a serious look.

"Boy, for someone who is carefree, she sure gets a lot of calls," Lily said. "What does she do for work?"

I contemplated and stopped. "I haven't a clue. And what do you mean?"

"Well, when you guys were in the kitchen, she had another call and did the same thing. Walked outside. She sounded pretty angry."

"Maybe she's having guy problems," I said.

"I asked her if she was in a relationship. She said no."

I shrugged. "It's been a while since I've seen my little cousin. I don't know what her world is like."

"Or why out of the blue that she's here?" Lily added.

I bumped her shoulder. "You've been conspiring with Saki again, haven't you? She's not a spy."

Foxy walked back into the main room. "What are you two talking about?"

I didn't hear her and jumped. "Oh, nothing. Just that we're ready to leave when you are."

"Sounds good. I'm done in the kitchen."

By the time we checked into the W, the ritziest Miami hotel, and made it to our suite, it was a little after ten. I was sparing no expenses and living it up my last night as a gazillionaire. My friends and family deserved it. Since I paid in advance for a three-night stay, there was no urgency to check out.

The Ambassador suite was a 9,850 square-feet ultra penthouse with five bedrooms, four full baths. Each of the bedrooms had a king-size bed. The lavish room had a fully equipped kitchen, dining area with a table and six chairs, plush sofa, multiple armchairs, and two private furnished terraces. Even though we were a couple of blocks away from the beach, the twenty-ninth floor gave us an ocean view. Of course, since it was dark, all we saw were lights. Luckily, the electricity was restored.

"Holy crap, cousin." Essie dropped her duffel in the grand entry way. "Sorry you have to give all this up."

"It wasn't mine to begin with." I bent to pick up Essie's bag, but she quickly snatched it from my grasp.

"The bellman could've taken it with ours." I studied her. "And what in the heck is in that? Weights?"

She shrugged. "Who am I bunking with?"

"No one. We each have our own rooms. But you might have to share a bathroom. There are only four of them." I gave her a cheeky grin.

Essie walked to one of the back bedrooms, while Foxy ran up and hugged me.

"Rose, this is ... way too much," Foxy said. "You shouldn't have. I mean you don't know me."

"That's just the kinda gal she is." Lily gave me a side hug. "And I concur, thank you."

Foxy and Lily walked over to the large bay window.

Foxy halted. "Oh no!" She furiously shook her head. "Can't do it. Afraid of heights. I can get up things, but not great at looking down." She spun and returned to the living room with me.

"I'm starved. Who's up for room service?" I picked up the menu.

"Um ... it's gotta be a fortune here." Lily plopped down on the couch. Sue joined her. She pulled the small note from Gil out of her pocket and set it on the table. I could tell the Sudoku baffled her.

I watched Lily furrow her brows as she picked up a pencil.

156

"I could try to give that a crack later," I said.

"I would, but my brain is fried." Foxy sat next to Lily and perused the menu. "Wow. These prices. I can help pay. Even though I haven't had a chance to talk to a lawyer, much less go to the bank and transfer the money my uncle left me."

"Dinner's on me," I said, writing my choice down on a note pad that sat on the ornate marble coffee table. "Can one of you call in our orders? I need a shower."

"I will," Foxy said. "And we can all try to give that number puzzle a crack later."

"Yeah, with a bottle of red." I laughed as I made my way down the hall. I stopped and turned. "Oh, Saki and the guys should be on their way. They're all going to stay here tonight. Saki can bunk with me and the guys can share a room. Unless you want Simon crashing in your room, Lily."

"Rose!" Lily giggled, her face and neck flushed. "I totally spaced. Saki texted earlier and said the house needed more attention than they thought. They'll see us tomorrow."

"Sounds good." I returned to the bathroom. As I scrubbed the day out of my hair, I had an *aha* moment. I hurriedly finished and pulled my hair in a turban and wrapped my body in a white Egyptian cotton hotel robe and bolted back into the living room.

Once I spotted my laptop bag I set it on the coffee table and sat next to Lily. I powered on my computer as Essie darted from the other side of the suite. She said she forgot sundries and needed to go to the hotel store before they closed.

At this hour? I considered and glanced at Lily. "I need to speak with Essie. But now that it's just the three of us, I have an idea."

"Go on." Foxy leaned in.

"Well, you know how they want you, Foxy."

"Mmm hmm," she said.

"I say we give them what they want." My fingers danced across the keyboard.

"Wh—what?" Foxy gasped.

"No, not like that," I said. "I was thinking earlier about a trap." I logged into the secret squirrel database and entered Gil Fox.

"Luucy," Lily said. "Didn't your gran tell you not to use that anymore?"

"Yep."

"Then why are you kicking the hornets' nest?" Foxy asked.

"She's got a plan," Lily said. "Just don't know it yet."

"That I do." I typed away.

Lily was looking over my shoulder and saw my message. She hopped to her feet. "Are you kidding, Rose? 'You know about X.' *That* is your trap? The whole darned Agency will be after you. After us." Her voice went up an octave.

"You didn't read the rest of my message. I told them to leave Foxy alone and deal with me. And that *I* would give them what they want."

Lily felt my head. "Nope, no fever. So, you have gone mad."

"Rose, I'm with Lily on this one." Foxy stood next to Lily.

Both stared down at me with crossed arms. Two matching angry bookends. Sue, who'd been sleeping on the opposite chair, picked up her head and stared at me with her judgy eyes. Okay, so maybe they weren't judgy. If she were a person, they would be.

"Sit, let me finish."

They re-joined me on the couch, and I told them my plan. "So, Foxy can you forge your uncle's signature and re-write the letter? Leave out the stuff about the USB, Lily, and the rest I just mentioned."

"On it." Foxy walked to the desk, opened her backpack, and pulled out a notepad.

"Not now." I laughed. "Shower and eat first. But we must leave Saki and Simon out of this, for the moment."

Just then someone knocked at the door. "Room service." A soft voice came from the other side.

I walked over and looked through the peep hole, confirming it was indeed room service and not someone pretending. The gal wheeled in our dinner on silver platters and set them on the dining room table. Just as she was on her way out, Essie sauntered in, all smiles. No bag.

"I thought you had to go to the store," I said.

"Uh … they were closed." She flashed her cutesy smile. "Oh, your yacht crew said they owe you a debt of gratitude. They're having a blast here."

"Huh?" I asked.

"You know, the chef, TJ, Khan. They were having a drink at the bar. They told me you have midnight cravings for chocolate-

chocolate cake, and they're having one sent to you." She laughed again. "Boy, did they have some funny stories about you."

"Thank you?"

I gave the room service attendant a hefty tip and shared a look with Lily who just shrugged.

How did Essie know so much in such a short time? Was there more to her visit than a reunion?

CHAPTER 38

◆

AGENT H SAT in his oversized recliner in his dimly lit study, enjoying his favorite jazz record, while his wife was upstairs doing her nighttime beauty routine of God knew what.

He closed his eyes, listening to Coltrane. He transported himself to a jazz club in Chicago. Times were less complex before his rise through the ranks of the CIA.

As he put his tumbler to his lips to take a sip of Bourbon, his cell vibrated with an alert text. He brought the phone to eye level and took a quick peek.

"What the?" He shot up to a sitting position. "No, this can't be," he mumbled, "it was disabled." H turned on the light to get a better look. Yep, it was correct. He stomped to the kitchen bar and opened his encrypted laptop, powering it on.

"That girl has some nerve," H grumbled as he called his analyst. "I thought you disabled that passcode!"

"S—sir I did. Hold on." H heard tapping away at the computer keyboard. "The user got in through a backdoor server. I don't know how."

"IP address?"

"Hotel in Miami. I'm sending you the address now. I apologize. It won't happen again."

"You bet your ass it won't." H disconnected, went to the stairs and looked up. His wife was still in the bathroom. Good. He telephoned Juno.

She answered with a sleepy hello. "What time is it?"

"A little after eleven. It's urgent."

"Yeah," Juno yawned. "What happened?"

"I'm sending you something. O'Brien's messing with me … with us." He forwarded the message.

"What the hell. Is Rose crazy? She must have a death wish. I had a feeling this was about X."

"I can't go into detail. But now you know the urgency. Personally deal with her and the Fox woman. I need this wrapped up. I have a meeting with the Director!"

"You want a bow on it, too." Juno scoffed. "But you're forgetting, I don't take orders from you. I'm no longer employed by the Agency. You *asked* me to do a job. While there's no excuse for the delay, I get that. But don't you ever bark orders at me again." The line went dead.

"What the frick?" H looked at his phone. Did she really hang up on him? She acted more like a scorned ex-girlfriend than a former colleague. But Juno was correct. He let his anger get the best of him. He inhaled and called her back.

"Don't hang up. I'm sorry. You're correct. I … I just need this contained and fast. Please, no loose ends. It's apparent Rose has taken it upon herself to come to the aid of the Fox girl. She's just like her grandmother. We could've used her. But now it's too late. Please, personally handle the situation."

There was a pause on the line.

"Juno, you there?"

"Yes. I'm looking at the address. And you don't think this is a set up?"

"I thought of that. I doubt it. She's offering an olive branch. And come what may, I trust your judgment. You were the best we had."

"I'm doing this for you, *not* the Agency. I don't owe them shit. They threw me under the bus and ran my ass over. Twice."

"I understand, you were treated unfairly. Had I been in the position I am now, that wouldn't have happened."

"I know, Hansel. Sorry, H. I'll personally handle it. You have my word. And none of this will lead back to you."

"Thank you. And I truly mean that." H disconnected and scrolled through his contacts until he found Lillian's number. It went straight to voicemail.

"I warned you what would happen if you didn't call off your

granddaughter. I'm sorry it has come down to this." He ended the message.

Agent H ran his hand through his salt and pepper thinning hair and tossed back his Bourbon. He moved to the bar and poured a double.

It was that kind of night.

Juno turned on her bedroom light, her sleep ended.

Why did H have to bring up how the Agency screwed her over?

Sure, she shared some of the blame. She fell in love with a double agent. But she put a bullet in his head. It was either that or be terminated by him. To make matters worse, her own agency turned their backs on her. She had to resign. It was the only option.

"Alexander was the mole. Not me! And they all knew it. Somehow, I got blamed." Juno seethed to no one as she opened her nightstand drawer. She tossed the contents. "Come on, I know you're here somewhere."

Juno rolled over to the other side of the bed and opened the other nightstand drawer. There they were, tucked in the back. A pack of cigarettes, with a lighter inside. She gave up smoking a year ago, so these were probably stale. She propped her pillows up, sat back with knees up and puffed away, like a schoolgirl sneaking a smoke.

Juno contemplated her next move. She took her laptop from the dresser and carried it back to her bed. She caught a glimpse in the mirror. Cigarette hanging out of the side of her mouth, hair disheveled, tank top and *his* boxers. How did she get here? Juno had felt that on some level Alexander loved her; she saw it in his eyes. She frowned and shook off the memories.

She logged into a search engine that H had given her the passcode to.

"She's registered there. Doesn't mean she's staying there. Rose is smart."

Juno spoke to the computer screen as if she expected it to respond. "And Hansel's right. Rose would've been an asset to the Agency. But then again, so was I. Look how that turned out."

Juno picked up her cell and called Captain.

"Yo. I was gonna call you. We got a plan."

"Yeah. Whatever. You're fired, you buffoon. You were supposed to deal with Foxy and now the O'Brien woman is a problem. I'm dealing with this myself."

"Hold on. Wait, a minute."

"What don't you understand. You. Are. Fired."

Captain kept talking and told Juno his plan. "So, whataya think? We deliver her and Foxy to you. We'll let you know when they're there."

Juno put out her cigarette and lit another. She contemplated, then texted Captain the name of the hotel.

"Fine. I just sent the hotel where she's registered. I'm pretty sure she's there. Unless it's a trap." Juno said the last part almost under her breath.

"She is. I confirmed it."

"How?"

"I got connections."

"You followed her, huh?"

"Yeah."

"When you snatch them, make sure there are no witnesses or cameras around. Don't use your own vehicle. There are CCTVs everywhere."

"I'm aware of that, Juno! I've done this before. And it's next to impossible to avoid cameras. We've got it covered. We'll be fine."

"Says you. I'm not impressed on how you've handled the job thus far."

"Screw you, lady. This is a solid plan. Hey, if you don't want us involved, we'll back off."

"No. But this is your last chance."

"Don't worry. We got this."

"And you're sure that area will be vacant?"

"Yep. They evacuated and won't return. Besides, they're backwoods hunters and turn a blind eye to stuff like this. People disappear out there all the time. For a fee."

"Very well. Call when you have them."

"Copy." Captain disconnected.

Juno hadn't been in the trenches like this in a while. She was looking forward to getting her hands dirty. She put out her final half-smoked cigarette as it was leaving a nasty taste in her mouth and walked over to the hall closet.

She took out her dresses and slacks and tossed them on the bed. Juno removed a panel to expose a hidden wall safe. She stood hand on hip trying to remember the combination. And then it came to her.

After she opened it, she beamed. "Hello old friends. Miss me?"

Her AR15, an assortment of handguns, and extra ammo just waiting to come out and play. She would take one of each, including ballistic vest.

Tomorrow was going to be a fun day.

CHAPTER 39

◆

DESPITE HAVING THE most comfortable bed to sleep in, I had a restless night. I rolled over; the time read 9:15 a.m. I threw off the covers.

We never slept in this late. No surprise, since we hit the sack at midnight. Even Sue, wiped out from the hurricane, was still conked out. She was lying on her back, belly up, snoring.

I gazed at her for a few minutes and sighed. I loved her more than anything. She brought meaning to my world. She must've felt me staring because she stretched with all four paws in the air, rolled over and cuddled next to me. Tail wagging, puppy kisses galore.

"Okay, Sue. I've got something to tell you. I have an important errand today, so you will have to ride with your auntie Lily. You see, it's sort of a trap for a very bad man. You need to be on your bestest behavior."

Sue licked my face and smiled as if she understood.

"One more thing, Mama is going to be poor as of midnight tonight. But I promise we'll be okay. I've got resources and a small amount of money saved."

"Don't forget, you have friends." Lily's voice came from the doorway.

I turned my head and smiled. "I know. I was just giving Sue a pep talk."

"Are you trying to convince her or you?" Lily walked over and laid down on her side next to Sue. "I'm serious, Rose. You can return to Montana with me." She caressed her necklace.

"Perhaps. I need to see where this latest venture leads us. It's more of a challenge without unlimited money."

"We should let your gran in on it. She has a ton of resources."

"I know. I'm just miffed she's kept us in the dark. I don't buy this you're in danger. Back down BS. She promised we'd get to the bottom of what happened to your parents."

"I appreciate that. But I may never know the truth. And if it means anyone else getting hurt, or even killed … well, maybe I need to let it go."

"Lily, stop that." I sat up. "I also vowed to see this to the end. And when *I* make a promise, I follow through."

"I know you do, Rose. But we need to come up with a less hazardous plan. A plan for *after* Foxy is out of danger." She rubbed her sternum.

"You still having chest pains."

Lily nodded.

"You don't have to do this today, if you're not feeling well."

"No! I'm fine." She stood. "I'd just feel better after my blood tests come back."

"You and me both." I joined her and brushed my hair, pulling it in a high pony.

"So, what's the plan?" Lily asked as she grabbed my brush and did the same to her hair.

"I thought about that. It's simple. A switcheroo. I put on this baseball hat." I held up a Miami Dolphins cap. "That blue zipped hoodie and those sunglasses." I pointed.

Lily looked at the leggings. "We're not the same height. And we have completely different hair color."

"I thought of that, too. He'll only see the top half. The hood and cap will cover our hair, and glasses will hide our faces. Besides, my Range Rover has completely dark windows. I'll hang around the lobby with Sue and Foxy for a while until we've been made."

"How will you know?"

"We were followed last night. I made sure of it. I spotted that turd's Cadillac. So, he knows we're staying here. I also left the IP address exposed last night when I logged on. I figured that's how they knew it was me the first time. Like a dumb dumb, I neglected to cover my digital trail."

"What about Essie?"

I moved to the door and peeked my head out. I heard Essie and Foxy having a conversation in the living room.

"I kinda told a fib to Simon," I said in a hushed voice. "I told him I think Essie has a thing for Tucker and that if he could pick her up and take her to grab protein shakes for us all. When they leave, we make our move. I'll leave a note telling them we had a quick errand and will meet them for lunch."

"What is Simon doing?"

"Hopefully still helping Saki. I kind of fibbed to Saki, too. Just to keep Simon with her for a while."

Lily tilted her head like Sue does when she's trying to figure out what I am saying.

"I told Saki we're going shopping this morning, and you want to surprise Simon with a fancy watch. I asked her to keep him busy."

"Oh yeah. Gil's GPS watch that you took off his body. I can't believe you wear it." Lily shuddered.

"I wear it only sometimes." I picked it off the nightstand and strapped it on my wrist. "It's a reminder to get to the root of things. And I'm serious about getting one for Simon as a parting gift for training me."

"You're a great friend … wait. It's Sunday, what stores are open?"

"The mall of course. I called and looked online to make sure the hurricane didn't impact it. We're good to go."

"Boy, Rose, a house of cards."

"I don't like lying any more than you do. And it's for the greater—"

"I know." Lily rolled her eyes heavenward. "Simon will be fit to be tied. He'd want to be involved."

"I just need to have a private conversation with Captain then give him what he wants."

"You mean that letter from Foxy's uncle? Then why the charades? Why not meet with him openly?"

"It's a game. They'll get suspicious if we just hand Captain that letter. It must be *coerced* out of us."

"So, you let him follow me, but I am you. And you corner him? What about Foxy?"

"She stays with me. And you keep Sue to make it look like you are me."

"What if he has help?"

"Don't think too hard about it. It'll be fine. Going by our last interaction, he works alone for the most part."

"I hope so, Rose." Lily exhaled.

CHAPTER 40

IT WAS ELEVEN O'CLOCK. Time to set the plan in motion.

Tucker took Essie in search of our shakes, while Saki kept Simon preoccupied with more honey-do-lists. It wasn't hard to do since her husband, James, was still working up north and I was not certain where my guy, Kevin, was. I was so busy strategizing that I didn't take O'Malley into consideration.

He'd offered for me and Sue to come live with him in D.C. until I figured out my future. Heavy sigh. I wasn't about to have a man take care of me. It wasn't in my genes. My mother raised Saki and me to be self-sufficient, independent women.

I shook it off as Foxy, Sue, and I exited the hotel. We waited for the valet to bring my Rover up and hopped in. I looked in my rearview mirror and spotted that worm's Cadillac across the street. I slowly drove into the underground garage, using my hotel key card where Lily was waiting in the silver Jeep Wrangler I bought last night off a transplant from Georgia.

The guy was desperate to sell the beater which had seen better days. Since I still had money to burn until midnight, I gave him full price, cash. No questions asked. He said he'd meet up tomorrow morning for the title, but I doubted I'd need it.

Initially, I was going to rent a vehicle, but given what I had in mind, that would not be a great idea. Besides, this one had a bumper guard on it. Go figure.

Sue stayed in my Rover while Foxy and I hopped out and jumped into the Wrangler. Lily slid behind the wheel of my vehicle. The minute I closed the door, Sue whined. She was a smart dog and knew something was up. I kissed her through the opened window and reassured her I would see her soon. I don't think that eased her much because she tried jumping through the window.

"Easy, baby girl," I cooed. "It'll be okay." The last time she acted this way, I was heading for a plane with a malfunctioning parachute. But I wasn't aware of that at the time. I considered her reaction and paused. Nah. She couldn't really know about my crazy plan. Could she?

"Lily, please roll up the window so she doesn't jump out."

Lily obliged and made her way out of the garage. I waited for a couple cars to pass and slowly followed. I had Foxy duck down in the back, so Captain didn't see her. The Jeep's windows were not as dark as mine.

A few seconds later Lily called my phone. "Rose, can you ease Sue? She has not stopped whining and is jumping from the backseat to the front like a crazy dog. I'll put you on speaker."

I cooed in baby talk and Sue seemed to quiet down.

Our plan was to head out of Miami, onto the Tamiami Trail. There would be fewer cars—and witnesses. Then we execute our strategy.

But sometimes plans don't go as expected.

Captain watched Rose, Foxy, and that mutt hop into the Rover. But why was she going into the underground garage? Oh well, he'd wait for her, nonetheless. His phone rang. Bo.

"Hey, where are you guys? They're on the move." Captain tapped the steering wheel.

"We're right behind you, numb nuts," Nevaeh said, so obviously the call was on speaker.

"Where? I don't see Bo's Hummer."

She sighed. "You didn't pay attention last night, did ya? If you recall, we're in my uncle's tow truck. No thanks to you, the Hummer still has no wheels."

"Damn, little lady. I forgot," Captain said. "I thought we were going to pick it up together. Don't blow a gasket." He shook his head and spotted the truck. "I see ya now."

Another call came in. Blocked number. Probably Juno. "I gotta take this. Follow me. When I give the word, hit em'."

"Fi—"

Captain didn't let Nevaeh finish and disconnected, answering Juno's call. "Yo."

"Where are we?" Juno asked.

"Jeezo, lady. I've been sitting on the hotel for two hours. She's just pulling out. What's with you impatient women this morning?"

"Don't use that tone with me," Juno snapped back. "I have been waiting for your call. You verified the drop off location? There's been flooding everywhere. Especially out there. Don't want to get stuck in the mud."

Captain sighed. "Yes, I don't need a micromanager."

"Says you."

"I confirmed this morning that the road is drivable. There's one lane, partially paved, then you hit dirt. That might be a bit muddy. There's a heavily forested area on one side, the other swamp. Remember, it's off the Tamiami Trail. Not Alligator Alley. After you leave the last residential area of Miami, it's about another twenty minutes on the Tamiami. Then turn North on Burny Lake Road. It creeps up on you. Take that road to the far end, past the campground and the lake. I texted you all this."

"I got it. And you said twenty minutes? Do you have something to keep them sedated that long?"

"I thought you people were all about plausible deniability."

"That doesn't apply to me." Juno paused. "You confirmed there's no one out there?"

"Affirmative."

"I did a satellite search last night. It looks like a couple of rundown buildings."

"Yeah. They belong to that hunter I was telling you about last night. He's out of there."

"Sounds like a good big game hunt for me. It's been a while. And you sure they'll keep quiet?"

"He doesn't give two shits about what we're up to." Just then Captain spotted the Rover pulling out. "She's on the move. Gotta go." As he hung up, he flipped on his turn indicator, so he could follow.

As he waited to pull into traffic, a Jeep pulled out of the garage.

It caught his attention because it was a beat-up, rust-bucket. How could that driver afford the W? Maybe a worker?

Captain shrugged it off and kept following Rose.

It appeared Rose and Foxy were heading out of the city. She was playing into his hands. Or was she? She must've been on to him because she was weaving in and out of traffic. Taking unnecessary turns. Either that or she was just a crappy driver.

He looked in the side mirror. The Jeep was behind him. He couldn't make out the driver. Female. Baseball cap. Dark glasses. Solo occupant.

He contemplated for a moment and called Bo. "Seems we have a little game going on here. You see the Jeep behind me?"

"Yeah. Georgia plates," Bo responded. "Who's in it?"

"Not sure. Let's see how this plays out. We only want Rose and Foxy, but if we need to, we snatch them all."

"You choose!" It was Nevaeh. "We can only hit one of them."

"Let me think a minute," Captain said. "I need to get a better look at the driver."

"What if Foxy is in one and Rose in the other?" Bo inquired.

"We have a lot of money riding on getting Rose." Nevaeh interjected. "So, don't screw it up!"

"Yeah, yeah." Captain studied the drivers in both vehicles. This was crucial and there was no going back. He couldn't mess it up, or not only would Juno have his nuts, so would Nevaeh. Both these gals made his cheeks pucker.

After carefully observing the driver of the Jeep, he knew the answer.

CHAPTER 41

———◆———

WE ZIPPED THROUGH Miami in just twenty minutes; Sunday traffic was surprisingly light. Then, twenty-five minutes later, we were out of the city onto the open Tamiami Trail. The hurricane missed this area almost completely.

No downed limbs. It looked like they'd gotten only heavy rain. Go figure.

Though traffic was easing, we were directly behind Captain. I slowed down considerably so he wouldn't see me. Not yet.

Foxy said she's prone to motion sickness and the back seat wasn't improving things, so she hopped in the front passenger, reclining as far back as possible. She must've seen me adjusting Gil's watch.

"What about my uncle's watch is it that you found intriguing?"

I told her we were able to determine the time of death using the watch. That was one way Lily was cleared of charges.

Not to mention I wanted to buy one like it for Simon. I took it off and handed it to her.

She inspected it. "There are so many buttons on this." She laughed. "My uncle was a genius and loved tinkering with things." She touched a red button on the back. "I wonder what this does."

"I wouldn't touch too much." I chuckled too. "It might eject some poison spray. You know, Inspector Gadget stuff."

Foxy gave me a sideways look.

"I loved that cartoon as a kid. Way before your and my time," I said. "He was my dad's favorite character."

She was about to hand it back when she said, "Uh oh."

"You didn't gas us, did you?" I looked at her.

She held up a USB flash drive in her palm. "It was inside the watch. Flush with the contours."

"Oh my God. My dad had one of those too. A spy watch. Why didn't I think of that? I found encrypted data on it," I exclaimed. "Foxy. This is awesome. It's a major break." I flashed a wide smile.

She reinserted the flash drive and handed the watch back to me. "You keep it on for safe keeping. I'm a jinx with watches. Every one I've owned has eventually broken."

I'd just put on the watch and was about to call Lily to tell her we were in position when my phone rang.

Grandma. I contemplated not answering but then changed my mind and put her on speaker.

"You need to *stop* at once!" Her irritation came clear through the phone.

"What?"

"They're on to you."

"Um ... Rose," Foxy said, pushing her seat forward.

I held my hand up to Foxy as I was just about to chew my grandma out for keeping secrets, when Foxy yelled.

"Tow truck is coming hot behi—"

The rest of the scene played out in slow motion.

First, we got slammed from behind. Then the Jeep fishtailed on the slick pavement. Damned bald tires.

We swerved left, then right, and left again, smashed against the guardrail. I needed to avoid the freshwater canal that ran adjacent to the highway. God only knew how many gators were in there. I attempted to correct and set us straight when we were hit again.

This time, I lost control. We spun an unknown number of times before we went airborne for what seemed endless seconds, until the front end contacted a palm tree and we flipped twice, maybe more. I couldn't be certain.

Foxy shouted something inaudible. My heart pounding muffled the sound. *Thump-thump, thump-thump.* My inner organs twisted like a pack of Twizzlers.

There was dead silence for a millisecond before the buzzing in my ears took over. I slowly looked over at Foxy and she appeared to be drifting in and out of consciousness. More in than out. I returned my gaze ahead, and it was then I saw beads of bright red blood plopping on the steering wheel. My last thought was "no airbags."

When I opened my eyes again, I had no idea where I was. The droning in my brain was deafening and my vision was blurry. I couldn't move. I looked over and spotted gloved hands and masked people removing Foxy from the upside-down Jeep.

"You idiot. Why did you have to hit them so hard?" A female with a Bronx accent yelled. "Quick. She's waking up. Tranq her."

"I got it. I got it." A male's voice I'd never heard of sounded behind me.

"Shit, water's filling the jeep. Hurry up. There're gators out here." The voice I remembered as Captain yelled.

"If ya didn't slam into them like you were in the fukin' demolition derby, we wouldn't be here, Bo!" the female exclaimed.

"I got the job done, didn't I, Nevaeh," the man named Bo replied.

Foxy mumbled something.

Glancing over, I saw a short man wearing a balaclava, who I assumed was Bo, carrying her. Grunting.

"Quick, Foxy's awake," Nevaeh said. "Where's the needle?"

"In my pocket," Bo replied.

Just as I shook my head to clear the blurred vision, my seatbelt was being cut away.

I slapped the gloved hand and attempted to release my seatbelt.

"Stubborn dame," the man who sounded like Captain said.

I felt weighed down as my attempts to fend him off were futile.

Captain freed me, lifting me out of the Jeep. First, they hit us and now they're saving us? Or were they? This was a nightmare I was ready to wake up from.

Captain grunted as he flung me over his shoulder. "Shit. My arm where your fukin' dog bit me."

My dog! "Where's Sue?" I slurred and flailed, kicking him until he dropped me in the canal. I fell backward into the water. Now I was awake. I bolted up, ready for a fight. I quickly looked around and remembered, Sue was with Lily. Thank God.

And another thought. Gators. Where were they? I was more afraid of alligators than this creep. I took him on once before, I could do it again. Couldn't I? And that's when my question was answered. He caught me off guard and grabbed me by my hood and slapped me across the face.

I stood on wobbly legs in water up to my waist, lily pads all around me, and then came that familiar iron taste in my mouth. This chum was going down. Using muscle memory, I quickly drew my Hellcat from my fanny pack.

"Back off, asshole." I waved my pistol.

"Easy. We just want to talk to ya."

"Bull shit." I jutted my chin. Just as the last word fell out of my mouth, I felt a jab to my neck followed by multiple gun shots.

Lights out again.

CHAPTER 42

"I HOPE YOUR mama knows what she's doing," Lily said to Sue, who'd finally calmed down. A bit. Sue was sitting in the passenger seat and kept looking behind them. It was obvious she was uneasy with this whole situation. Lily gave her a reassuring pat behind her ears.

She was about to phone Rose when Simon called. Lily braced herself for a butt chewing.

"Seriously! You guys leave us a note. Not as much as a phone call. Exactly what kind of errand are you running?" He said it all without pausing.

Lily was a terrible liar and told Simon the truth.

"Are you absolutely insane … never mind. It's Rose we're talking about. And you went along with her? I swear, you two are a lethal version of Lucy and Ethel."

"We just want to chat with the guy. That's all. Rose figured we could give him what he wanted and he'd leave Foxy alone. Then we'd deliver him all wrapped up in a bow for you and Tucker."

"Jeez. You're starting to sound like your partner in crime." He paused. Lily assumed to come up for air. "So, you set a trap … with a hit man hired by the CIA?"

Lily hadn't thought of it that way. She looked over at Sue for support, but by the expression on the dog's face, she probably agreed with Simon.

Okay, so maybe Lily had been hanging around Rose too long. Not only did she buy into this crazy plan, now she was reading emotions into a dog.

177

"Lily. Are you still there?"

"Sorry. And I really mean that."

"Fine. Just tell me, where are you?" Simon's voice was calmer.

"We're west on the Tamiami Trail. About twenty minutes outside the city. We wanted to get him out in the open."

"And feed him to the gators?"

"No. Although that would get rid of him."

"Lily Cazier!"

"Just kidding." Kinda of …

Lily kept her eyes trained on the side and rearview mirrors. Waiting for Rose's signal or even a phone call.

Then she saw Rose swerving all over the place, spinning wildly out of control. The Jeep rolled over multiple times and landed in the canal.

Lily gasped. It happened so fast; she couldn't believe her eyes.

"No!" Lily let out a blood-curdling shout and slammed on the brakes.

"What?"

"Sh—they were hit and … and they ro—Gotta go." Before Simon could utter a word, she disconnected the call, released her seatbelt, and dashed from the Rover. She'd forgotten to close the door, and Sue was on her heels in a flash, wildly running, passing her.

"Sue. Stop!" Lily shouted, but the dog didn't listen. Sue loped at full speed.

Rose's Jeep was approximately a hundred yards behind.

And that's the moment she saw them.

Captain hopped out of the tow truck, slipping on a balaclava. And then she saw two more jump out, but they already had on their face coverings, so she couldn't get their descriptions.

Lily stopped dead in her tracks. She was no match for them. She had no weapon, not to mention she couldn't keep up with Sue. So, she bolted back to Rose's Range Rover, hopped in and made a reckless U-turn, catching up to Sue.

"Dog! Stop," Lily demanded.

Sue halted, her tail tucked, head down. Panting like no one's business. Since Rose rescued Sue, the dog had never known an angry tone. While Lily felt awful for raising her voice, she was heading toward danger. Slowing down, Lily opened her door. Sue hopped onto her lap, settling right into the passenger seat.

Lily quickly scanned Rose's Range Rover. Surely, she would've left one of her guns hidden.

Eureka. Lily located Rose's Smith and Wesson, 9mm tucked away in the center console. It took but a couple minutes for Lily to catch up to Captain and his mangy accomplices. But now what?

It was then that Lily answered the numerous calls from Simon.

"We're en route. Tell me what's happening." Simon's voice was calm and even.

This helped Lily. While Lily was no stranger to stressful situations, she'd never witnessed someone this close to her attacked.

"Captain just pulled Rose out of the Jeep. And they're fighting. The other two have Foxy. I have a gun."

"Under no condition should you engage."

"I can disable his Caddy."

"Fine."

Pop … pop … pop … pop.

Lily was an expert shot and won awards for mounted shooting back in her rodeo days.

"Got 'em. Now the tow truck."

Lily continued driving. As she was about to shoot the truck's tires, Captain flung Rose over his shoulder with one hand, while he returned fire with the other hand using a .40 caliber handgun.

Simultaneously, the shorter person from the tow truck opened fire on Lily, while a third person carried Foxy. The Range Rover's windshield shattered.

"Sue! Down." Lily ordered again.

The dog hit the floorboard. Fearing for her and Sue's safety, Lily slammed the car into reverse and floored it. Her left index finger, injured in a roping accident, limited her ability to continue firing back with her left hand.

Lily watched as they sped off west on the Tamiami Trail. As Lily was aiming at the tires, the back passenger-side window rolled down. Through the window, a black semi-automatic was brandished by a woman with long, bright red nails.

Rat-Tat-Tat. Rat-Tat-Tat.

Lily immediately ducked as the Rover was turned into Swiss cheese.

CHAPTER 43

———◆———

AN HOUR AND a half later, Lily and Sue were safely back at the W.

Lily slumped on the couch as Simon pulled out his first aid kit.

Sue wouldn't leave the front door and kept whining and pacing, echoing what Lily felt.

"Ouch, Simon."

"You're lucky these cuts are superficial. She used a semi-automatic? Must've been a terrible shot."

"Not helping, Simon." Lily winced as Simon applied antiseptic spray on the scrape and contusion on her left forearm. From when Lily shielded herself and Sue from flying glass.

"All I'm saying is that it could've been a lot worse. I can't believe you gals. Going in like that."

Lily pulled away and shot to her feet. "Are you done lecturing me?" She stood fists on her hips. "We need to find Rose and Foxy. Or have you forgotten they were taken?"

"I haven't." Saki paced the living room, biting her nails. "She lied to me. My sister lied to me. Again. Boy, when I get a hold of her …" Saki paused and dropped to her knees, crying. "If I ever see her."

Sue ran over and put her head in Saki's lap and whined.

"What do we know so far?" Essie entered from the kitchen where she grabbed everyone some bottled iced tea. She passed out the bottles and sat on the couch.

"Rose and Foxy were taken by Captain and two unidentified masked people. But why?" Saki stood again. "I need you to level

with me. What was Rose up to?" Saki shot squinty eyed glares at Lily and Simon.

Lily looked at Simon for help. She couldn't keep a secret well. However, Rose was adamant that Saki shouldn't be involved in Project X, and Simon and Lily concurred.

Simon walked over and waved to the couch for Saki to have a seat again. She obliged.

Tucker walked in and inclined his head to the door for Simon to join him.

"Brother, you can speak freely," Simon said.

"I just got off the phone with my contact at the Miami-Dade Sheriff's Department," Tucker said. "I provided them with the tow truck company's name, the one Lily mentioned. Mafia owned. They only tow when it suits them. They don't have GPS tracking on their trucks and are tight-lipped."

"Makes sense," Simon said. "By Lily's account, the gal in the back had a semi-auto."

"Yeah. Her name is Nevaeh," Tucker said. "She's wound up as they come. Her guy is none other than Bo."

"Oh, you mean the little guy that we ... uh, had a talk to?" Simon asked.

Tucker grunted.

"So, is it Rose or Foxy they want?" Saki asked.

"Looks like both," Essie interjected.

Everyone looked at Essie.

"How would you know?" Lily asked.

"If they only wanted Foxy, they would've left Rose for dead," Essie said matter-of-factly. "And because they didn't kill either one, it appears Rose has something they want. And it sounds like they're not the shot callers. By what you described, Lily."

Silence filled the room.

"Essie, aren't you in the least bit worried about them?" Saki asked. "You sound cold and detached. And as a matter of fact, what are you even doing here?"

"Easy, Saki." Simon stood between them. "Don't tell me you're suspicious of your own family."

"You show up out of nowhere. Ask a ton of questions. You know a lot of shit." Saki shook her head.

"Stop." Lily stood and put her palm to Saki.

"Look," Essie said. "I am worried. But given what I know about my cousin, I'm confident she can handle herself."

"Essie is correct," Simon said. "I just wish she had her phone on her. But we found it in the jeep with her Apple watch." Simon scratched his head. "Actually, why wasn't she wearing it?"

"Apple Watch?" Lily asked.

"Yeah. I might've put a tracker app on it," Simon said.

The room was still again.

"Hey, it was Kevin's idea, not mine." Simon shrugged.

"Her boyfriend was tracking her?" Essie narrowed her icy blue eyes.

"Not what you think. Given the hit that was on her, he wanted to keep track of her. She knew about it and could disable it when she wanted to. They have a mutual agreement."

Essie nodded. "Did you find her fanny pack?"

"Yes, along the canal," Simon said.

"So, she doesn't have any weapons." A pit opened in Lily's stomach.

It was almost five, and Tucker had his law enforcement buddies look at the security footage from around where Rose and Lily got abducted. No luck, as they were out in the wide open.

A beeping sound came across Rose's phone.

Lily jumped to her feet and inspected it. She spotted something on the screen that caught her attention. She darted her eyes to Simon and back to the phone.

Simon must have picked up on the fawn in the headlight stare. He grabbed the phone and looked at the screen. "Oh … just Kevin." Simon cleared his throat. "I'm going to return his call in the other room." He shot Lily a "come with me" look.

Lily had been with Simon long enough to know his nonverbal cues and followed.

"Why can't you call him in here?" Saki crossed her arms.

"I need you to call your husband. Can you tell James what's going on?" Simon asked.

Lily and Simon walked back to Lily's room and closed the door.

"Care to explain?" Simon asked.

"You remember Gil's watch?" Lily asked.

"Yes."

Lily took the phone back and scrolled. "It's obvious Rose paired it with her cell phone. The app says Gil's watch. I have no idea why, or how but it's tracking her. We were looking at the watch just this morning. I noticed there were all sorts of buttons on the side. She must've activated something. Looks like an SOS signal."

Simon snatched it back. "You mean, it's tracking her ... in real time?" he exclaimed.

Lily nodded.

"This is amazing." Simon kissed her. "But how do we tell the others that we have their location?"

"Can you *really* call her boy toy, Kevin? Make something up?"

Simon shook his head. "He's out of the country again. He doesn't have access to coms right now either. And I don't want him to worry. Not yet."

"It's probably for the best," Lily said. "He'd blow a gasket."

"Exactly. He'd kill me, too. I'm supposed to keep an eye on her."

"That's impossible. You know that." Lily looked at the cell. "We need a plan. What do we say to the others?"

"We use Kevin. Tell them he had another secret squirrel tracker on her." Simon shrugged. "He is on the FBI/CIA's joint terrorism task force. Should we bring Lillian in on this?"

"No. Rose is still sore at her for keeping secrets. Besides, her grandma would be furious if she knew we still had Gil's watch. You don't want to be on her bad si—"

The ringing of Simon's cell phone interrupted their conversation. He peeked at the caller ID. "Speak of the devil."

"Oh shoot," Lily said. "She called me right after Rose was hit. A few times actually. But in the chaos, I didn't answer."

"Yes, Lillian." He pulled the phone away from his ear as her shouts were loud and clear. "I have Lily right here. I'll put you on speaker, but please keep your voice down. We have other ears in our conversation."

"I warned my granddaughter. She's so damned stubborn. I was on the phone with her when I heard a loud crashing sound. I've been calling for the last couple of hours. None of you have picked up! Is she okay? Put her on the phone."

"I'm sorry," Lily said. "They took her."

The phone went silent.

"Are you there?" Simon asked.

"Yes. Yes, I am." Lillian let out a muffled sob.

Lily had never heard her cry before. She covered her mouth to hold in her own howl.

Lillian cleared her throat. "I warned her. She's playing with fire. It was a matter of time before she got burned. These people are ruthless."

"You understand you can't keep your granddaughter out of any—wait. You *know* who has her?" Simon asked.

"Yes."

"And you can't do anything about it?" Simon inquired again.

"This time … no." Lillian paused. "For once, it's out of my hands."

"What if I tell you we're tracking her?" Lily said.

Simon put the phone on mute. "Are you crazy? You can't tell her that. She's not supposed to know about the watch."

"We'll simply say we're not at liberty to tell her how and leave it at that. Turn the tables on her."

"How are you doing that?" Lillian asked.

Simon took the call off mute. "You don't need to know." Simon stood his ground. "We'll keep you posted."

"What do you need?" Lillian asked.

Rose's phone chirped once more.

"Lillian, we'll get her back. For now, don't talk to anyone. Just stand by." Simon disconnected.

"I can't believe you hung up on her."

"Change of plans. We tell everyone Lillian is tracking her. Let's go get them."

CHAPTER 44

◆

WHEN I CAME to, my world was hazy. I was damp and zip tied to a chair.

But why? I blinked to clear my vision. My brain pounded as if I was hit with a sledgehammer.

That's right. The accident. We were hit from behind. We rolled into the canal and were freed by Captain and two others.

Who were they? Why didn't they just kill us? I also remembered being jabbed with a needle and that's it.

"Where are we?" a slurred voice sounded behind me.

"Foxy?" I turned my head, but she was out of my field of vision. "Hold tight."

I shifted my weight forward to loosen the plastic ties off my wrists. I looked down to find my feet bound as well. Yet, rope secured each leg to a chair leg. So, I did what any reasonable person would do, I scooted my chair around and fell, immediately coming face to face with an alligator.

"Ahh!" I squealed like a schoolgirl.

I still had nightmares of the time I shot a couple of crocs in the Florida Keys. Another crazy story for another time. At least this critter was already dead.

"Rose." Foxy shrieked. "Are you okay?"

"I'm better than this guy." I nodded to the taxidermized alligator with his mouth opened. Teeth and slitted eyes, the whole shebang. I shuddered again and slithered on my belly like a … well, like an alligator.

"Where are we?" Foxy asked, interrupting my thoughts.

"No clue."

Lying on the floor, I searched for a sharp object to cut the ties. The gator. I wiggled back to him and used his teeth to cut the plastic. "Thanks buddy."

As I sawed my wrists back and forth on the tooth I must've hit a button on Gil's watch, because it started beeping.

"What was that?" Foxy asked with wide eyes. "I've read this book, Rose, the ending sucks." Her voice was shaky.

"Don't know. But I need to get you lose."

After my wrists were free, I hurriedly unraveled the rope around my ankles and did the same for Foxy. But the watch continued to beep. I quickly looked to make sure we weren't going to go kaboom. Who knows what Gil put in his Inspector Gadget device.

The scratched crystal had a blinking red light. It read: *tracking activated.* I showed Foxy. She looked at me with big eyes and gave a thumbs up.

I scanned the dilapidated shack. Alligator skins and skulls hung on the walls and the filthy, splintered rickety floor was covered with dead roaches and other insects. I then noticed rusty saws, chainsaws with dried bloodstains, cans, and jars. Even a generator. Whoever evacuated must have brought it inside.

We were in an illegal hunting camp. Which meant they'd be back soon. Could they have been the ones with Captain?

"We've got to hurry, Foxy. Who knows when they'll return for us … unless they never left." I darted to the dirty, hazy windows and tried peering through them. No cars or people were present. "I think we're alone."

Foxy joined me at the window. "Where are we?"

"Not sure. But I aim to find out," I said and opened the door a crack. "Oh boy." I flung it wide.

Foxy and I stood there in disbelief. We were some place in the swamps.

"Are we in the Everglades?"

"I'm not sure." I reached for my fanny pack, but it was gone. I fumbled around in my sweatshirt pocket for my phone. "My cell's missing."

Foxy checked her pockets. "Mine, too."

I stepped onto the rickety porch and looked up at the sky. The dark storm clouds had passed, leaving only wispy gray puffs behind. Although it was five o'clock and sunset was still hours away, an unusual darkness had settled. The density of the forest behind the cabin may also be a factor.

"We've been missing a while." The watch kept beeping. While it was maddening, I didn't want to shut it off in the event someone—anyone—might receive the SOS.

I heard a hissing noise.

I jumped. I knew that sound. An alligator. Even though they don't usually attack people without provocation, it freaked me out anyway.

"Foxy, remain calm. He or she won't attack."

"Um, Rose. There are three of them." Foxy pointed to marshy swamp land on the south side. "Will they gang up on us?"

"No, but they're probably pissed that their deceased relatives are hanging on the walls."

I quickly stepped back inside and closed the door, scanning the hovel. I spotted a Whelen rifle in the corner. I know hunters or in the case out here, poachers, used this weapon for hunting gators on foot. Odd for hunters to leave their rifle, I considered as I moved over and picked it up.

As I assumed, it was unloaded. I flung open drawers of a wobbly, antique desk looking for ammo. "None on this side." I went to the other. Still none.

"This sucks. It's no good without bullets." Okay one last drawer. As luck would have it, a Smith and Wesson .38 revolver was tucked away at the very back.

"Please be loaded, please be loaded." I chanted as I opened the cylinder. "Sweet. It's full. Six rounds are better than nothing." I slipped it into my pocket. For kicks I removed the bottom drawer completely and lady luck smiled on us again as I found a box of .38. I opened it, hoping to find at least a few in there. The box of fifty had twelve bullets.

"The revolver won't kill an alligator," I said.

Foxy scrunched her face.

"Don't worry. I'm only going to pop them if they attack first. You know, buy us time. I'm not into hunting. Unless you're a person. Then it's game on."

Foxy looked sideways at me. "O.M.G.!"

"Just kidding." I shrugged. "Sort of," I mumbled the last part under my breath, as I emptied the contents of the ammo box into my pocket.

I heard the door open. "Rose."

"Yeah." I spun.

"They're gone."

"They'll be back. In the meantime, let's look around the north side. I wonder if there are more buildings. Or better yet, maybe we can find a swamp buggy or something else to get the hell out of here."

"Not unless that watch alerts someone to our location first."

"Yeah. The bad guys." I looked at her. "For giggles, I paired it with my cell phone. I wanted to see how it worked. Unfortunately, if Captain took it, we're screwed, unless …" I removed the watch and discovered a "silence" button. I hit it. The chirping stopped. But thank God, it seemed to still be transmitting. "It worked." I showed her.

"Yeah, but we're still stuck out here." She hung her head.

"Let's not give up hope. On the positive side, the gators have retreated to the saw-grass marsh area. Look." I pointed.

We walked six hundred feet along a muddy dirt road, with overgrown pines and oaks on one side and a swamp on the other. A building peeked out from behind some trees, with more forest.

"Remember, keep a lookout for any mode of transportation. A side-by-side or swamp buggy," I said. "Now that the hurricane has passed, the owners of this place are bound to return."

"Is that a good thing or bad? Have you heard about the people that hunt out here? They wouldn't take kindly to us crashing their illegal hunting site. I mean look at all the no trespassing signs, trespassers will be fed to alligators, etc."

"They could be with Captain, too," I said. "But we'll cross that dilapidated bridge when we get to it."

We picked up the pace to the second building, a shanty too. I held my breath opening the fractured windowless door. It wasn't any better. At least there was a refrigerator, table, and a couple of cots. The cabin had two front-facing windows and a back door leading to God knew where. We stepped inside. It was muggier in here than the other cabin.

My sweatshirt was sticking to my body, and I assumed Foxy's was too as we simultaneously peeled layers. I was careful not to have the gun and bullets come flying out, so I put them on the chair. The humidity was at an all-time high and so were the mosquitoes and other flying insects. Gotta love Florida in the summer. Especially near swampy areas. We each took a chair to drape our sweatshirts. Our only saving grace was that we were quickly drying from our dip into the canal.

Foxy approached the refrigerator and opened it. "Shoot. Just beer." She made her way to the opened cabinet. "Baked beans and crackers." She picked up a can to show me.

"And pretzels." I pointed to a bag on the counter.

"All that's missing is a game to watch." Foxy slumped on the cot.

I stood at the center of the shack, removed my hair tie, running my hands through my tangled, wet waves. I shook it out and twirled my hair back up in my pony and contemplated. I had no idea where we were or how long we'd be stuck. And we most likely had to wait till the morning.

I wasn't sure if there were deadly snakes out there as well as alligators. Wherever *there* even was.

Another thought occurred. Tonight was the deadline to tell my attorney I declined to be inseminated. Could this day get any worse?

And then my question was answered.

CHAPTER 45

"IT'S FIVE-TWENTY." LILY paced the hotel room, playing with her necklace. "Where's the rest of the crew?" She stopped and looked at Simon who was drinking coffee at the breakfast bar.

Simon tapped away at the computer, then turned. "We only just found their location. Essie is getting Khan and TJ up to speed. Good thing they were still around the hotel. Saki and Tucker are fueling up his truck. They're going to meet up with us." Simon walked over and embraced Lily.

She buried her face in Simon's broad chest. Without a doubt, he knew how to calm her. Sue, who'd been staring at the door, stopped and scampered to Lily. She started whimpering, pawing at her leg.

"I'm sorry, girl," Lily cooed, scratching behind her ears. "You're feeding off my emotions. We'll get your mama back." She drew a deep breath. "I still can't believe Essie was able to find a drone."

"Yep. It turns out, when she was at the bar last night with Rose's crew, she discovered TJ enjoys flying drones in his spare time." Simon returned to the computer screen. "Like you do."

"If I had my drone, we'd be there. And have you noticed how Essie has a crazy way with people? She asks lots of questions and you just feel like you want to bare your soul to her."

"Indeed. I checked Rose and Foxy's location, again," Simon said with unruffled assurance. "They haven't moved. Still around fifteen miles off the Tamiami Trail."

"I'm glad you're calm." Lily sat at the bar next to Simon,

fumbling around with her necklace. "Oh shoot! I broke it. It just popped open." She inspected it. "Oh my gosh!"

"What?" Simon inquired.

"A computer chip." She handed it to Simon.

"Where did you get this necklace?"

"Not sure of the sender, but I received it in the mail. I thought it was from Lil—wait a minute. In his letter to Foxy, Gil told her he mailed me something. But I never received anything from him." Lily looked at Simon. "Or did I? Simon … this computer chip must be it. I just need a reader."

"I have one in my computer bag—"

The front door flung open and in walked Essie, Khan, and TJ.

"We're ready to roll." Essie smiled.

Lily surreptitiously took the chip back from Simon and returned it to her necklace.

She and Simon shared a look of understanding; no one was to know about this.

"Hey guys, thanks for coming." Lily approached TJ and embraced him. Since he towered over her, she stood on tip toes.

TJ handed Khan his black backpack as he returned Lily's hug. "Are you kidding? There isn't anything we wouldn't do for Rose. She was the best boss we ever had."

"I concur. Ms. Rose was a delight." Khan gently placed the pack on the bar. "Now what is the plan?"

Essie approached the bag. "TJ, do you mind?"

"By all means." TJ removed the drone.

"I'm impressed. This is a heavy-duty law enforcement model. It's used to find missing people, deliver supplies, track targets." Essie glanced at TJ. "How did you get your hands on it?"

Everyone stopped their side conversations and stared at Essie.

"Essie, how do you know all this?" Lily asked with a head tilt.

"Oh … um. I have a friend in law enforcement."

"Hmm. You'll have to tell me about him or her sometime," Lily responded.

"This model can carry up to four payloads, deploys in under a minute. Can lift a thirty-three-pound payload." TJ picked up the drone. "Look here, concealed landing gear ensures 360-degree visibility for each payload. Infrared camera." He paused. "Ms. Rose gave it to me for my birthday," TJ said with a sad tone.

"We've got to find her. And if I get a hold of this … what did you call him, Captain? I'll crush him like a bug." He slammed his fist on the bar.

"You and me both," Simon added. "For now, let's focus on getting our ladies back." He turned his computer screen around. "They're in this area off the Tamiami. Glad your drone is an LE model with thermal imaging. It can find a person's or animal's precise location by detecting heat signatures. It'll also determine how many people are out there with our gals. I take it, this thing is fairly quiet?"

TJ nodded.

"Okay then." Simon looked around. "Are any of you handy with weapons?"

"I'm not a fan. But I can kick butt," Essie said, standing tall.

TJ grabbed his groin. "I can attest to that."

"Sorry about that," Essie replied. "It was a reflex."

"You guys make up later," Lily said. "I'm a good shot."

Simon nodded. "How about you, Khan?"

"I served in the Royal Air Force. So, yes."

"I know Saki has been training. And I can personally vouch for Tucker," Simon said. "Tucker and Saki will meet us." Simon pointed at his screen. "Right here." He looked around. "Let's roll."

CHAPTER 46

◆

I HEARD A vehicle in the distance. Foxy's eyes widened so she did, too. We darted to the windows and peered out through the dirty film.

"Hmm. It's not Captain and his team. At least I don't think. I only see one person." The time on my watch read 5:45 p.m. "It's unclear if this person is friend or foe. But I don't want to risk the latter." I spotted the table. "Quick, help me move this to the door. There's no lock so we'll improvise."

I adjusted the table and peeked out the window.

The sole occupant, a female with cropped brunette hair, exited the SUV. She wore desert-colored fatigues, an olive-green long-sleeved t-shirt, and tactical boots. The icing was her ballistic vest and the forty caliber in her thigh holster. She was taller than me with legs past her ears. She had a brawny upper body, but not in a body builder way. Just someone who pumped iron and could probably kick my ass.

This woman obviously knew what she was doing. When she exited her vehicle, she didn't slam the door. With her gun drawn, she moved in a combat glide, weapon extended. She peered up at the trees and behind her, her head constantly turning, eyes scanning. She must be here for us because she headed directly for the cabin where Foxy and I had been held.

But who was she? The woman did not look familiar.

Foxy's eyes widened, and she lowered her body to the floor and yanked me down with her. "Ro—Rose." Her words were breathy. "She's here for us." Her eyes were watery with fear and her bottom lip trembled.

"My thoughts exactly."

I swallowed hard. But all that was there was cotton. I was thirsty.

For the first time since this all started, I was scared. This woman was a soldier of sorts and would smash me like a bug.

Pull yourself together, Rose. Snap out of it.

My attempts to talk myself down weren't working.

I trembled as I crawled to the chair to get my measly revolver and our sweatshirts. I threw on mine and stuffed the ammo in the pockets. I crawled back to Foxy and handed hers to her as well.

There I was, more concerned about gators. How I would have welcomed those cold-blooded, vacant eyed, slithering critters over this … this woman. Xena Warrior Princess. Although, I'd never call her that to her face.

Gulp again. I would've even preferred Captain and his gang of misfits.

I crept up to the window and slowly peeked out. Waiting for the angry giant to exit the cabin without her targets.

A few minutes later the door opened.

"Are you sure they're here?" Juno asked Captain over the phone as she stood in an empty cabin. Empty except for a few knocked over chairs.

"Yeah," Captain said. "We tied them up and put enough tranq in them to keep them sedated for a few hours."

Juno walked over and found the zip ties on the floor. She picked one up. "Well, moron. They're gone. You obviously didn't give them enough." She kicked a chair. "I didn't see any tire tracks going out, other than yours. Where could they have gone? Wait. According to the satellite view, there are two structures."

"How could they have gotten away? We tied them up and they were knocked out."

"I gave you fair warning about her. You're certain there are no weapons out here?"

"Not that cabin. We checked."

"And the other cabin?" Juno paced. "Did you check it? You

know these places are used for hunting. Hell, even poaching." She looked at the alligator's heads on the wall, staring back at her.

"There was no reason to. Look, there's no place to go out there. If they left on foot, you would've seen them. Don't forget the gators out there."

"I'm aware of that. I'm staring at one on the wall right now." Juno rubbed the back of her neck. "For your sake, she better be in the other building."

She disconnected and opened the door, then peered around the property. Ah. There was the second building.

Juno jumped back into her SUV and drove off. She needed another vantage point.

And if Rose was watching, she wanted Rose to think she left.

Juno drove up a slight hill and found the perfect spot to keep eyes on her targets. She backed up and parked. When Juno was in the cabin, she'd noted its weak construction.

To confirm her targets' position, she pulled her thermal imaging monocular, complete with strap, from her duty bag. Bingo. Two heat signatures were acquired. They appeared to be moving around the cabin.

Juno hung her monocular around her neck and checked her watch. Six o'clock. Although sunset wasn't until 8:30 p.m., it seemed dark already.

So, she grabbed her ballistic helmet equipped with night vision from her duty bag. She put it on and adjusted the chin strap. For the heck of it, she snatched up her red-light flashlight.

After getting her equipment ready, Juno sat back and munched on a power bar. The second she put her water bottle to her lips, her satellite phone dinged.

"Yes," she answered abruptly.

"Update," Agent H asked.

"What happened to plausible deniability?"

"Spare me. You no longer work for the Agency."

"Currently I have eyes on them. Ready to engage."

"As we discussed. I want what information Foxy has, then take care of them."

"I'm aware of the mission. Did you call to check on me?"

"I thought you'd be done by now and on your second beer."

"There was a slight delay."

"What?"

"Apparently, they had a plan of their own. They almost got my guy first."

"I cautioned you about her capabilities."

"I know, H. Just like her grandmother." Juno tapped the steering wheel as she drank from her water bottle. "This will be a piece of cake. I almost feel bad for her. She doesn't have an equal playing field."

"Don't underesti—"

"Yeah, yeah. Gotta go." Juno disconnected.

She took a quick peek to confirm her targets were still there. After she verified, Juno grabbed her AR15 with extra magazines and conducted a press check. After she was fully loaded, she exited the SUV, gingerly shutting the door and then slowly approached the cabin.

Time was on her side.

CHAPTER 47

———◆———

"YO," CAPTAIN ANSWERED his cell. He removed the phone away from his ear as Juno chewed him out. He placed the call on speaker to let his other two accomplices hear her rant, too. They were headed to fetch his Caddy from where they left it when they nabbed the two women.

The three exchanged bug-eyed glances.

During Juno's tirade, he put the call on mute. "You guys didn't by chance check the cabin for a weapon, did ya?"

Nevaeh, who was seated between Bo and Captain, whacked Captain on the arm. "We didn't have time. So to answer your question, no. I didn't."

Bo, who was driving the tow truck, looked at Captain. "Me neither. But we zip tied them gals good. And you're right. They should've had enough of that sedative to keep 'em knocked out a while."

"Do you think your buddies left any weapons behind in the other cabin?" Captain asked.

"Don't know," Bo replied.

Captain listened as Juno continued to chew him up. She finally disconnected.

"Ain't our problem now." Nevaeh looked at her phone. "We did our job and got paid. It's Juno's issue."

"Yeah," Captain said, the truck slowing as they approached the spot of the abductions. "There's my car. Shit! Look at her! All shot to hell. If it wasn't my Caddy, I'd be impressed. She's got mad skills. Kinda turns me on, too."

"A cool breeze turns you on," Nevaeh chimed.

"True that." Captain nodded.

Bo stopped the truck and the three of them exited.

Captain and Bo went to work, hooking the Caddy to the tow truck when Nevaeh's phone dinged with a text message.

"Who is it?" Bo asked. "Better not be notification that payment didn't go through."

"Nah, we received money from that gal who had a hit on Rose. This is my contact." She paused. "It's not our problem a tree fell on that lady's rental car. She's loaded and can get another one. I'll tell her to forget that. We did our part."

"What?" Captain inquired.

"She wants us to sit on Rose and her friend until she's freed up." Nevaeh tapped away on her iPhone, her acrylic nails furiously hitting the screen. "I'm telling her someone else took care of her problem."

"At least we hope." Bo stopped lowering the ramp and looked at Nevaeh. "What if they want proof?"

"I took a picture of them after we tied them up. And just sent it!" Nevaeh snapped. "We got our mullah from both parties. End of story."

"Easy, tiger. I'm on your team." Bo blew her a kiss.

"Gross you two." Captain scrunched his face and tapped the hood of his Caddy. "I agree with you. Now let's get her on the bed."

"What's the hurry?" Bo asked.

"I have an errand to run later," Captain replied.

"A hot date?" Bo inquired.

"Something like that. I plan on getting reimbursed for that dog bite. And my girl, here." He nodded to the shot-up Cadillac.

"Ain't you forgetting, the dog's owner is incapacitated at the moment and won't be able to pay. Probably forever," Bo replied.

"Someone at that swanky yacht will be there. And somebody's got that dog too." Captain replied. "Bo, I still need your tranq gun."

"Anything else? A ride perhaps? Seeing how you don't have any wheels." Bo laughed.

"Screw you! But no. A guy owes me." Captain narrowed his eyes.

CHAPTER 48

$\blacklozenge$

I PEEKED MY head up. It had been a few minutes since the Amazonian left. Something was off. Why didn't she check the area? That's what I would've done.

"What's that look, Rose? I don't know you well enough, but your furrowed brows have me worried."

"I was just thinking. We get kidnapped right? Our abductors leave us. Leave us for what?"

"Or who." Foxy finished my thought.

"Exactly. And then Xena shows up and leaves? And she has a satellite phone. Judging by this woman's appearance, she's obviously a pro. Perhaps former military? And that got me thinking."

"She'll return? Maybe with reinforcements?" Foxy exhaled.

"No. Why wouldn't she have brought them with her? She was expecting to find us tied up in that cabin. She must've seen this shack on her way out. She drove slow enough." I paused. "No, my spidey senses tell me this woman is not far. She's watching and lying in wait for us." I stood and looked out the window again. I walked to the back door and then back to the cabinets.

"What are you looking for?"

"Anything that we can make an explosive device with. In the other cabin I saw jars filled with God only knows what. And a generator. There's got to be something here. This thirty-eight—" I patted my pocket— "Is no match to that forty on her hip. And my guess is she has a much bigger weapon." I took the revolver out of my pocket and opened the cylinder and double-checked it was loaded. I closed it, put it back in my pocket, and resumed my search. A Grand Canyon size hole opened in my stomach. "What else can we use? These hunters must've left something."

"Perhaps bug spray?" Foxy joined me.

"I doubt they'd be concerned about insect repellent out here. Look at this place."

A few minutes later, Foxy and I had opened every cabinet twice, and turned the cots upside down. That's when I heard branches breaking outside.

Foxy must've heard it too.

Our eyes met.

I didn't have to, but I put my index finger on my lips to hush Foxy. I pointed to the floor hoping she'd understand dropping. She did. We both crawled to the back door.

We hadn't checked it, so we didn't know where it led. Or if it even opened. But it was our only option. I hoped the woman out there didn't see it on her earlier visit.

I delicately turned the knob, praying to God it was unlocked and would open. He heard my prayer. I pushed on the door and remained on the floor, peeking my head out.

Okay God, you answered one prayer, here's another. Please don't let there be gators back there throwing a welcome to the swamp party.

Phew again. None. And neither was our two-legged predator.

I scanned high and low. A tree grew right outside the back deck. I wasn't sure how adept Foxy was at climbing trees. But she was a stripper, and a pole couldn't be that much different from a tree, right?

Rose! I scolded myself briefly for thinking that way. Saki would be proud though. I jutted my chin to the tree and looked up. Foxy returned my nod. I waved to her to go first. She obliged, and I gave her a boost. Foxy was able to get to the first branch until it gave way and she fell. *Crash.* On her backside. I rushed to her, and she gave me a pained grimace.

I mouthed *sorry* to her and whispered if she was okay to try it again. This time, I wanted her to jump from the tree to the roof.

She emphatically shook her head. *No.*

Thinking she didn't understand me, I gestured towards the roof.

"Afraid of heights, remember." She whisper-yelled back to me.

Of course she wouldn't do something so stupid, because that's what I would've done. Heavy groan. And then I heard the door open and slammed against the wall.

Out of instinct, I flung Foxy off the deck.

Crap! Alligators.

CHAPTER 49

———◆———

LILY SAT IN the second row of Khan's Suburban, jiggling one leg while Sue's head rested on her other leg.

"It's okay." Simon put his hand on her knee. "We'll find them. Safe and sound."

"I know … it's just." Lily put her head back and drew a deep breath. "What if … what if we're too late? She doesn't have a weapon … of any kind."

"You mean other than her mouth." Simon gave Lily a crooked smile.

"Point well taken." Lily gave a half-smile in return.

"I've been training her for a while. She's resourceful. Have faith."

"I do." Lily looked to the heavens.

"Have faith in your friend, too."

Sue nuzzled the crook of Lily's neck and whimpered.

"She's picking up on your mood." Simon scratched Sue's scruff. "Can you be a little more upbeat?"

"Sorry, girl." Lily turned to look at the last row.

Essie had her head back, eyes closed.

"How can you sleep, Essie?" Lily snapped.

"I'm not sleeping. I'm processing. I heard every word." Essie opened her eyes. "Come, girl. Sit with me." She motioned for Sue.

Sue obeyed and jumped in the back.

"Sorry, Essie. I … I'm just," Lily sighed and faced front again.

Essie leaned forward and put her hand on Lily's shoulder. "No need. I understand."

Lily toyed with her necklace.

Simon gave her a wide-eyed look and shook his head. Oops. There was a chip in there that could easily fall out. She nodded and rubbed her sternum. Lily found a roll of antacids and popped a couple of Tums.

"Lily." Simon touched her shoulder. "I'm worried. Any news from the concierge doctor?"

"That's been the last thing on my mind today," Lily replied. "But ... no, not yet."

Simon's phone rang. "Yeah, bud. Uh huh. We are twenty aw— copy. No, we'll proceed ahead." He disconnected. "That was Tucker. He had a flat. They aren't far behind."

"We ... we can't wait. We've got plenty of people in this vehicle to rescue them." Lily's speech was pressured.

Simon grabbed her hand. "We're not waiting. This isn't the first time Tuck and I've had a delay. We've got this." He kissed her hand. "I've never seen you this frazzled."

"Me either. I don't like feeling this helpless. I was more involved in the last rescue mission."

"Would it help if you had a horse?" Simon chuckled.

Lily joined him. "Yes, it would. I could do anything on my horse. Include fly that drone."

"I'd like to see that," TJ said. "This one might be hard to maneuver on horseback."

"Oh, you underestimate her, TJ," Simon replied.

"Yep," Lily said. "I could ride backwards and still fly."

"As a matter of fact, it was nighttime when you and Rose rescued Saki and their half-sister, Kaylee, from the mountains in Montana."

"I wasn't riding backwards." Lily grinned.

"But you scared that bear away from them with your drone."

"For someone who wasn't there, Simon, you certainly know a lot about what went down."

"Rose told me. She was so impressed by you. She said you and she hit it off instantly."

"Yes, we did. We were instant besties." Lily's eyes welled up with tears. "We've got to find them." She leaned forward. "Mr. Khan, can you go any faster?"

"Madam. I have, how you say, 'pedal to the metal.'"

"Good one, Jeeves," Essie chimed from the back seat. Her phone vibrated. "Yes?" She answered like she didn't know the caller. "Mmm hmm. Neg—no, it's not a good time."

Simon looked at Lily and mouthed *negative? She said that earlier.*

Lily gave him a quizzical look. She knew where Simon was going because Lily also overheard an earlier conversation. Essie used terminology such as "affirmative" and "negative." Did she work for an agency?

Essie disconnected as quickly as she answered. Then she started cooing to Sue. "Your mama's okay, baby."

Simon cleared his throat. "We should be getting close." His phone rang again. "Yes. I see. *Negative.*" He gave Lily a wink. "They're not our priority. Rose and Foxy are." Simon handed the phone to Lily. "Tell Saki to take it easy. Talk her down."

"What's up, Saki … Mmm hmm … Well, like Simon said, Rose takes precedence." She looked at Simon with her big eyes. "Yes, Saki. We'll get those mother sucking S.O.Bs."

"She didn't say *sucking*, did she?" Simon asked.

Lily shook her head and kept talking into the phone. "See you soon. Yes. You get first crack at them. I promise."

She disconnected and handed the phone back to Simon.

They shared a look and a laugh.

"My cousin was unhinged, wasn't she?" Essie asked.

"I've never heard so much swearing. And I was in Special Forces." Simon shook his head.

"What's got her in a tizzy?" Essie asked.

"When Tucker was changing the tire, the tow truck I described to them drove past. Saki's out for blood," Lily said.

"They'll get theirs." Simon's jaw clenched. "And don't get me started on your 'bestie.'" He air quoted the last word. "Her damned need to control the narrative."

"Cut her some slack. She's got to control something," Lily said.

"How do you mean?" Simon asked.

Essie leaned forward. "She doesn't have a career. Soon will have no money. Her identity has been stripped away."

"She has us," Simon said.

"Not enough. I've known people like her. She's independent," Essie replied. "Simon, put yourself in her shoes."

"They'd be a tight fit." Simon smiled. "But I get it."

"Is that why Ms. Rose is so determined to save Ms. Foxy?" Khan looked in the rearview mirror.

"Uh … I believe so." Lily looked at Simon with raised brows. "She's committed to getting to the truth, too."

"Here I thought it was her hero—or in her case, superhero—complex," Simon said.

"Oh, how can we forget that one?" Lily knew Simon was changing the subject. Of course he was. Only he and Lily were privy to what was really going on.

"It's not so bad to be in control or have that complex, as you say," Essie chimed in.

"In Rose's case, sometimes it is," Simon sniped.

"Hey, going by what James said, she's improving," Lily said. "Remember her solo journey to the Keys searching for Saki."

"Right after she was almost mortally wounded. Again, going by herself." Simon huffed.

"One thing is certain, my cousin is a survivor," Essie said.

"True. That's what Simon has been working on with her." Lily patted Simon's leg. "But at least this time Rose brought someone along."

"Hmm. Was it intentional or accidentally?" Simon asked.

"We'll soon find out." Lily nodded and sighed. "Hopefully," she muttered.

CHAPTER 50

———————◆———————

AFTER ROLLING FOXY like a log away from the door, I quickly pulled out the *pew pew*. The .38 and I bolted to the side of the cabin. I stood, back to the worn wood siding.

"Come on, Rose." The woman scoffed.

I peeked through the doorjamb.

As I suspected, the woman I'd called Xena, was wearing a ballistic vest and armed with an AR15.

Boy, she wasn't wasting time. She went for the big guns. Literally. She also had a military-looking helmet with goggles resting on top. And what looked like a thermal imaging monocular hanging around her neck. That's how she knew where we were.

"It's not fair. You know my name, but I don't know yours."

"My name's not important. I want to speak with Foxy. I'm not here for you, Rose. Don't become a statistic."

"One of us is wrong. I think you are here for me. Why else would you bring such a high-powered weapon if all you wanted was to *talk*."

"Give me Foxy and you walk."

"Who do you work for?"

"Not your concern."

"It is. I've taken it upon my—"

A bullet whizzed past and splintered the door frame. It appeared to have been shot by her handgun.

"Thanks for using your suppressor," I called out. I chose not to return fire. I had limited ammo and needed to make my rounds count.

"Told you, Rose. I'm not here to do harm. We can't communicate with our ears ringing."

"What do you want?" Foxy shrieked, joining me.

"The info your uncle mailed you."

"It's just a letter," Foxy replied. "Like I told the other guy, he sent me nothing else."

I peered in both directions away from the cabin. Either way, it was a crap shoot.

"Don't think so." The woman fired a few more shots.

Crap! I felt a familiar searing pain in my left tricep. I quickly clutched my arm and pulled my hand away. Blood.

Thankfully, Foxy didn't hear my whimper, nor did she see me grab my arm. I've unfortunately been shot before, so I knew this was a simple graze. I'd live.

And then a crazy thought occurred. I knew sharks were drawn to blood but were gators as well? I dismissed it and looked over at Foxy. She had pure terror in her eyes. Crap again. She'd obviously never been fired upon before.

Foxy and I hit the deck as the crazy woman continued to shoot at us.

"You're not helping the situation, lady!" I yelled.

"I thought you'd been in a fire fight or two, Rose O'Brien."

"I have, *bitch*. But Foxy has not." I pulled my thirty-eight and contemplated.

"I've been called worse." I heard her walking on the deck on the other side of the shack. The floorboards creaked with every step she took. "But you can call me Juno."

"That's brave, *Juno*. Shooting at unarmed persons." I scoffed and contemplated why she purposely missed us. It's apparent that killing us wasn't her immediate intention. She was toying with us, like a cat with a mouse before the final kill. "I'd gladly go fist to fist with you." I sized her up. We were similar in height, give or take an inch.

"That can be arranged. Let's save it for dessert," she taunted back. "Listen Foxy, just give me what I want, and I'll leave you two ladies alone."

"Why don't I believe you?" I responded.

I motioned for Foxy to go to the left as I heard Juno stepping to her left, our right. Foxy obliged and stepped off the deck and into the mud. She stopped and her mouth dropped. She pointed at me. She must've seen fluid dripping down my torn sleeve. I motioned for her that it was okay and to keep moving. With a head shake, she pointed down.

I heard the familiar hissing and looked.

Shit! Gator. I retrieved my gun. My understanding, though little, is that they aren't aggressive toward humans, despite common belief. Unless they have babies nearby, are super hungry, or in this guy's case, curious. So, shooting wasn't my plan.

I've heard that kicking or punching them works too, but I wore tennis shoes. I also heard making oneself appear big works. Or was that for bears? I couldn't remember.

And that brought me to my gun. If his hissing and grunting continued, I'd give him an old-fashioned bonk on the head. As I feared, Mr. Gator continued towards me. So, I responded as any rational person would do in my situation. I took the barrel of the gun in my right hand and raised it over my head and whacked him once on the head and once on the snout with the butt. "Bad swamp pup," I mumbled.

It worked because he retreated.

Foxy stood there, mouth still agape. She was frozen with fear. I closed the gap and shook her.

"Foxy! Snap out of it."

"S—sorry." She looked at my arm and tilted her head. "You're bleeding."

"Just a graze." I shrugged and pushed her forward.

I had barely uttered those words when Juno fired again. This time it was from a longer distance. The round that zinged past was not the forty, but her AR.

"Just a warning, Rose."

I believed Juno. She undoubtedly was an expert shooter.

We picked up the pace and quickly ducked to the right, into the thick of the trees. I heard her run too, mocking.

I had a sense of déjà vu. Just a few short days ago, I was in the forest up in Tallahassee being hunted by Simon and Tucker during training.

Think, Rose.

I scanned the area. And while I didn't have a higher-powered weapon, I had my wits. I needed to lure Juno into the dense woodlands behind us.

It was time for Juno to become the prey.

CHAPTER 51

"KHAN, I THINK this is the spot," Lily said.

"Indeed, madam." He shifted his vehicle into Park.

The five of them piled out of the SUV as Sue wildly ran with her nose in the air.

"Is she a tracking dog, Lily?" Essie asked.

"No, but I wouldn't put anything past her. She knows we're looking for her mama," Lily replied.

Essie and Lily followed Sue.

"Sue, stop," Lily ordered. "Come!"

The dog obeyed and was next to Lily on a dime.

Lily saw Essie inspecting the ground. "What is it?"

"Fresh tire tracks." Essie swatted at mosquitos.

Lily mirrored Essie. "Yeah, from Captain ass wipe and his crew."

"No, these were made by an SUV. You said Captain was in a tow truck. The spacing and tire size are completely different. Not to mention, they had a flat bed. Which uses—"

"Okay, okay. I get it Rain Man." Lily held up her palm. She paused and marched up to Essie and looked her in the eyes. "Who do you work for ... really." Lily's tone was serious.

Essie stared back at Lily. "We've got to track down Rose and Foxy. It appears our ladies have company, and I doubt they're here to have a tea party and a gentle chat."

"Fine. But I want the truth," Lily said. "I don't buy that you just dropped in out of nowhere."

"Later," Essie calmy replied.

They trekked back to the Suburban in silence and spotted the guys all inspecting the drone that was now on the hood.

"I saw fresh tire tracks, headed that way." Essie pointed.

"Yeah, where the watch was ping—"

Lily's eyes widened.

"What watch?" Essie inquired and shot looks between Lily and Simon. "I'm not the only one with secrets, Lily, am I?" Essie mumbled to Lily with squinted eyes.

Lily paused. Essie and Rose squinted their eyes alike when peeved.

"That's not what I meant," Simon said. "Anyway, according to the satellite image, the gals' location is a couple miles up there. If you think they have company, then we can't wait. I'll let Tucker know he can be on the outer perimeter." Simon looked around. "I think we can handle any trouble."

Essie looked up. "I doubt we'll have cell service. Simon, I assume you have a sat phone?"

"Affirmative," Simon said, patting to his pocket. "But how did you know?"

"Oh, she knows *a lot* of things." Lily glared at Essie as she opened the door and folded down the back seat for her.

"What did I miss?" Simon said to Lily before they got in.

"Tell you later," Lily replied, taking her seat in the middle row.

Essie leaned forward and whispered in Lily's ear. "It's not what you think. I promise. I'm on your side."

Lily turned her head to face Essie so quickly, she almost gave herself whiplash.

Essie just nodded and put her finger to her lips.

Lily gave a small nod and softened her "look."

Ten minutes later, Lily rolled down her window. "Essie, you're correct." She pointed. "The same tire tracks are deeper here."

"I have the drone recalibrated," TJ said.

"We should pull over," Simon said.

Essie leaned forward. "I see your firearms back here. Enough for all of us?"

"I thought you weren't a fan of guns," Simon said.

"Poor choice of words. I don't use them as often as you do," Essie replied. "But I'm a good shot."

Simon gave Lily a quizzical look.

Lily replied with a shrug and threw her hands out.

CHAPTER 52

IT WAS NINETY degrees with at least 84% humidity. The mosquitoes were out with vengeance. The pain in my arm was now accompanied by oozing and increased bleeding.

Compared to this, the earlier surface burn felt like a paper cut. One thing was certain, if I didn't get it treated sooner rather than later, it could get infected.

But hey, if Juno killed us, the mosquitoes would feast off our corpses for days. They were unbearable. I threw the hood over my head attempting to block out the buzzing around my ears. I think they were also drawn to the blood.

"What's our next move?" Foxy mirrored my motion and jammed her hands into her pockets. "That's if we don't go mad from these things." She shook her head.

"You see the overgrown pine and oak trees covered in moss on that side." I pointed. "And the towering cypress over there?"

"Yes. It's quite eerie now the sun is dropping below the tree line," Foxy said. "I thought sunset was around eight thirty."

I peeked at my watch, it was 7:30 p.m. Foxy was correct, the swampy forest land had a creepy feel to it. Deliverance meets the Glades. I considered. "We head that wa—"

Five AR15 rounds hit a tree a few inches from my head. It splintered a tree branch in half.

Foxy and I became one with the ground. If we could, we would've dug a hole, too.

"She missed," Foxy exclaimed.

"No, she didn't. Still warning shots. Crazy has arrived," I said.

213

"We run, zig zag, not in a straight line."

We sprang to our feet and ran deeper into the forest. My heart felt like it was going to beat out of my chest. And then the shooting ceased.

I ducked behind a large oak tree.

Foxy plunked down next to me. "What now?" Foxy's green eyes were wide with fear as she threw her hands over her head.

Juno was behind us somewhere, still taunting, urging us to come out.

Then all was quiet. No shots, no shouts. The silence was deafening. She was planning the last take down. I felt it.

I peered around. Then I spotted it. Just fifty feet from our faces. Brown and green paracord trip wire. It blended into the forest floor. The second thing I saw was a wire noose. I was surprised to see a basic snare trap set by hunters. It was non-metal, rather humane for the poachers that hunted out there.

We were lucky. Or was it a God thing? If we'd kept running, Juno would've found us dangling. At least one of us.

All we needed was for Juno to fall into it.

I snapped my fingers. The Simunition training I did with Simon and Tucker in Tallahassee. I still had a bruise on my leg from it. I put my hand up to Foxy and rolled over to her, ignoring my pained arm.

"See that paracord over there?" I jutted my chin.

Foxy nodded.

"It's a snare trap. The animal steps into it. You see, the hook up there." I pointed. "It unhooks the hook, the branch straightens, yanking the animal in the air."

"How do you know this?"

"Simon showed me when we were training up north," I said. "I was planning on setting a trap, anyway. But it appears one came to us. I'm going to throw leaves over it. We need to lure Juno over here."

She concurred again.

I army-crawled, swiftly covering the trap. It was perfect. I slunk over and motioned for Foxy. She joined me and we laid there, heads against a tree.

I counted on Juno falling into the trap, thereby incapacitating her. Then Foxy and I would drive her vehicle out.

That, or we'd be dead and alligator cuisine before anyone discovered us.

I shuddered.

"Are you cold, Rose?" Foxy asked.

"Uh, no. Just hoping Juno falls into this. I think we can take her and drive off in her vehicle."

"I'm sorry I got you into this mess. If it wasn't for me and my uncle … well. I'm just sorry." She patted my arm.

I pulled away so fast it made her jump.

The sound of leaves breaking beneath footsteps hushed us both.

"You're out here some place, ladies. It's getting darker. Don't know about you, but I have night vision."

"Not good," Foxy leaned in and whispered.

"What makes you think we don't?" I yelled hoping she would follow my voice.

"Highly doubt hunters or poachers or whatever you call these backwoods people would have them out here."

"What do you want, Juno?" Foxy shouted.

"She speaks. Like I said earlier, any correspondence from your uncle. We know he penned a letter to you, telling you about X. I've got a feeling he gave you a flash drive too. Or something of that nature."

I remembered the letter. "Foxy, where's the letter?" I asked in a hushed voice.

She drew her head back. "Are you crazy?"

"Not that one. The one you wrote."

"Ooh. I forgot." She reached into her pocket. "Our dip into the canal likely got it all wet." She handed it to me.

"Let's hope some of it is legible." I examined it in the remaining light. It appeared to be okay. I returned it to her.

"Don't have all night, ladies. Hmm, maybe I do." Her voice drew closer. And then five more AR15 rounds.

Giving Foxy a nudge, I gestured toward the trees and leaned in. "I'll zig zag again and give you more time. But you'll need to be ready to drop to the ground. She won't shoot you until she gets what she wants. I'm disposable," I whispered, wincing.

"Rose, your wound is getting worse. That's it." She stood and stepped out from behind the tree. "Hey, lady. If you want the letter. Come and get it."

"Foxy! No." I tried to grab her, but she pulled away and waved the letter.

That wasn't part of the plan. Or should I say trap.

This was going south, fast. Juno was not there only to retrieve the letter and then let us go.

No, she knew about the letter and X. So that meant the Agency sent her. And they don't leave witnesses.

By the time I reached out to pull Foxy down, it was too late.

Juno jumped out, grabbed Foxy by the arm, snatched the letter from her hand, and threw her to the ground. Juno quickly pulled out what looked like a red-light flashlight and began to read.

"You expect me to believe this is all your uncle gave you? There's nothing here."

"It's everything," Foxy said.

"Bull shit."

"He didn't give me anything else. I swear." She put her hands up in surrender.

"Maybe so, but you know too much. You both are a liability. Rose had to stick her nose into places she shouldn't have," Juno yelled. "Rose, you woke a sleeping giant. You don't know what you've gotten yourself into."

"You *are* going to kill us!" Foxy jumped to her feet like a ninja and kicked Juno in the stomach, then turned and made a run for it.

I watched in awe. She'd obviously had martial arts training. Where had this Foxy been the last couple of days?

Juno got the last word as she fired twice at Foxy. This time the suppressor was off the Glock and the ear-piercing decibels of a double tap of the forty echoed through the forested swamp land.

Why didn't she use the AR?

CHAPTER 53

◆

"OVER THERE," LILY exclaimed. "I see an SUV. Doesn't look like anyone is inside."

Khan pulled alongside it.

"Tucker is on the way," Simon reported. "He just texted."

"I had no idea sat phones can make or receive text messages." Lily exited the vehicle and folded down the seat for Essie.

"Oh, yes," Essie replied as she too jumped out. "I'll bet Saki is fit to be tied."

"I can almost hear her rant from here," Simon said.

"The drone is ready for lift off," TJ said, standing next to the vehicle.

"I've got our gear ready, too." Simon opened the back of the Suburban.

Shots echoed around them.

The five of them all shared wide-eyed looks.

"Sounds like a high-powered weapon," Khan said.

"AR15," Essie and Simon said at once.

Lily looked at Essie.

Simon removed his Glock from his hip holster, conducted a press check and reinserted it. He then took the M4 out of the back and slung it across his body. Handed Lily the medical bag and a Glock .40.

"Choose your weapon, Khan," Simon said.

Khan walked to the rear. "Very well, sir. I'd be honored."

Essie, Lily, and Sue walked to the SUV, looked at the back and marched to the front. "No plates," Lily said.

Essie stood on the running board of the SUV and peeked into the windows. "Doors are locked. But looks like there's only one person."

"What makes you certain?" Lily inquired.

"One duffel bag. One water bottle, one power bar wrapper. And a pair of ladies' tennis shoes. This woman is tall."

"Again, how do you know?"

"Look how far away the seat is from the steering wheel."

"She could've been leaning back."

"Her size eleven sneaker, too."

"Good to know," Lily said.

As they were returning to the guys, Essie crouched. "Fresh prints in the mud." Essie put her foot next to the imprint. "And based on the stride length she's about five feet, nine inches. Give or take. These look like military boots." She stood. "There's a limp to her gait."

Lily nodded watching Essie. "Okay, Sherlock. You're a freaking walking computer search engine."

"Sun will set soon. Here are LED head lamps for everyone," Khan called out.

Five more shots rang out.

"That person is toying with our ladies," Essie said.

"What makes you say that?" Lily asked with a scowl.

"No pained shouts from either Rose or Foxy."

Simon looked at Essie and back to Lily. "She's got a point. But ho—never mind. We'll talk later. Let's load up and get down there."

Two more shots rang out.

"Forty caliber," Essie and Simon said at the same time again.

Sue whined and made like she wanted to run for the shots until Simon swooped her up in his massive arms. "No, little girl. We need to keep you safe."

"Either Rose got her hand on a forty or whoever is after them has two weapons," Essie said matter-of-factly.

"Sir, if they are hit ..." Khan paused. "We may need a chopper."

Simon nodded. "TJ, I need eyes now," he calmly ordered. "Tell me what you see."

TJ followed, flying the drone. "Both buildings are clear. But as we suspect, the heat sensors are picking up three people in the forest right behind the second building. That's obviously where the shots rang out ... two of them are on the ground."

"Khan, you're correct about a chopper. When we came back from Tallahassee, Tucker flew the chopper to the private airport because of the incoming storm."

"Yes, it's in the hangar," Khan said.

Simon dialed. "Tuck, change of plans. Pick up the chopper. Multiple shots fired. We have people down—copy." He disconnected. "They're a couple miles away from that airport."

He looked at Lily. "Good thing I restocked the medic kit. Let's roll."

Without another word, Khan jumped into the driver's seat. TJ sat in front, while Simon put Sue in the back seat. "Stay." He ordered the dog with his palm out.

Lily placed the medical bag next to Sue, while she, Simon, and Essie hopped on the running boards. They looked like a SWAT team making their way to a call.

In a manner of speaking, they were.

CHAPTER 54

I YANKED THE revolver out of my pocket as Foxy shouted, grabbed her left arm, and fell to the ground. She rolled over and threw her right hand up in surrender.

"You're just grazed. You'll survive. Now where did you put the data?" Juno leveled the gun. "I know there's more."

I jumped out and unloaded six rounds into Juno's arms and legs. I avoided center mass as I knew she was wearing body armor. I would've attempted a head shot, the kill shot, but I selfishly wanted her alive. I needed to question her. Juno knew more about Project X and its dirty secrets. She had to.

I retreated behind a tree as I fumbled to re-load the stupid revolver. I longed for my semi.

"You bitch!" Juno yelled. "You shot me."

"I can tell you were with the Agency. And that's who hired you," I bellowed in hopes to buy time and lure her into the snare.

Silence

"You know as well as I do that once you leave, they won't protect you," I said.

"If they ever did." Juno returned rapid fire with her AR.

I lost track of how many rounds hit the tree where I once stood. I dropped and crawled, but it didn't do any good as Juno was now determined to hit me.

"Here's the deal. I'll triple your fee of what they're paying you." I quickly rolled in time for her to miss.

"I heard you're broke, Rose." She fired more rounds.

"I have until midnight. It's still mine." I popped out and fired the six rounds again. Not sure where I hit. But I only had six more bullets remaining.

"I have money too, Juno," Foxy yelled from her corner of the abyss.

"Too late. If I don't complete my mission, there'll be someone right behind me." Her voice trailed.

"Sure, they'll send in housecleaners. Don't you think they will, anyway?" I made my way to Foxy.

"No. No, you're trying to get into my head. I was warned about you … O'Brien."

I heard the squishing of mud beneath her boots again. Darkness was falling fast. Stupid trees. And Foxy was whimpering. The first time I was shot, I believed I was going to die too.

"You okay?" I patted her leg.

"I think so," she said. "Not to sound ungrateful, but she only hit me once." She clutched her arm and groaned. "It's you I'm worried about."

"I'm good. Sadly, not the first time I'd been shot," I said. "At least it was her forty. Unlike the AR she's peppering at us." I reached into my pocket. Only three rounds. I must have dropped the rest. I loaded the remainder and readjusted my body. "Not to alarm you, but I only have three bullets left."

Sitting beside Foxy, I could almost count the breaths between us. It felt like an eternity. And our huntress was too quiet.

"Don't think she's falling into the trap." Foxy sighed. "We need a Hail Mary."

"Just thinking the same thing." I peered at the forest floor, making a mental note of where the paracord trip wire was. Fortunately, a bit of light filtered through the trees. I stood.

"What are you doing?" Foxy asked.

"Call me Mary."

I knew Juno was a good shot. But I figured I'd catch her off guard. She was wounded and moving targets are a bit more challenging to hit when one is compromised.

I had to get her into the trap. No matter the cost. This time when I fired back, I wasn't going to be concerned with bullet placement.

"Here I am. Do your best!" I jumped out, wildly running zig zag. The pain in my arm was the last thing on my mind. If I didn't lure her, we'd be dead.

Juno fired. She didn't use the AR.

Either I wore her down or she didn't have time to re-load.

I heard her footsteps behind me.

I tried to run but it felt as if I were swimming against a current. Then the rounds hit the back of my left thigh. At least I think that's where they hit. I couldn't tell. Adrenaline surging, I dropped to the ground, rolled over and shot one-handed.

Juno stepped into the snare.

I watched her get wrenched off her feet, sending her helmet flying through the air. In the shadowy light, I saw the whites of her eyes. It was like watching a slow-motion picture. She continued shooting with her Glock.

One thing was certain, the last round hit my already wounded arm. I writhed in pain on the ground.

CHAPTER 55

POP … POP … POP.

"There's a gun battle out there," Lily yelled to Simon and Essie.

"Sounds like our gal has a .38. Not a high caliber, but at least she's in the fight," Simon replied.

"I've counted fifteen rounds of a thirty-eight, lost track of the AR, not sure who has the forty," Essie said. "My guess it's not Rose."

Khan stopped the vehicle and the three of them hopped off.

With the touch screen tablet controller in his hands, TJ continued flying the drone. "Don't mean to alarm anyone, but how far out is the chopper?"

"A few minutes. Why?"

"There's something you need to see." TJ showed Simon the tablet.

"Get the drone closer. Closer. Perfect. A woman, who is the obvious shooter, is dangling by her ankles."

"Let me see her." Essie walked over. "Yep, that's her. She has an AR15 strapped to her, wearing a ballistic vest."

"She just flipped off the drone," Simon said.

"We'll take our time taking her down," Essie said. "I'd like to have a chat with her."

Lily looked at Essie, shaking her head. "Who are you?"

"She messed with my cousin."

Simon tapped TJ's shoulder. "Get closer to Rose and Foxy … Rose looks badly wounded. Let's move now ladies." He motioned for Essie and Lily. "Khan, you hold back with TJ. Not sure if we're going to have any more company out here. You'll need to engage them if we do."

Khan nodded to Simon.

"Does this drone have a powerful light?" Simon asked.

"Yes," TJ answered.

"Keep it on us," Simon said.

"You got it, boss."

"Khan, please make sure Sue stays put." Lily yelled over her shoulder. "She's a sneaky one."

"Yes, madam," Khan replied.

Lily, Simon, and Essie beat feet as fast as they could with the drone's light guiding their way. Each had their own head lamp for extra illumination.

"Look! Over there," Simon said, picking up the pace as they approached the scene.

"Hurry up." Foxy's rattled voice reached them. "She's been shot pretty bad."

"Who?" Lily asked, speeding up.

"Rose."

"No' tha' bad."

Lily heard Rose's slurred words and leaped over branches, rushing to her friend.

"Lily, she'll be okay." Essie said.

"You don't know that!" Lily snapped.

"I know my cousin," Essie responded, loping next to Lily.

"Me too," Simon concurred as he caught up to the gals. "Lily, give me the bag. Please call Tuck on the sat phone. Check the chopper's status." He handed her the phone before he charged ahead, coming to a stop next to a body on the ground.

Lily drew a deep breath. "Okay." She was fine handing over the reins to Simon especially since he was the medic. Even Essie seemed knowledgeable. Heck, Essie could probably perform a heart transplant just by watching a tutorial video.

She sucked back a strangled sob as she dialed. Lily knew what Simon was doing. Keeping her occupied. She loved him for that.

"Saki. We need the chopper now. How far are y—it's Rose, she's hurt."

"Foxy too," Essie yelled.

"I was only hit once. Just grazed." Foxy rushed to Lily. "Rose was shot worse. She needs help now," she yelled into the phone.

Lily covered the mouthpiece. "I wasn't going to tell Saki Rose was shot yet." She returned to the call. "Okay, okay. She'll be fine."

Saki yelled profanities over the phone.

"Yes, yes. The f'n shooter is incapacitated. Gotta go." Lily disconnected and dropped to her knees next to Rose. "They'll be here in five. Tucker is looking for a place to land."

Rose wore a pained grimace, as Lily stroked her face.

"You're lucky, Rose, it looks like it's a through and through," Simon calmy said. "The exit wounds look good, too. No shrapnel left behind. And the bullets missed your arterial veins."

Rose nodded.

"I want to help," Foxy said, settling next to Rose.

"Foxy, you're bleeding," Essie said. "Let me take a look at that." Essie grabbed some gauze from the first aid kit. "You should be okay. It's a graze." After she finished treating Foxy, Essie stood and walked away.

Lily watched Essie scan the forest. And then it occurred. The woman. The shooter.

"She's gone. Must've cut herself down," Essie said coldly.

"She had a knife in her boot. She used it just before you got here," Foxy said.

"She couldn't have gone far," Lily said.

"Does someone have an extra gun?" Foxy asked. "It would make me feel better, with her on the loose."

"We've got you covered," Essie said. "But my guess is she took off, especially seeing how she's outnumbered and outgunned."

Rose let out a moan.

"Rose, do you want something for the pain?" Simon asked.

"No, K," Rose whispered.

"Okay, a baby dose of Ketamine it is. And some Fentanyl." Simon administered it to Rose.

Out of nowhere, Sue came charging on to the scene, whimpering and panting at the same time. She plopped beside Rose, profusely licking her face.

"Sue," Khan's voice sounded in the distance.

"She's fine," Lily yelled "Sue's here."

"My apologies. She jumped out of the window."

"That's okay. The chopper will be landing. Keep a lookout." Lily hollered through cupped hands.

"Sue," Rose said with a breathy voice. "I'm k," she slurred.

"Rose, Rose." Lily dropped to her knees again. "We're here."

Peace and calmness returned to Rose's face as her head lolled to the side.

"We're ready to transport her out," Simon said.

"How are we going to carry her out of here?" Lily looked at Simon.

"We can make a stretcher," Essie said. "All we ne—"

"In the bag," Simon said.

"I should've known you'd have a portable foldable stretcher in your kit." Essie peeked inside and removed the bag. "Here, Lily, you grab the other side."

As the gals laid out the stretcher on the forest floor, the drone flew closer to Simon and his phone rang.

"Lily," Simon said.

"On it." She answered the call. "We're coming out now."

Simon, Lily, and Essie eased a brave and wounded Rose onto the nylon stretcher. Simon took one side while Lily and Essie took the other. They hefted her up and walked out of the forest. With Foxy and Sue in tow.

CHAPTER 56

JUNO DANGELD FROM the tree long enough. She heard what sounded like a low humming, but the closer it drew, she realized it was a drone buzzing, like an insect. After she flipped it off, she knew it would be a matter of time before they arrived. Whoever *they* were. Rose and Foxy's rescuers. But how were they discovered?

"I'm not waiting around to find out," she murmured as she held her arms in front of her, swaying left and right, then forward and backward. Ignoring the pain, she gained enough momentum to do a crunch. Then she grabbed hold of her boot and removed a folding knife.

"You're not going to get away with this, Juno." Foxy bellowed and then addressed Rose. "I see a drone, Rose. The watch worked. They found us."

"Watch? So that's your secret." Juno shouted while cutting herself down.

"Forget you! And if you think you're going to finish us off, you better think twice. They're coming," Foxy snapped. "Over here … over here."

"It wasn't personal. You were just a job." Whoomph. Juno landed onto a pile of leaves. She found her helmet unscathed and put it on, adjusting it so she could see in the dark.

"Screw you. You're a coward," Foxy shouted. "Hunting helpless unarmed women."

"You weren't helpless or unarmed. You had Rose." Juno's voice dripped with disdain.

"Fox—" Rose groaned.

"Save your breath. Help is on the way," Foxy soothed.

Juno clutched her side and quietly winced. She felt along the wound, fortunately the .38 grazed her. Juno couldn't say the same thing for her upper left thigh. That one was lodged inside. Nothing new for her. She'd been wounded by a much larger round and lived to talk about it.

In the distance she saw the headlamps, three of them. She quickly ducked behind a tree, waiting for them to pass. The minute the coast was clear, she gimped away. The closer she drew to the clearing, she spotted two men looking out by a Suburban, one of them the drone's operator. She glided behind the first cabin. As she peeked through the trees, she spotted a dog jumping from the vehicle.

One of the men ran after her, calling her name. "Sue." What kind of name was that for a dog?

Juno shook it off as she made her way to the second cabin. The person flying the drone would be too preoccupied to go after her. Juno crouch-walked to her SUV, unlocked it and tore off down the mud packed road.

Close to the highway, she spotted a helicopter flying low toward Rose and Foxy. Maybe Rose was telling the truth and still had all that money?

As she hit the Tamiami, Juno's phone rang. It would be H looking for an update.

What would she tell him? The letter she read didn't have enough information to be noteworthy. And since Foxy and Rose knew about Project X, they should've been terminated.

"Not gonna answer." Juno tossed it out the window. Sooner or later, Hansel would send in a clean-up crew. She would rush back to her condo, clean her safe, get her bugout bag, set her SUV ablaze, and disappear. Although she possessed several passports, she opted for her Canadian one. She'd make her escape that way. There wasn't anything left for her in Florida.

Juno punched it and hauled ass back to Miami.

CHAPTER 57

＊

I AWOKE TO the smell of bleach and the beeping of machines, my nose tingling. After I blinked a few times to clear the cobwebs, I realized I was in the hospital. I turned my head and Foxy sat in a chair, feet up, sleeping. Her arm in a sling. Saki stood next to me, grinning, with tears in her eyes.

"What? No flowers?" I snorted.

"Ah, music to my ears," Saki said, pouring water from a plastic pitcher. She handed it to me.

"Thanks, sis." I took a sip and handed it back to her. "I know I'm not dead, nor did I even have an NDE this time. No bright lights, no mother or my beloved husband." I peeked down. Phew, no catheter either. But I did have an IV attached to my right arm, and my left was in a sling. Mental head slap.

A gut-wrenching thought occurred.

"Where's Sue?" I yanked the covers off and sat, but the room spun.

Saki eased me back. "Essie took her out. She wouldn't leave your side but was also doing the pee pee dance."

Foxy woke and joined me.

"You shouldn't be up." I raised the bed with the controller.

"No, it's you who shouldn't be up. I'm good. Butterfly stitches. They didn't do surgery on me."

"How many holes this time?" It was Essie walking into the room holding Sue's leash.

"Baby girl," I cooed to Sue. "Thanks, Essie."

Sue gently hopped on the bed with the grace of a gazelle and inched her way to me. Showering me with kisses. She whimpered as she lay beside me.

"I was so worried about her," I said, stroking her with my right hand.

"She was equally bothered," Saki said. "But Lily took good care of her."

"Speaking of, where is she and Simon?" I asked.

"They just went to get us all take out," Foxy said. "Lily is fine, by the way. Doctor Ryan called. She wasn't um …" She looked at Essie. "Sick. Just stressed." I know Foxy wanted to say "poisoned."

"Oh, thank God. I'm not surprised though. She's been through a lot."

"You guys will have to tell me what that was about," Essie said, scratching behind Sue's ear.

I nodded. But that conversation would not take place. Essie wasn't in our inner circle of trust. She had her own secrets. Whatever they were.

"How about Tucker?" I asked.

"He returned the chopper and had to go back north," Essie replied.

I nodded again. "And Juno?" I asked.

Foxy's jaw tightened. "She escaped."

"How? She was in that trap," I said. "Now she's in the wind."

"Hopefully she crawled into a dark hole, never to resurface," Foxy said with a scowl.

I almost mentioned the letter. Phew, stupid pain meds.

"I don't understand why this Juno person was after Foxy and you?" Saki asked.

"It's obvious it has something to do with Foxy's uncle." Essie said. "Foxy, you said he was a scientist, correct?"

Foxy nodded and looked at me.

"Jeez. By the way someone was after you all, you'd think it was a hit squad sent by a deep covert agency." Saki snickered.

Foxy and I just stared at one another and said nothing.

"Wow, guys. I'm just kidding." Saki said. "Or am I?" Her laughter ceased.

Silence filled the room again.

"One thing was certain, Juno was a professional," Essie said.

"And my guess is that since she didn't terminate you gals, she disappeared."

"Wait! What?" Saki asked with her fists on her hips. "And why exactly would you come to that conclusion?"

I stared at Essie for a spell. "Because she's one of them ... aren't you, little cuz?" I put my hands to my mouth. Stupid drugs.

Essie said nothing and pet Sue.

"We have to chat, Essie Lee," I said.

"What am I missing?" Saki asked. "Damnit, Rose. No more secrets. I'm tired of it. You almost died, again, tonight. You, Lily, and Simon have been cryptic for days." She paced. "And don't get me started on Essie, here." Saki snapped a look at Essie. "You take secret phone calls. So, I'm inclined to agree with Rose. You work for the Agency!"

"Gee, will ya look at the time," I glanced at my watch, but I wasn't wearing it. "Where's the watch," I quickly scanned the room.

"Easy, Rose," Foxy said. "It's safe. I have it." She gave me a wink.

"See! Cryptic. All of you. Even Foxy is in on it." Saki headed for the door. "You can all suck it!"

"Saki," I called out and planted both feet on the floor, practically yanking the IV tubing out of my arm. But I was dizzy, again, and almost fell back. The cardiac monitor I was attached to sounded off as if I were an escaped convict. Sue sat upright, ready to chase after me.

"Rose, stop," Essie put her palm to me. "I'll chat with her." She left the room.

I turned off the machine as the intermittent beeping was driving me mad. I looked to make sure no one else was in the room. "Foxy, you sure the watch is okay?"

"Yes," Foxy whispered. "Before you went into surgery, I grabbed it. The flash drive is intact." She pulled it out of her pocket and showed it to me. "I don't want it. Nor do I want to know what's on it. It's yours." She attached it to my wrist.

"Thanks," I said. "Boy, the tension in the room. I'm inclined to agree with Saki. I think my cousin has deep deep secrets."

"I'm sure you'll find out," Foxy said. "Oh," she held up my fanny pack. "They recovered it for you." She paused. "Are you really going to let Saki in on it? I thought you were worried about her and Violet's safety."

"I am worried. But you see how my baby sister reacts to being kept in the dark. I think it's time to read her in. If she knows the severity of the situation, she can take extra measures. Kevin and James will need to be briefed, too." I looked at the time. 11:30 P.M. "Shoot, I really need to make that call to my attorney. I have half an hour left. And I'd like to retrieve something off the yacht. It's in the safe in my stateroom. I almost forgot about it."

"No, Rose. I'll get it. Considering all you've done for me. I discovered courage within myself *because* of you. Meeting you ignited a flame inside of me I didn't know was there. Uncle Gil would've adored you."

I smiled and patted her hand. "Your uncle's bravery and self-sacrifice ... well, it's admirable. And I see his likeness in you."

A moment of silence passed between us. We were both most likely contemplating his valor.

"It's getting kind of sappy." Foxy cleared her throat. "I insist, Rose."

"You can't."

"If you're worried about me having the combo to your safe ... after all we've been through!"

"No. It's not that. I put in a new safe. Equipped with a biometric iris scanner."

"What's in it? Can you get it later?"

I shook my head. "My mother's diamond engagement ring. It also contains my fine jewelry. What little I have ... besides." I lowered my head. "I want to say goodbye to the crew. They've all been wonderful to me."

"No kidding," Foxy said.

"Huh?" I tilted my head.

"TJ and Khan helped rescue us." Foxy then described the entire series of events. "They returned to the yacht this evening to check on things."

"I was in and out of it. I thought I heard Khan's voice." I wiped tears from my cheek. "Then it's imperative I get there. Will you help me?"

A nurse came in. "Ma'am, sorry for the delay. But it has been incredibly busy tonight." She reset the machine and readjusted my

IV bag.

"That's not necessary." I smiled. "I'm leaving."

The nurse gave me a skeptical look. "Rose, the doctor wants to keep you overnight for observation. You underwent surgery."

"Not the first time. Besides, I have a medic with me. I'll be fine." Once again, I put my feet on the floor. "With all due respect, I'm leaving. So, either you can take the IV out of me, or I can. I've done it before." I gave her a cheeky grin.

"Trust, me. She's not kidding." It was Saki returning. She walked up and gave me a hug and kiss. "Sorry, sis. And why do you want to leave?"

"I have a half hour left before … ya know."

"Yeah, you turn into a freakin' pumpkin." Saki turned to the nurse. "Please help my sister."

"You'll need to sign the AMA form." The nurse sighed and removed the IV line. "Hold here," she said, applying pressure to my arm.

"Can I get that form now? I seriously need to be somewhere before it strikes midnight."

The nurse threw her hand up and left the room mumbling something inaudible. But I could've sworn she said something about a glass slipper and me being a princess.

I scanned the room again. "Where's Essie?"

Saki laughed. "She had a phone call."

I nodded. "I can't wait to have that chat."

Saki stared at me with a serious look. "She gave me a condensed version of the truth. Said we'd talk later when all interested parties were present. Whatever that meant."

CHAPTER 58

◆

THE SECOND I got dressed, we left without the AMA paperwork. No time. And there was no time to grab crutches, so Saki did what any normal sister would do. She stole one from another patient's room. Since I had one arm in a sling, taking both would've been pointless.

We had to hurry as my attorney, Keith, would undoubtedly be waiting at the Max One at midnight sharp to take ownership, locking me out.

I called Lily on the way and told her what I did. Simon chimed in, giving me a butt chewing. Before I disconnected, I told them we'd meet back at the W since the room was paid for two more nights.

Simon said no, they'd meet me at the yacht and then take me back to the hospital. He added that he'd picked up a bottle of whiskey each for Khan and TJ. He wanted to reward them for helping with our rescue mission. I concurred 110%.

It was 11:57 p.m. when Foxy, Essie, Sue and I arrived at the marina.

Saki sat in her vehicle, updating James on the day's events.

The sky was clear, and the moon was almost full. It turned into a spectacular evening. I could finally relax. But the second I stepped onto the docks, I heard Sue ferociously growling. I looked down. Her hackles were raised, and she was baring her teeth.

I spun around so fast I almost fell off my crutch. Had it have not been for Foxy and Essie catching me on either side, I would've ended up in the bay.

I saw a tall shadow advancing closer from the north.

"Who's there?" Because my left arm was immobile, I used my right hand to draw my pistol from my fanny pack, keeping it low.

Sue crouched and started stalking the person.

"Sue, stop!"

But she didn't listen. I'd never seen her act like this. Today's events must've shaken her, causing her to be extra protective of me.

"No!" I yelled.

This time she partially obeyed. Still growling, she moved back a little and then stood next to me. Trembling.

"Whoever you are, you better stop. I'm armed and my dog wants a piece of you."

The shadow moved closer to us. Neither Foxy nor Essie had a weapon, but they stood on either side of me; my guardian angels, fists up, ready for a fight.

"I warned you. Stop now."

Out of nowhere, another person appeared, but to the south. What in the world? That one I recognized. It was Captain. He had what looked like a long gun held to his side.

"Captain, you back for more?" I yelled.

"Something like that. Here I thought you were dead."

"Surprise!"

The other figure, who I now knew was female by her long hair, was also packing heat. Was that Juno? No, she had short hair.

"Was she part of the crew that abducted us?" I softly posed the question to Foxy.

"I was incapacitated," Foxy replied.

The three of us were now surrounded, and we formed a triangle, each having one another's backs.

"Where's the security officer?" Foxy asked.

"No clue," I replied.

"Roosie," the lady jeered.

That voice. She sounded familiar, but from where? Was I hallucinating this whole thing? Was I still in surgery? Or did I die? Maybe it was the pain meds coursing through my body. If I wasn't certain, perhaps being armed wasn't such a good idea. I shook it off as we looked left, then right, then left again.

"Who are you?" I directed the question to the woman.

"Aw, forget me so soon?"

"Shilo!" That's right. She'd escaped.

"I was here first, lady." Captain shouted. "Where's your freakin' mutt?"

That was a good question. I looked down. Sue was gone. "Sue!" I shouted her name. But she didn't come to me. "Come, girl." I tried to sound happy and not irritated.

Nothing.

Both Captain and Shilo inched closer to us. We were literally stuck between two crazy people. I looked toward Captain then snapped my gaze to Shilo.

Shilo for sure wanted me dead. What did Captain want?

"Ladies, when I say the word, we drop," I said.

With my double vision and inability to get a clear shot, I re-holstered my weapon into my fanny pack.

"Okay," Foxy and Essie said at the same time.

No sooner had they replied, than the next thing I heard was a vicious growl. Sue's shadow looked larger than life as she stood next to Captain.

"Now," I yelled.

I braced myself for excruciating pain as we hit the deck. Literally. Another slow-motion picture played out.

But Sue had a plan of her own. The second Captain leveled his weapon, Sue jumped up and bit his arm.

Once again, fueled by adrenaline, I grabbed my crutch to stand and quickly hobbled in Captain's direction just in time to see him punt Sue like a football into Biscayne Bay.

"No!" I shouted.

I spun to dive, but Essie was already in the water.

I returned my attention to Captain, striking him in his nose with my good arm. I would've kicked him too, but I would've fallen.

A quick second later, Essie yelled. "Sue's okay."

Upon hearing the good news, I sucker punched Captain in his nuts. "That's for my dog. Asshole."

Captain doubled over, holding his groin.

I turned my attention to Shilo. Finally, security was on her.

"She doesn't deserve to have his baby," Shilo shouted, flailing her arms, followed by the sound of glass shattering.

A comedy of errors unfolded as she ran toward the parking lot with three huge security guards chasing her. Seconds later, Miami-Dade PD arrived with their red and blues flashing.

I stood, unsteadily, in a state of shock.

Now was I dreaming? The answer to that question was immediately answered as my leg was kicked out from under me. I fell backward onto the deck, hitting my head. I literally saw stars.

And then his boots came toward me.

CHAPTER 59

AS I LAID there dazed, I quickly pulled my arms to shield my head and face, bracing for that kick. Out of the corner of my eye, I watched Simon charge Captain like a linebacker, slamming him to the ground.

"You want to beat up on someone, shit bird," Simon shouted. "How about someone your own size?"

"I wasn't going to kick h—"

Simon didn't let him complete that sentence before he jumped on Captain, straddling him. He yanked Captain's shirt and knocked him out with a punch.

I stared at the stars in the rapidly moving sky and pondered what just happened when I was ambushed by a wet dog.

"Sue!" I cried, hugging her. I didn't care about the pain I was in or that it was now after midnight, and I was poor. All that mattered was my friends and family were okay. Especially my baby girl.

More sirens wailed in the distance as I sat rocking Sue. Law Enforcement and paramedics, each had their unique sounds that I'd heard a lot in my career.

"Rose." Lily dropped next to me. "Are you okay?"

I nodded.

Essie and Foxy rushed over. Simon too. Even Khan and TJ came out from the yacht during the commotion. It was too much for me. I never liked people fussing over me. This moment was no different. And then came the EMTs.

"Stop! Please." I inhaled deeply. "I'm okay. I don't want to go back to the hospital." I looked at Simon. "You can restitch me."

Everyone's voices became muffled. That's all I remembered.

When I regained consciousness, I was in the hospital. Again. With the same nurse, flashing a shit-eating "I told ya so" look on her face.

I peered around the room. It was just the two of us.

"What happened? Where is everyone?" I asked.

"They're all giving statements to the police." She checked my vitals. "You've torn your stitches, and you've had substantial blood loss. But you'll survive. You're stubborn, you know that?"

"So, I've been told," I faintly said.

"Are you always on a crusade?"

"Meh." I shrugged. "What time is it?"

She looked at her watch. "Two."

"A.M. or P.M.?"

She smiled. "A.M.," the nurse replied softly with a gentle touch to my shoulder.

"Wait! Where's my dog? Is she okay?" I tried to sit up but couldn't move.

The nurse pointed to a chair. Sue was curled up on a blanket, sleeping away.

"Is she okay? She was kicked in the water," I cried.

Sue heard me and jumped off the chair onto my bed.

"Does that answer your question?" The nurse scratched behind Sue's ears and left the room.

"Little dog. You can't go off like that by yourself. You're gonna get yourself killed. You had me worried."

Sue lay beside me and cuddled. I think she understood.

"Exactly!" Simon said.

I turned my head and Simon, Lily, and Saki stood there, arms crossed.

"I hope you just heard yourself," Simon said. "That's how we all feel."

I pondered that for a moment. "I'm sorry."

Silence filled the room.

"Well. Giving the cops my statement. That was fun." Saki laughed. "After I spoke to James, I watched crazy unfold. So, I called 9-1-1. You should've seen yourself, Rose. Hobbling over to Captain. The whites of his eyes were huge. And Bam! Right in his balls." She giggled again.

I chuckled, but it hurt. "Thanks. This broke woman needs a laugh."

"About that." A man said from the doorway. I turned my head. It was my attorney.

"What? Do I have to give you my blood now too? Or keys to the yacht and car." I groaned.

"Um ... no," Keith said. "May I?" He pointed at a chair.

"Sure," I coldly replied.

He dragged a chair to the bedside. "So, about the whole being poor thing."

"Did you come here to rub my nose in it?"

Simon walked up and stood over Keith, arms crossed wearing his resting bitch face.

Keith drew his head back and put his hand to Simon. "That woman, Shilo, who attempted to shoot you at the marina?"

"Yeah," I said. "Where are you going with this?"

"Well, after she escaped from federal custody, she searched for you," Keith said. "She put a hefty bounty on you."

"So, she's the one who sent Juno and Captain ass hat?" Saki inquired.

Keith stared with a perplexed look.

"No," Essie said entering the room. "Captain said Juno hired him at first. And then his friends Bo and Nevaeh were paid off by Shilo to take you to the swamps."

"Wait, wait, wait." I raised my bed. My head was spinning again. "They were paid by Juno *and* Shilo? Two different hits? Then who wanted Foxy?"

"Juno. You just happened to be in the way until ... you know," Essie said.

I cocked my head.

"You had to save the world," Simon, Lily, and Saki said at once.

"Sheesh, guys. Okay, I got it." I scratched my head. "So, Captain worked for both Juno and Shilo?"

"In a manner of speaking," Essie said. "As we suspected, Juno works for ..." She shot her eyes around the room. Everyone but Keith was allowed to hear it.

I nodded at her and returned my attention to Keith. "Then why are *you* here?"

"As I was saying. Shilo had it in for you. After she escaped, she found her way to Miami looking for you. After she put the hit on you, she, well." Keith looked at his feet. "Stole Max's sperm from the … um bank."

I scrunched my face. "And?"

"When she was arrested. She … uh smashed all the vials of his … stuff." Keith shook his head. "She said if she can't have his babies, then no one can." Keith stood. "There are no more vials. Therefore, you're in the clear. You keep the money. The yacht. Everything."

I was stunned hearing this. I'd been preparing myself physically and mentally. "And you're certain that all his … stuff, is gone?"

"Positive." Keith paused. "The sperm fell into the bay."

We all gasped.

"Holy shit balls, there's gonna be some strange-looking fish." Saki laughed. "Remind me never to swim in that body of water again."

"Saki!" I chuckled too.

Essie's phone rang. "Sorry, I have to ta—"

"Take it. I know." I smiled.

Essie walked out and Keith started for the door.

"One more thing, Keith," I cleared my throat. "After hearing that you were the executor of Max's estate if I failed to come through with the whole baby thing, I felt … betrayed that you didn't get me to really understand what I was signing."

"We covered all that, Rose. You were aware what you were signing."

"Well, I didn't and as you know, I was in a similar situation that I am right now. Heavily medicated." I growled.

"That wasn't my problem," Keith snapped.

"You're absolutely correct." My grin was tight and closed-mouthed.

"I'm glad you see it my way." He turned for the door.

"One last thing." I cleared my throat. "You're fired."

"Yo—you can't fire me."

"I can and I just did."

"But—but."

I glared.

Simon moved closer to Keith and pushed him out the door.

"Bye, bye, now." And he slammed it in his face.

Lily, Saki and Simon looked at me.

"Well, how does it feel to be rich again?" Lily asked.

"Like I just won the lottery." I closed my eyes.

CHAPTER 60

$\blacklozenge$

"HOLD ON." CLOSING Rose's hospital room door behind her, Essie spoke into the phone. She walked down the hall and out the front door.

"Yes, Justice." She rolled her eyes, "Agent Stormi—jeez, Stormi. Does it matter what I call you? And to what do I owe this displeasure?"

"Agent Q. Why haven't you returned my calls?" Stormi asked.

"I've told you, don't call me that. I'm just Essie." She spun as the door behind her opened. Hospital staff wheeled a patient outside.

"Your papers were never filed, and we own you, remember?" Stormi said. "Nice way to change the topic."

"It runs in the family," Essie said. "And negative. I'm done. Like I've been telling your people, I'm out of the spy business. Not my problem you all *lost* my paperwork."

"What do you assume you've been doing?"

"I'm here for protection. For. My. Family."

"We sent you for recon."

"You mean spying? I thought the Agency wasn't allowed to do that on American soil."

The line went still. Essie looked at it to make sure the call hadn't ended. "You bribed me here to ensure the safety of my family. And, they are, no thanks to Juno."

"Juno hasn't been with the Agency for quite some time. Not sure who hired her."

"I heard that too. Speaking of." Essie walked further away from the hospital. "My family suspects *I'm* with the Agency."

"You just said you're not anymore." Stormi said. "How much have they uncovered?"

Essie pulled the phone from her ear. A deep pit opened in her stomach. She was sent to keep them safe. Not investigate them. She cleared her throat. "Nothing."

"I find that hard to believe. If they were targeted for termination, they know something." Stormi sighed. "Last time. What is their knowledge of X? And has there been any chatter on locating the data or the scientists?"

"Negative. They don't trust me yet. They're very astute. I've also promised to tell them something about how and why I've suddenly appeared into their lives. And if I don't, their suspicions will grow."

"You were with the Agency long enough to make up a cover story. Or tell them the truth."

Essie pondered that for a moment. She was pressured into joining the CIA. They told Essie her country needed her. Didn't it always begin that way? But Essie was exceptional. The Agency recruited her at eighteen due to her innate observational skills, incredibly high IQ, and eidetic memory.

By eighteen, when her classmates were entering college, Essie had completed her first PhD. Because of her age, she was assigned the role of analyst. She was the best they'd ever had. When she turned twenty-one, she began working in the field.

"Essie, are you there?"

"Yeah. And are you kidding? I can't tell my family the truth."

"Tell them you're with MI6."

"I'm not. That was a one and done joint operation," Essie growled. "And I'm not going to lie. They'll see right through it."

"Do what you will. But don't forget our arrangement." Stormi paused. "Aren't you the least bit curious about locating Agent A?"

Silence fell on the line. Essie looked up and tears formed. Her heart shattered.

"He has a name! Say it!"

Stormi exhaled. "Angus."

Angus Hamilton. Essie last saw him during an undercover assignment. They had an instant connection. She and Angus posed as married scientists in a joint agency operation. Angus was MI6,

Essie CIA. The information given to them was the general location of the last lab making Project X. Since X was a rogue experiment, MI6 and the CIA sent Angus and Essie to do some house cleaning and shut it down. But it was a ruse.

Upon landing in Paris on the last leg of their trip, Essie and Angus were drugged and abducted. When Essie awakened, Angus was gone, and she was back in her hotel room with no memory of the last forty-eight hours. Only an odd, raised mark appeared on the back of her ear that vanished before she could question its origin. When Essie contacted her handler, his number was disconnected. She called the Agency, but they denied knowledge of her mission. It wasn't until Essie was ordered to return to Langley and given a desk assignment that she tendered her resignation.

Essie spent the greater part of six months in Ireland with her mother. Leaving the CIA in the rearview mirror. Heartbroken, Essie was determined to find Angus, no matter how long or how far it took.

After telling her mother everything, Mum encouraged Essie to reach out to her Aunt Lillian, who had inside contacts at the Agency. However, she was reluctant to involve more people in her entangled web.

While Essie was in Ireland, she was contacted by an Agent Justice Stormi. Someone she'd never heard of. But then again, the CIA employed countless people. The agent told Essie an anonymous tip led to Angus' whereabouts. When Essie asked why the Agency had amnesia when she called the first time, Stormi told her she was not at liberty to give her the specifics.

And for Stormi to reveal any more details, Essie had to do one thing. Head to Florida and watch her family. Under Stormi's orders, she couldn't tell a single person, her aunt Lillian included. How did Stormi discover Essie even considered calling her Aunt Lillian? Was her place bugged? Perhaps even Essie's phone?

She changed her number and purchased a new cell. But that was futile, as Stormi still found her. Essie knew the Agency had ears and eyes everywhere.

Now she was expected to spy on her family. She felt a surge of anger.

"Essie … Essie. Agent Q. Are you there?"

Essie cleared her throat again. "It's Essie." She answered sharply. "What do I have to do?"

After hearing her new mission, Essie disconnected, put on her happy face, and rejoined her family.

CHAPTER 61

THREE WEEKS LATER and I was healing nicely.

I decided to inspect the Max One. It was beyond repair, so I opted for a simpler way of living. I ordered a smaller yacht. I planned on naming it Salty Sue with dog paws on either side. It was a no brainer. I had grown accustomed to living on the open seas. But I decided only part time, when it wasn't hurricane season. Since I downsized, that also meant fewer crew members. But I kept on Khan and TJ and some of the close-knit folks.

As Sue and I walked into the lobby of the W, followed by my former Special Forces security entourage that my entire family insisted I hire, the front desk handed me a box that was sent via overnight messenger. It was an encrypted laptop with extra secret squirrel stuff that my grandmother's IT guy, Rayo, set up for me. It was odd that Grandma offered it up to me, no questions asked. All she said was she had an upcoming project she needed my help with. And under no circumstances was I to use her passcodes ever again. So, I graciously accepted.

I entered my room, and eased onto the couch, giving Sue her usual dose of belly rubs. Sue was exhausted as we'd just had a two-day visit with my sweet niece Violet and Saki. They couldn't wait to go home to greet James properly, who'd been working his tail off. And while Saki visited, I told her everything, and I mean the whole enchilada. No more secrets.

Just as I suspected, she flipped a lid and was concerned about Violet's safety. Not to mention James did too. I assured them, we would not be involving Saki or her family in our quest for the truth about Project X and what really happened to Lily's folks.

As for my guy, Kevin O'Malley, he too had paid me a long visit but returned to D.C. I could tell living apart was wearing on him. But work sent him overseas most of the time. Since he wasn't around much, Kevin said he was going to bubble wrap me, ensuring my safety. I told him the truth, too. I was determined not to be secretive with my family anymore. Except Essie, she was not in our circle of trust, yet, since she showed up out of nowhere.

I leaned back, removed the boot from my foot, and closed my eyes, embracing the stillness of the room to contemplate my future. With the money unconditionally mine, a relief washed over me, no thanks to Keith.

Interestingly, my finances improved considerably after firing him. As a result, I engaged the services of a forensic accountant to investigate. The results showed Keith had been skimming from the wounded vet foundation. The nerve of him.

After the accountant was finished, I hired a carefully vetted attorney, and we reviewed every aspect of the trust together. I was determined never to be taken advantage of again. And surprisingly, I also discovered that I did not have to be personally involved in the fundraisers. Therefore, I delegated the task to someone else who was better suited. Stella. We didn't fault her for what occurred. And if Foxy forgave her friend, then so did I.

Speaking of Foxy, with her newly inherited money, she gave up her job at the Dancing Flamingo and was headed north to finish her education. She opted to change her major to pre-med. I think her Uncle Gil would've approved. Even though she was moving away, she'd always be a part of our lives. Plus, there was Harlee and Nala.

"Penny for your thoughts." Lily stood in the entry. "Actually, a million." She smiled.

"Hi." I returned a cheeky grin.

"I see you finally got the laptop." Lily joined me.

I opened it, powered it on, and waited for it to boot up. I set it on the couch for Lily.

"Let's wait for Simon," Lily said. "He should be up in a few minutes." She opened her locket and pulled out the computer chip. She then removed the note with the Sudoku puzzle. "I can't believe how fast Essie solved this thing."

"Yeah. Ms. Genius did it in a matter of minutes," I said. "Good thing there wasn't anything else on it."

Lily looked around the room. "Speaking of. Where is she?"

"She went to Saki's gym to work out."

"Do you believe her reason for being so secretive?" Lily asked.

"You mean men problems? Not completely," I replied. "I've got the feeling there's something she's still not telling us."

"Is she looking for work?" Lily asked.

"No. Taking time off. Spending time with the family. She has money socked away from her inheritance when her grandfather passed. Something I know a little about."

Just then Simon used his card key and entered. "Sweet. It's here. Let's get this game going." He looked around. "Are we alone?"

I nodded and patted to the couch.

"I'm too nervous, Rose." Lily held up the chip. "You do it."

I shook my head. "Lily, it was sent to you."

Lily drew a deep breath and inserted it into the chip reader. She typed in the passcode from the solved Sudoku.

After a few moments of reading, Lily sat back with her mouth opened, staring straight ahead. She went to the large bay window and said nothing for what felt like an eternity.

Simon stood and joined her. "Are you okay?"

When she turned, Lily had tears in her eyes.

"What's wrong, love?" Simon asked with softness to his voice.

She just pointed at my computer and dropped her hands on her knees. "Read it."

"Are ... are you sure?" I asked.

She nodded.

I read it and read it again. "Oh my God, Lily." I looked up. I would've run up to her, but I was still on the mend.

"Tell me!" Simon said impatiently as he walked over to the screen. He too scanned it. "These are test subjects and their real names. Including your father." He looked up.

"Keep reading." Lily fanned her face and drew a deep breath.

Simon returned to the screen. "Your mother is alive. Ho—how can that be? And Gil was certain?"

Lily rejoined us at the couch and stared at the screen. "It's all right here." She looked at me with a scowl. "How could my mother keep this from me?"

My heart ached for Lily. "I'm not making excuses." I turned the computer around. "It says that Maisy had to keep you in the dark."

"For five years, Rose!" Lily yelled. "I buried my parents." She shot me a look. "Wait! Do you think my father is alive, too?"

"It says no. I'm sorry. But Mai—wait. M for Maisy." I stared at Lily. "Grandma was communicating with an individual called M, a few weeks ago. She asked M if *they* were in Florida. When I confronted her, she got nervous. I wonder how long she's known."

"Probably from the beginning. Now that I think about it, there was a letter from my mother that Lillian had in her possession. After I got abducted, she acted oddly toward me. And then insisted I come out here." Lily paused. "When I was visiting my parent's grave, you know the day I was kidnapped, someone was watching me. Rose, do you think it was my mother? Where has she been all this time? I've got to find her and tell her I know she's al—"

"You can't. Not yet. We've got to play along with the charade. For now."

"Why?" Lily asked.

"Too risky."

"Rose is right," Simon interjected. "According to this, your mother's life is still in danger. Hence her playing dead. Not until X is exposed, including all the moving parts."

"My grandmother said there was a project she needed my help with." I pointed to the laptop. "It could be this."

Lily sighed and nodded. "Okay, Rose, now your turn."

I took the USB flash drive out of Gil's watch, which I was still wearing, inserted it and waited eagerly for the computer to decode.

The three of us sat back and read with opened mouths.

I scrolled down. "There are so many scientific formulas." I looked at Simon and Lily. "Do you think the rest of the formula is in there? We need Foxy for this. She's the only scientist we know who we can trust."

"And look at this one. Another damn puzzle," Simon said. "They look like coordinates of sorts. At least we know the state."

I continued reading. "But according to this, there's one last source. The documents of the original experiment."

"That is what Gil gave me that my kidnapper took." Lily scratched her head. "Why would he give that to me first? Isn't that backwards?"

I shrugged. "Maybe these were supposed to be handed to you first." I continued scrolling. "Wait, there's one last attachment." I opened it. "According to Gil these two agents were the last involved. He spoke with an Agent A. But the agent was abducted mid-conversation. The line went dead. He never met with an Agent Q."

We sat back and stared for a spell.

"Okay then," I finally said. "You guys asked what I wanted to do when I grew up? Well, right now, it's this. To solve this mystery."

"Oh, not alone, you aren't." Simon gave me his best big brother scowl.

"Don't worry. I know."

Continue the adventures of Rose O'Brien in Book Three-Saving Angus.

AUTHOR'S NOTE

I have been asked how I draw inspiration for my characters. The answer is simple: dogs, dogs, dogs. My dogs, friends' dogs, heck even ones I've just met. And like any dog lover, I wanted to pay homage to my two original fur babies, Saki and Rose. So, instead of writing about my devoted K-9 companions, I bring them to the human world by creating characters drawn from their unique furry personalities.

List of characters and their K-9 identities.

Rose O'Brien

Saki O'Brien-Powers

Lily Cazier

Essie Lee Quinlan

Simon Rae Rose

Foxy – a.k.a. Francine Fox

Stella

Tucker Fite

TJ Hooker

Captain

Juno

Nevaeh

Agent H-Hansel

Nala

Harlee

"M." a.k.a., Maisy   Justice Stormi, a.k.a., Stormi

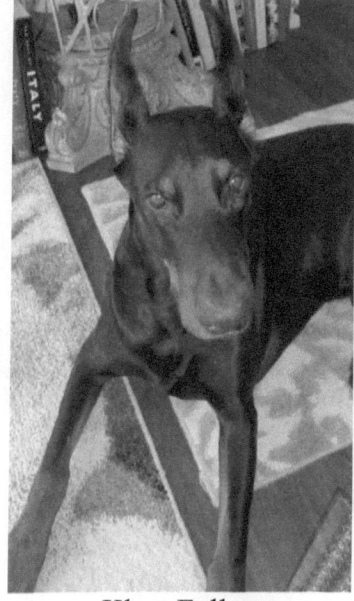 

Khan Fullerton   Bo

Last, but not least, Grandma Lil. Lil is the only character in my stories based on a real person, my mother-in-law, Lillian Weinstock. Lillian, the real-life inspiration for Grandma Lil, shared her fictional counterpart's spirited personality. She is greatly missed.

RIP LILLIAN E. WEINSTOCK

ABOUT THE AUTHOR

S.S. Duskey retired from law enforcement with over 20 years of experience. She lives in the Bitterroot Mountains of Montana with her husband, Steve, and fur babies, Essie and Lilly.

When she's not plotting mischief for her characters, Sharon enjoys spending time with her family, friends, and furry children in the outdoors of the beautiful Bitterroot.

Included in Sharon's early works is the three-part Rose O'Brien Trilogy: Secrets in the Keys, Deception in the Bitterroot, and Redemption in the Tahoe Basin. Book One-Saving Lily is part of the new Rose O'Brien Series. These are all available on Amazon.

Sharon invites you to contact her at ssduskey@yahoo.com or visit her website www.ssduskeyauthor.com. She can also be found on Facebook at www.facebook.com/ssduskeyauthor and on www.instagram.com/ssduskey

NOTE TO READERS:

I hope you enjoy reading my stories as much as I have writing them. For an indie author, reviews can have a tremendous impact on reaching more readers like you. So, if you like *A Rose O'Brien Series, Book Two: Saving Foxy,* or any others, please visit Amazon and Goodreads and leave a review.

If you are reading this on Kindle, click here to leave a review on Amazon. Thank you!